What the critics are saying...

4 stars! "Gray delivers a warm, funny, sometimes poignant look at a young woman who has her prince, but is afraid he will turn into a frog any second." ~ *RT Bookclub Magazine*

5 coffee cups! "Ms. Gray has a way with words that give her characters depth and makes the reader want to read more..." ~ *Coffee Time Romance*

5 Angels! Fallen Angel Reviews Recommended Read "These characters just jump off the page and into your life, making you not want to put down the book until you know how it all comes together." ~ *Fallen Angel Reviews*

5 stars! "The characters pop off the page..." ~ *Ecataromance*

"...an immediate attention grabber with its fresh writing and crisp dialogue." ~ *Romance Divas*

"The World According to Ali is just what romance readers are looking for." ~ *Joyfully Reviewed*

Also by T.L. Gray

 හ

Object of His Affection

About the Author

 හ

   T. L. Gray loves romance and mystery, writing and reading it. She's an active member of RWA, loves to travel, hates being politically correct, and tends to view the world with a slightly skewered sense of humor—but that could be because she's married to a police officer. She lives in Kentucky with her husband, sons, and dogs.

T.L. welcomes comments from readers. You can find her website and email address on her author bio page at www.Cerridwen.com

T.L. Gray

The World According to Ali

Cerridwen Press

A Cerridwen Press Publication

www.cerridwenpress.com

The World According to Ali

ISBN #1419955136

ALL RIGHTS RESERVED.

The World According to Ali Copyright © 2005 T.L. Gray

Edited by Pamela Campbell

Cover art by Willo.

Electronic book Publication October 2005

Trade Paperback Publication July 2006

Cerridwen Press is an imprint of Ellora's Cave Publishing, Inc.®

Trademarks Acknowledgement

The World According to Ali

80

Dear Reader

Enjoy!

Dedication

∞

For my mom, Pat.

Your courage and faith in me to the very end makes me stronger.

I love you.

Chapter One

છૈ

Ali slipped on leather pumps that matched her midnight blue dress, stood back, and gave herself one last look in the gilded cheval glass mirror. Something was missing, other than the accompanying blackwatch plaid jacket. The sleeveless crepe sheath had a zip-back closure with princess seams and a hemline that skimmed just above the knee. Only just, she noted with a sigh. The outfit was sedate in a classic, thirty-something sort of way. Perfect for her dinner date with Gil Moorland.

So why the hell did she want to rip it off and set it on fire?

"Deep breaths, Ali," she told herself, fingers itching to yank out each and every pin holding her French twist in place. "The attack will pass. Remember what happened last time."

She reached for the plaid jacket and slipped it on, closing the single button at the waist. Matching purse, a last minute spritz of perfume, and she was ready when Gil rang the doorbell.

Gil Moorland was thirty-five with thinning brown hair, blank eyes, and a body most any woman under forty would covet. But he was...well, boring. Only the dating gods knew why she had agreed to go out with him. Her last disastrous date—two months ago—had only recently begun to fade from her memory.

"Ali." Gil greeted her with a proper peck on the cheek. "Don't you look nice."

Nice. She looked *nice.* The evening was already ruined and she hadn't even made it out the door yet. "Thanks."

Gil didn't wait for her to lock the door. He walked ahead of her to his car, parked along the street, dropped into the driver's seat, and started the engine. Ali was left to open her own door and slide into the passenger seat. Gil was a terrible driver, she'd been warned, so snapping the seatbelt into place wasn't only law-abiding but a matter of self-preservation. She feared for her life through three yellow lights, four no-turn-on-reds, and one busy intersection where the light was out and it was every man for himself. What stop sign?

In the foyer of the restaurant the waiter greeted them with a smile on his beautiful Italian face. "Table for two?"

"Yes," Gil answered.

"Smoking or non?"

"Smoking," Ali said before Gil could disagree.

Gil raised an eyebrow at her. "I didn't know you smoked," he said somewhat stiffly. "Do you mind if we sit in non-smoking? I simply can't eat with all those choking fumes up my nose."

The olive-skinned waiter looked from Gil to Ali, back to Gil, his expression one of mild distaste. It was plain to see he thought Gil might have taken the time to learn about these pesky details before he asked the lady to dinner.

Ali forced a smile. "Non-smoking is fine." When they reached the table the waiter held back, expecting Gil to hold her chair, but stepped forward to do the deed himself when he saw no such pleasantry was to be observed. He was further miffed when Gil waved away the offer of a wine menu, marching away to give them a scant few minutes to peruse the menu.

But only a scant few. Anton—as the name on his badge announced—sailed back to the table, pen poised to take their order. "For you, ma'am?"

"I'll have the linguini in clam sauce."

"Ah, a very good choice. Very good. And to drink?"

"Gin and tonic."

"You wouldn't rather have iced tea?" Gil lowered his menu to ask. He might as well have asked if she'd bothered to look at the prices of cocktails.

No, I need to be drunk so I can pretend my date isn't cheap and generic. "Why didn't I think of that? Of course," she told Anton, "iced tea it is."

Anton gazed at her sympathetically over his order pad, then turned to Gil. "And for you, sir?"

"The spaghetti. House salad."

"To drink?"

"I'll just have water."

"Appetizers?"

"No, thank you." Gil cleared his throat and took a sip from his water glass.

Ali wanted to scream. Instead she jiggled her foot, thought about kicking Gil under the table, and listened as he launched into hair-raising tales of life as a real estate agent, with himself, naturally, as the hero who solved every starry-eyed homeowner's problems of pestilence and contractual bidding wars.

She almost wept with relief when the food arrived, curbed the urge to check her watch, and picked up her fork. She was about to take a bite of the delicious smelling concoction when a horrible slurping sound migrated across the table, freezing her fork midway to her lips.

Please, God, tell me it's not possible he's sucking that strand of spaghetti from the plate. It was all she could do to swallow the linguini and keep it down.

* * * * *

By ten o'clock Ali was pacing the black and white tiled kitchen floor of her condo in her underwear, swigging down a bottle of Busch beer, her date with Gil Moorland playing grotesquely and repeatedly through her mind with startling clarity. The man had actually sucked spaghetti from his plate then expected her to invite him in for a nightcap!

Nightcap her ass.

With each swallow the urge to call Franny became stronger. Why was she fighting it? She and Franny hadn't had a girls' night out for almost two months. Granted, she'd come away from the last one with a tattoo on her left hip. But what the hell? Life was made for living and she wasn't going to end up bitter and prudish like her mother.

Her mother had lied. It wasn't a sin to want to be noticed by the opposite sex. Lord, if her mother ever found out about the tattoo she would be hogtied to the kitchen chair and given that all-too-familiar lecture about nice girls.

If her mother was speaking to her, that is. Which she wasn't.

Nice girls didn't wear tight clothes. Nice girls didn't wear makeup, or flirt with strange boys, or call boys, or stay out until eleven o'clock at night. Nice girls didn't talk about sex or admit to certain bodily functions. They wore skirts below the knee, sensible shoes, and never, never teased their hair. Nice girls didn't get asked to the prom by the high school hunks, either. They didn't let a boy kiss them on the first date, date fast boys, and certainly never let the heathens touch their breasts. This word would be whispered, almost as if it were a sin to have breasts.

Not that Ali considered herself a "bad girl". Far from it. But sometimes she just had these...*urges*...to enjoy a little freedom. A little fun without feeling guilty. Urges Franny Demato, whom she'd met in college, was only too willing to help fan into a fire. Ali had tasted alcohol for the first time under Franny's tutelage. She'd had her first makeover one week after discovering her college roommate was what men referred to as "a looker", and learned which shades of eye shadow and lipstick complemented her coloring. She'd bought her first pair of high heels after seeing a professor on the sidewalk outside the Science Building come to a dead stop to watch an older female student in spiked heels walk past him.

After that she had bought dozens of fashion magazines and learned which clothes flattered her slender figure, shunning her wardrobe of baggy jeans and clunky shoes and sack dresses in favor of the classic, sophisticated, sometimes outrageously trendy apparel. She had let her mousy brown hair grow out past her shoulders, tinted it with a subtle shade of honey blonde, and experimented with new hairstyles.

They had gone to war over her hair, her mother and she. But Ali had determinedly pushed on, selling reference books and cookbooks and children's books for Southwestern to pay her way through college when her mother announced she wouldn't be financing "the whore" through another three years.

So her hair was blonde instead of the dull brown she'd been born with, and she wore makeup and clothes that actually fit. Those things didn't make her a whore. Thank God Franny had been able to drill that into her head over the years.

The tattoo—a way of letting off steam, assuring herself she wasn't falling back into old habits or diving headlong into the blackened pit of the three P's. Prim, proper, and prudish.

The navel ring—well, she had to admit to a moment of insanity there.

But she'd gotten used to them eventually, these moments of insanity. Like now, when she traipsed around the house in her Victoria's Secret panties and matching bra just for the heck of it.

She only smoked occasionally. Could take it or leave it, but hadn't been able to resist baiting Gil at the restaurant after he'd so obtusely decided she was so hot to trot to go out with him that she wouldn't mind opening her own car door. She supposed she should be shocked he had agreed to pick her up. The fashionable way to date nowadays was to meet at the hot spot of your choice, go Dutch, and if the date was a flop you could drive yourself home.

Fashion designers were pushing the Sixties and Seventies look as new and innovative. Please. Ali hadn't liked the hippie look in its heyday. No way was she going to wear baggy, wide-legged jeans and tacky flower prints and platform shoes that made her slim legs look like toothpicks so a man with the same fashion handicap would ask her out on a date that wasn't really a date.

Finally, she gave up and called the only person who understood her. "Franny?"

"Uh-oh. I know that tone. What's up sugarbuns? Another nose-picker sabotage your dessert course?"

"No. This one had a talent for sucking spaghetti off his plate."

"So you thought you'd go home and put on your sexy underwear and throw down a few, eh?" Franny knew her so well. "Cheer up, honey. You must have been reading my mind. I was just about to call and tell you about a party my firm is throwing tomorrow night. We just finished up a big job and the money's in the bank. Now it's time to boogy."

"Sounds like a lot of bosses pinching their secretaries' asses to me." Ali peeled the cellophane off a spare pack of cigarettes from the kitchen drawer and tapped one out.

"I wish. You haven't seen my new boss. Fresh from South Carolina. Looks like he just stepped off the cover of GQ. The man's a babe magnet."

"Grow up, Franny."

"This from thirty-year-old Allison Geraldine MacPherson, who wears a navel ring. Come on, it'll be fun. What have you got to lose?"

"At a party with you?" Ali lit up and inhaled, blowing out a stream of smoke. "Only my self-respect."

"Hey, who taught you the meaning of life?"

"My mother. Then I had to learn it all over again from you."

"Speaking of your mother…"

"We aren't speaking of my mother."

"Ali, you have to talk to her at some point. It's not healthy to hate your own mother."

"I don't hate her, Franny. But I'm not going to put myself against the wall to satisfy her bloodlust. If you want to know the truth, I think she's happy with the way things are. She pretends I don't exist, I pretend she's not really my mother. If you'll shut up about it, I'll go to the damn party."

"Great. I'll pick you up at the boutique after work. Take something sexy to change into. We'll knock their socks off."

"Wouldn't it be nice if someone knocked our socks off for a change?"

"Yeah," Franny said wistfully. "It would be. Alas, you have to kiss a lot of frogs."

"I'd settle for a toad with table manners."

Ali was smiling when she hung up. Franny could always lighten her mood, even after one of her mother's more stringent lectures had knocked her down a couple of notches.

Franny was the sister she'd never had. Her parents were warm and loving. They had opened their hearts and their home to Ali the first time she met them. Gladys and Don Demato knew their daughter had a bit of a wild streak in her, but loved Franny no less for it.

Ali could still remember the first time she'd worn lipstick home in her freshman year of college. Gladys Demato had assured her the peachy shade suited her. Ali's mother had dragged her to the bathroom sink on sight and tried to scrub it off.

She didn't hate her mother. Really. But honest to God, sometimes it was very, *very* difficult to love her. Maybe if she hadn't been forced to wear ill-fitting clothes and plait her hair until she'd made it out of the house and into college, into *freedom*, she wouldn't be so resentful now. Maybe if her mother hadn't made everything fun seem like a sin, she wouldn't be so impetuously irresponsible during those insane moments when the urge to do the outrageous gripped her.

She hadn't done so very badly for herself, after all. She had a degree in marketing and business. Ran her own fashion boutique in the heart of one of Chicago's busiest shopping districts, which was doing well. Was even thinking of expanding into one of the better malls with another store. She owned a spacious two-bedroom condo, which she'd decorated herself, various coveted stocks and bonds, which would see her into to old age if managed responsibly, and her health. What did she need with one bitter old woman's outdated opinions and fiery sermons? It seemed the more successful she became, the more her mother scorned her efforts to succeed.

If she needed a dose of family, Gladys and Don Demato would be happy to oblige. It had been Franny's parents in the crowd, cheering her on when she graduated college with Franny. The Dematos who had gifted her with a maroon leather briefcase, her initials embossed in gold. The Dematos who had taken her out for a celebration dinner, and helped paint and paper her and Franny's first apartment—until Ali and Franny decided they both needed to live on their own, like real adults, instead of clinging to each other like two old-maid sisters.

It was Don Demato who went with her to sign loan papers, and agonized over which commercial property best suited her needs, and helped fill out thousands of small business forms. Gladys taught her how to cook, and made her feel like a second daughter at Christmas, birthdays, and Easter. Both, along with Franny, had shown up for the grand opening of Spangles, her clothing boutique. They'd been her support, her surrogate family, for going on thirteen years.

And dammit, whores did not drive a brand-spanking-new Park Avenue with plush leather interior.

Her mother lived just across town in one of the older neighborhoods, but had the woman ever once bothered to come and see the boutique? Had she ever once called to say she'd like to see where her only daughter lived? Or congratulate her on making something of herself? No. It was always Ali who made the first move. Ali, who sent her mother an invitation to the opening of her boutique and received no R.S.V.P. Ali, who called and gave her new phone number, but never received that first call. Ali, who sent money but could wait 'til hell froze over if she thought she was going to get a thank-you note. And up until their last quarrel three months ago, Ali who drove across town every couple of weeks or so, only to be greeted with insults and recriminations about her loose lifestyle.

It was Allison Geraldine MacPherson who didn't understand why her mother couldn't love her for the person she was instead of the person she was expected to be. But Ali MacPherson—she refused to give two good damns anymore.

Stubbing out her cigarette, she padded to the bathroom and began the nightly ritual of washing her face, applying a retinol-based cream to keep those nasty fine lines and grooves from wanting to appear on her forehead, the side of her mouth, and nose. She applied another special cream beneath her eyes, flossed, brushed, inspected her roots for new growth, then donned her favorite Victoria's Secret nightgown and crawled beneath the covers.

She was up at six, soaking over coffee while listening to an early morning newscast on the small TV in the kitchen. After wolfing down a glass of O.J. and a bowl of corn flakes she dressed in a chic lime green silk suit, the skirt several inches shorter than the sedate blue crepe she'd worn to dinner last evening. She liked her hair up during business hours for the most part, so twisted it into a chic chignon at the nape. It wouldn't take more than a little fluffing and some hairspray to wear it down tonight if she chose. For tonight's party she packed a simple short black knit dress and sling-back heels.

By seven-thirty she was at the boutique and had time to organize her thoughts and her day. Deanna, her one full-time employee, arrived at seven forty-five. Between the two of them Deanna waited on customers while Ali placed merchandise orders over the phone, to be followed up by computer-generated forms faxed and signed, checked on back orders, glanced over sales figures from the day before, unpacked new orders, and tagged new merchandise.

She ate lunch on the run, then settled in her office to go over the books. Franny suggested she get an accountant, but Ali preferred to keep her finger on the pulse of her business, thereby decreasing the risk of waking up one sunny morning to find her accountant had absconded with all her money to Bermuda where he would spend it on ugly flowered shirts and frothy drinks and sand umbrellas. She'd also been toying with the idea of a catalog. She alone decided which lines to buy from or pass on, and her sales over the years proved she was right to stick with the classic, chicly smart clothes that never went out of style, as opposed to going with the trends—which changed every year, the over-abundance of which had to be marked down and placed on a clearance rack. Clearance racks annoyed Ali. It was a sign the store's buyers weren't gauging customer interests as well as they should.

Spangles didn't just sell chicly smart clothes, but accessories as well. Scarves, tasteful costume jewelry, bangles, bracelets, stickpins, cocktail rings, and a variety of hair combs, bows, clips, stylish barrettes, belts, and an assortment of evening handbags. Last year Ali had added an evening gown collection. She'd thought about shoes, but decided there was too much competition in that area for a specialty store to make a profit that would be worth the extra headache.

Her most cherished duty was setting up the store displays. These she did after hours or on Sunday, after the shop closed at six p.m. She loved creating the illusion of romance and beauty with a stunning outfit and coordinating accessories. In her opinion women were feminine at heart and wanted to feel that way. Not that she didn't cater to the power executive—she did—but those displays required sleek, no-nonsense lines that said "look me in the eye when I speak to you", whereas the evening and casual wear needed that softer touch, the one that said "look all you want from head to toe then eat your heart out."

Women who didn't take pains with their appearance annoyed Ali worse than clearance racks. After all, a dress was a dress was a dress unless a woman fixed her hair and her face and took time to manicure her nails. Then, and only then, did that dress come to life as part of the whole package.

Later that afternoon a young girl came into the shop, browsing in the evening gown section. She was tall, with hazel eyes, coltish legs, and a natural profusion of curls that rioted to her shoulders. Ali walked over to where the girl was frowning over a spangle and satin number.

"Can I help you find something?"

"Yes," the girl sighed. "Got anything that gives the illusion I have breasts?"

Ali couldn't help but laugh. She knew the feeling. "Honey, you're talking to a woman who didn't develop breasts 'til she was almost eighteen. What's the occasion?"

"Prom."

"Ah. Big deal, huh?"

"The best-looking guy in school asked me."

"Wow."

"Okay, he only asked because his girlfriend came down with mono and can't go, but still…"

"You want to knock his eyeballs out."

"I want him to go blind."

"Then we'll just have to make sure he does." Ali took the gown the girl was fingering out of her hand and hung it back on the rack. "You don't want something that binds at the top and spreads out at the bottom with your body build. Too heavy. Curves like yours need only the merest help."

The girl looked down at herself. "What curves?"

"If you were wearing the right styles of clothes for your build, you'd know you had curves." Ali eyed the girl's oversized T-shirt and baggy jeans balefully. "They're in there. Somewhere. Let's try this stretchy black knit with the jeweled straps."

"But it's so…I don't know…plain."

"Sometimes less is more. The knit won't bind you around the breast area like heavy sequins. Go try it on. I promise you'll be amazed."

The awkward colt emerged out of the dressing room a few minutes later and stood before the mirror, her eyes wide with disbelief as she stared at herself. "It's…it's…wow! I really do have curves."

Ali tipped her head and opened her hands as if to say *viola*! "And breasts. How will you be wearing your hair?"

"Um, down?"

"With all these gorgeous curls? Please, my heart. I bet you try to straighten them too, don't you?" The girl's mouth worked in a circle. "Don't move. I'll be right back."

Ali went behind one of the glass counters, slid the panel open on the case, and selected three small one-inch gold clips. Standing behind the young woman who wanted to blind her date, she lifted three handfuls of hair, twisted, and clipped, leaving small cascades of curls trailing around her ears, neck and temples.

"Oh, my God!" she girl whispered almost reverently, placing a hand to her heart. "How did you do that?"

"It's nothing you can't do if you take the time to practice. I mean, look at all this lovely hair, and with natural curl most women would give their left ovary for. Wash, air dry, fluff, and clip. Heck, you're done while all the other girls are spending a fortune, not to mention a good portion of their day, sitting in a salon chair. And darling, you won't need a drop of hair spray to hold it in place or stay the curl. Soft hair is every man's dream. Have you ever seen a boy try to run his hands through a stiff wad of sprayed hair?"

"Well…no," the girl admitted.

"You want this guy to run his hands through your hair instead of his girlfriend's?"

"You cast spells, too?" Hazel eyes lit up at the thought. "Cool."

"No." Ali shook her head. "*You* cast the spell. Just by wearing the right clothes and the most flattering hairstyle. I know it's the trend, but those," she shivered visibly, pointing to the discarded clothing lying on the dressing room bench, "are not flattering in the least."

The colt shifted on her feet. "But everybody's wearing that style now."

"Yes, and everybody looks the same. Stand out. Be different. Get noticed in a crowd. Women are not made from a mold. Certain body builds require a certain type of cut. You aren't going to look good in the same outfit as a shorter, wider-hipped girl. You have to go with the flow of your body lines, the shape of your shoulders, hips, legs. Believe me, the sack dress is highly overrated even on the best of models. Not everybody is built like a square. Now, what's it going to be? The knit or the box?"

"The knit," the girl decided after a deep breath and one last glance in the mirror.

"Smart girl."

"What about jewelry?"

"You don't need much with that gown. A ribbon cameo choker—which I just happen to have in the case—along with a small black clutch, and black heels should round things out nicely. Not the fussy, glittery ones. Wrapped satin, I think. Tell you what," Ali said, walking back to the accessory case to extract the choker. "If your dad's eyes don't fall out on the floor when he gets a load of you, you can return the dress for a full refund."

The girl jerked a shoulder. "Aw, my dad doesn't notice things like that on me."

Ali felt almost like Franny must have when urging her to go with the new, the forbidden, the outrageous. God, what a rush! "So what have you got to lose, honeybun?"

"Okay. Deal."

"Great. Now, change out of the gown and I'll wrap it for you. You want the choker and the clips, too?"

"Sure, why not. Satin heels, you said?"

"Mmmm hmmm. And no wild earrings. Something plain and sedate." *I can't believe I just said that.*

Ali took the gown and the accompanying credit card when the girl handed them over the top of the louvered door. She placed the gown in layers of tissue, wrapping it carefully. When the girl came out dressed in her formerly drippy shirt and jeans, Ali had another one of her urges. Thankfully, this one wouldn't have her up pacing the floor at night. "If you can't get the hairstyle down pat after practicing, give me a ring. Here's my card."

"You really don't have to go to all this trouble," the girl mumbled self-consciously. But Ali glimpsed a strange light in the girl's eyes that said she was grateful.

"Oh yes, I really do." She put the choker and the clips in a small velvet box and snapped it shut, fitting it between the layers of tissue next to the gown. "I was you once. Only skinnier. You want to pay me back in kind, spread the word I'm a miracle worker. When's the prom?"

"Next Friday."

Ali slipped the wrapped box into a snazzy little shopping bag bearing her logo and handed it over the counter. "Let me know how it goes, huh? Maybe I can live vicariously through you."

"Yeah," the girl snorted. "Like you'd ever have a hard time getting a date."

"My last date made me open my own car door and sucked spaghetti off his plate."

The girl stared at her in horror. "No way!"

"Way. What's your name, honey?"

"Susan."

"Well, Susan, I'm Ali. Have a great time at the prom and be sure to keep a quarter between your knees."

"You sound like my dad."

"If he lets you out of the house in this dress I'll be amazed and delighted." Ali wagged her fingers as the girl pushed through the shop door, glancing one last time over her shoulder.

"Good show," Deanna remarked. "What are you going to do when her father comes charging through the door?"

"I'll do what every smart businesswoman does who's just transformed a duckling into a swan. Dive for cover."

Chapter Two

ᔕ

"Tell me why I agreed to come here again," Ali said as they climbed the steps to the main entrance of the swanky apartment building.

"We were discussing your mother," Franny reminded her wryly.

"Oh, yeah." Ali readjusted the thin straps on her dress in the mirrored door of the elevator.

"Relax." Franny gave her red locks one last puff job, punching the elevator button with a lacquered nail. "We look great. Penthouse," she told the older gentleman manning the elevator controls, leaning closer to whisper loudly. "My friend has a navel ring. You'd never know it to look at her, would you?"

"Franny!"

A fascinated gleam came into the man's eye as his gaze dropped to her stomach. Ali's hand curled into a fist at her side to keep from slapping Franny.

"Sounds painful," the porter remarked.

Franny wiggled an auburn eyebrow. "You should have heard her scream when she woke up and saw it."

"Franny, I swear, if you don't close your mouth you're going to need false teeth."

"She's a little touchy about it sometimes," Franny informed him.

"Here we are. Penthouse." The elderly man held the doors open with his gloved hand, winking as they stepped past him. "You ladies have a nice evening."

"Now you've done it." Franny told him, taking her by the arm so she couldn't bolt. "You've gone and said the 'N' word. It'll be on your head, mister, if my friend here does something tonight that is totally inappropriate for a woman her age."

"I want to go home."

"Too late for that, sugarbuns." Franny dragged her further down the hall to the double oak doors and rang the bell. "It's party time. John! You big hunk of architecture you. This is my friend, Ali. Lead us to the booze."

And so it went, Franny dragging Ali all around the art deco penthouse, introducing her. Music blared loudly from the entertainment center on the far wall. Drinks included everything from bottled water to bottled beer, champagne and mixed cocktails. People draped themselves on the furniture, snuggled into dark corners where recessed lighting didn't quite reach, and sat on the spiraling iron staircase leading to the second level, while others stood out on the balcony enjoying the late spring weather, talking, laughing, smoking, and smooching like teenagers. Those who'd had too much to drink danced like heathens in an area cleared of obstacles—writhing, groping, whispering.

During it all Ali's butt weathered more than its share of pinches. Her eyes were burning from the smoke, and her eardrums pounded against the inside of her brain from the punk rock blasting in surround sound. She took refuge in the kitchen, found it empty, and sighed gratefully. Setting her beer down, she flipped the paper towels hanging from the under-the-counter dispenser for no other reason than it was a peeve of hers to have to reach beneath the roll.

"Thank God," a throaty male voice said from behind her. "Someone else who realizes the importance of tearing off a paper towel from the front."

Ali turned, leaning a hip into the counter. The intruder was a good six feet tall, with tawny, gold hair and intellectual features. Hazel eyes regarded her from behind round, gold-rimmed glasses. A straight, aristocratic nose, strong, square jaw, and a killer mouth gave way to perfectly straight, white teeth. Broad shoulders, encased in a polo knit, tapered to a firm, trim waist. Pleated trousers and leather loafers completed the picture of casual wealth.

When he tipped his imported beer up and took a swallow, Ali couldn't help but notice his hands. Long fingers tipped with blunt nails. Clean nails. His grip was warm and firm as she took the hand he extended in introduction. "I don't believe we've met. Jordan Finch."

"Ali MacPherson."

"You're hiding out, right?" He chose the counter opposite her, lined with louvered doors, to lean against.

"And you just came in here to see if the paper towels were hanging correctly."

"Okay, *we're* hiding out," he corrected with a smile. "What now?"

She scooped up her own beer, and took a swig. "I have to tell you up front, I don't go in much for charming, good-looking men."

"You and every other woman under the age of thirty," he grunted. "Nowadays, if you don't have stringy hair, pierced eyebrows, and tongue studs that clack against your teeth, you can forget dating."

Stuffed shirt, she decided. Professionally and socially uptight. Stuffed, she could handle, possibly. Uptight—no way. But neither was she a fan of tongue studs and ringed eyebrows. "What do you say we get the painful part over with right off the bat?"

"As in?"

"As in we hide out in here and tell each other our bad habits so we won't be tempted to date, only to be disappointed later when those wretched little details unveil themselves. Or we could go back out there and mingle."

He considered the alternative. "You don't give a guy much choice, do you?"

"Your call." She crossed her arms, waiting. He'd bail. She was almost sure of it. "Look at it this way. We can date right here in the kitchen, forget the pretense, and walk away winners without the battle scars."

"I'll stay. But you go first."

"How gentlemanly of you. I smoke."

"Nasty habit, but not one I couldn't make myself get around," he countered. "There are worse things."

"Yes, but sometimes I flick my ashes into my plate instead of the ashtray."

"Now that's disgusting," he agreed.

"Okay, your turn."

He thought for a moment in silence, then said, "Every once in a while, when I'm at a stop light, I get the urge to hawk and spit out the window."

Ali waved away the thought. "That's not necessarily a bad habit. More of a guy thing."

"Not with my family. There's no hawking, spitting, or discussion of bodily functions allowed at the dinner table."

She grinned over that. "What more could a girl ask for?"

"Moving on. What other nasty habits do you have, Ali MacPherson?"

"I'm fidgety. I jiggle my foot a lot."

"I'd never have guessed." His gaze dropped to her feet, admiring the sling-backed heels, then the legs attached to them, right up to the hem of her short cocktail dress. "You look normal."

"Ah, but you see, that's the catch. I *look* normal, but underneath I'm not what I seem."

He raised a tawny eyebrow. "How far underneath?"

She hesitated for a moment, deciding she wasn't quite ready to shock him into running for his life. "We'll cover body parts later. Right now let's stick with habits."

"Okay." He crossed one loafer-clad foot over the other. "I squeeze the toothpaste tube from the middle."

"Naturally."

"Come on, admit it." A twinkle lit up those hazel eyes behind his glasses. "You've squeezed from the middle, you just don't tell anybody."

She tossed her head in denial. "Never."

His gaze roamed over her figure again, more heated than before. "Quick, tell me something really disgusting. I'm beginning to get hot under the collar."

"I love to say outrageous things at the wrong moment, just to shock people."

"Like what?"

"Like the time I looked up to find my date carefully trying to conceal the fact he was picking his nose at the dinner table. I asked him if he'd like to use my fork."

He put a hand to his stomach, wincing. "Sounds like a real winner. But I can top that. My last date flossed at the table and flicked goop from between her teeth on my face. I'm thinking of going celibate."

"Ah, sex. Now, there's where you really get into trouble. Swapping spit, bad breath, clammy hands."

"My hands are never clammy," he informed her. "And we've already established I don't make spit."

"Bad breath, then."

He lifted his bottle of imported beer, shifting to the other foot. "It would only take a moment to find out if my mouthwash really does all the things it claims on the label."

"No can do. I might enjoy kissing you only to find out later that you're secretly married."

"Divorced," he said in a clipped tone.

"Oooh, that's a sore spot, huh?" she noted wryly. "Okay, give it up. What'd you do, step out on her?"

He stiffened. "Maybe it wasn't my fault."

"Then why are you getting so defensive?"

"Because I don't consider professional commitment a flaw. It helped pay for the house she's currently residing in."

"Depends how you look at it. Were you living in the house with her, or just breezing in and out the door between meetings?"

A faint scowl marred his forehead. "When someone pays a quarter of a million dollars for a prime piece of property, he doesn't like to wait until it's convenient for me to develop it."

"You miss out on the fun in life when you stick your nose in blueprints every waking hour. But that's another good reason for us not to consider dating. You're a workaholic, obviously."

"And you pay the bills how?" He quirked a brow at her.

"I own a fashion boutique, put in my share of sixteen-hour days, but always, always, make time for a night out with friends. Think you might look at me when I'm talking to you, or would you rather I stripped naked so you can see the tattoo on my ass?"

He colored profusely, ripping his gaze from her legs to concentrate on finishing off his beer.

"Can't say I didn't warn you," she reminded him sweetly.

"Yeah. You did." He twisted at the waist to discard the bottle on the counter behind him.

"Cheer up, Finch. Now you can go home grateful you didn't make the mistake of asking out a loose broad like me." He really was too cute for words the way he searched the steel and glass kitchen for something, anything, to fix his eyes on.

"My mother warned me not to date fast girls."

"My mother warned me not to *be* a fast girl."

"How fast are you?" he hedged, shoving his hands into his trousers pockets.

"You'd have a hard time keeping up," she predicted smugly. It was true. He would. Jordan Finch was one of those "nice boys" who expected a lady to act like a lady at all times. He would be uncomfortable, perhaps even revolted to discover a woman her age had a navel ring.

"Then I shouldn't ask you out for next Friday," he surmised.

"No. You shouldn't." *But ask anyway.* "I don't, however, floss at the table," she added as he vacillated between voicing the invitation and ending the encounter with a drab nice-to-meet-you.

"What kind of tattoo?" he asked haltingly.

"Sorry. That's privileged information. Only men I go to bed with get to see it."

He paused to clear his throat. "So it's in a strategically hidden place."

"Not hidden," she corrected. "Just not flaunted for public scrutiny."

Franny chose that moment to swing through the kitchen door. "There you are! I've been looking all over for you. So what are you two kids doing in here?" She sidled up to Jordan Finch and stood admiring the view. "Is Ali responsible for those red cheeks, darling? And whatever she said about me isn't true." Then she turned to point a warning finger at Ali. "If he fires me, I'm coming after you."

Great. She'd been swapping sexual innuendo with Franny's new boss. "This…is your boss?"

Franny pursed her lips. "Didn't I introduce you two earlier?"

"No." Killing her would have to wait until later.

"I could have sworn I did," Franny insisted.

"Franny, repeat after me. I dragged my friend Ali to this party and forgot to introduce her to my boss, who now knows more than he'd like to about certain aspects of my friend's personality."

Franny sucked in a breath, darting surprised green eyes at Jordan. "She told you about the navel ring?"

"Franny!"

"Navel ring?" he almost choked on the words. "No. No, she didn't."

"Uh-oh." Franny ducked her head and did an about-face, practically running for the door. Both Ali and Jordan stared at the swinging panel until it clumped to a stop.

His expression was almost comical. "She made that up just to see what I would say. She does that a lot at work."

"And yet you continue to pay her a salary." Ali wasn't worried that he could see the ring's circular outline through her dress. She had an innie bellybutton, which perfectly caverned and camouflaged what outies couldn't.

"You could give me your number," he said finally.

Her heart did a strange flip-flop in her chest. "I warned you I have moments of insanity, right? I don't want to be responsible for you having a heart attack and plunging facefirst into your soup."

"I'll be careful not to order soup on the first date," he assured her.

"Are you sure you really want to do this, Finch?" she asked pulling a tube of lipstick from her clutch purse.

"No, MacPherson. I'm not." He moved closer, watching over her shoulder as she snapped a paper towel from the rack and wrote her number across the quilted surface in flaming red.

She got a whiff of his aftershave. Expensive, woodsy, stimulating. Very GQ, as Franny would say. "There's just one more thing."

"What's that?"

"I'm a sucker for Brut."

"Brut?" he echoed blankly.

"Yeah, you know, the cheap stuff. Comes in a green bottle. It's a quirk. You can't get it at the better department stores. Try the drug store. Last chance, Finch," she warned turning to face him, dangling the paper towel from matching red-tipped fingers.

"I have one request," he said, watching her mouth.

"Shoot."

"Stick out your tongue."

She grinned, complied, rolling it upward so he could see the underside as well. "No studs. No holes where studs have been. Whatever else I am, I'm not a sadist."

He tugged the towel from her fingers. "Will this lipstick smudge if I fold it?"

"I guess you'll find out if you get home and can't read the number, huh?" *I wonder what he'd do if I wrapped my arms around his neck and kissed that adorably sexy mouth.* "Finch."

"Mmm?" He was still studying the numbers on the paper towel.

"I'm getting one of those insane urges. You'd better step back. It involves groping." He did, rather quickly if she did say so, more startled than surprised.

"Well." He checked his watch. "It's getting late. I'd better get home."

"Hey, Finch," she called out as he pushed through the kitchen door. He turned back, pausing. "Maybe you'd better not mention anything about this to Franny just yet. I promise, she'll make your life hell."

"Yeah. Good idea."

Ali was satisfied that Jordan Finch would think about her on the drive home. He'd wonder what her tattoo looked like. Try to decide if she really did have a navel ring. Then probably talk himself into not calling. But he *would* think about her.

* * * * *

"So, how'd it go with you and Jordan?" Franny asked once they were in the car and on the way back to the boutique.

"I'm not speaking to you."

"Aw, come on, Ali. I'm sorry I let it slip out about the navel ring."

Ali knew better. "No you're not."

"Okay, I'm not. But the suspense is killing me. What did you two talk about?"

"Nothing."

"Nothing?"

"Dating in general. Very boring."

"Please," Franny snorted. "Staring at the man is a national pastime. Don't even try to convince me you didn't find him attractive."

"I won't, because I'm not speaking to you."

"Fine. I'll make up my own fantasies."

"You usually do."

* * * * *

It was never a good idea to date your secretary's best friend. Jordan Finch had himself convinced of that all the way up until Thursday of the following week. The woman had a tattoo, for Christ's sake. She admitted to being moralistically liberated, carefree, sleeping around, and he was more than a little terrified if he went out with her he would discover she did, in truth, sport a navel ring.

He had an image to uphold in the community. Not to mention his teenage daughter was at that very impressionable age. Ali MacPherson was just the kind of woman he didn't want his baby girl associating with.

So why was he staring out the window, brooding over whether or not to call her for the hundredth time this week? Why had he committed her number to memory for fear the flaming red lipstick would indeed smear if he folded the paper towel she'd written it on? Why did he wonder what the tattoo on her ass looked like? How big it was? Where, exactly, it was permanently etched?

"Jordan?" Franny poked her head around the door of his office. "Line two."

He swiveled in his chair to pick up the phone, punching the blinking light, grateful to have something to take his mind off Ali-outrageous-MacPhereson.

"Hi, Daddy."

"Hi, baby. What's up?"

"Listen, I've been experimenting with this new hairstyle for tomorrow night and I just can't get it right. The woman at the shop where I bought my dress—"

"You mean the dress I'm not allowed to see until prom night?"

"Daddy. It's a surprise. Anyway, she's the one who showed me what to do with my hair and offered to give me a hand. I'm going to stop by her shop after school and have her show me again, okay?"

"What's wrong with your hair the way it is?"

"It's little girl hair," she complained.

"You are a little girl," he grumbled.

"Daddy, I'm fifteen, practically a grown woman."

Jordan pinched his nose between thumb and forefinger. He didn't want to be reminded his little girl was growing up, starting to date. Oh, God, the dating thing. Could anything be more tortuous than watching some punk kid drive away in a souped-up hot rod with his innocent, virginal daughter?

He didn't bitch about her wearing the baggy clothes that were so trendy these days because they hid the curves Susan was starting to develop. Damn Gloria anyway! She should be here to smooth Susan through this difficult transition into adulthood, not off gallivanting around Europe. But she wasn't here to do those things. There was only him to deal with the highs and lows of hormonal cataclysm.

"I like your hair down," he said.

"I'm not going to the prom with you," she pointed out. "I'm going with Randy Peters."

The name alone made him break out into a sweat. Randy Peters. *Sounds like a fucking machine in Reeboks.*

"I want to look sophisticated," she pouted. "Please don't make a big deal out of this. It's important that I make a good impression. He only asked me to the prom anyway because his girlfriend has mono, and darn it, I'm not going to be left to stand in a corner all night."

It suddenly became very hot in his office. *Mono. Jesus.* "I'd advise against kissing a boy who gave his girlfriend mono."

"He didn't give it to her. She got it from some other boy. Randy doesn't have mono."

He has a penis, that's all I'm concerned with at the moment.

"Daddy, please," she used that little girl tone that always twisted his insides. "There's nothing worse than being a wallflower at a school dance. Nothing."

"How can you be a wallflower if you have a date?"

"Forget it," she said sullenly. "You don't understand."

"Honey, I'm trying to understand. This…Randy," he forced himself to say the name, "asked you to the prom. Why would he ask if he were going to dump you the minute you hit the door?"

"Because he's only going with me to save face and once he gets there he'll spend most of his time at the punch bowl bragging to his friends how he didn't have to go stud."

"The correct term is stag. Never mind. Tell him to take a hike."

"I can't believe you just said that! He's the cutest guy in school!"

"Fine. If he's so cute he won't have any trouble getting another date on last minute notice."

"I've already bought my dress!"

"Take it back."

"No!"

"Dammit, Susan, have a little self-respect. The kid's a punk. He's using you."

"I know that, Daddy. That's why I want him to eat his heart out when he sees me dressed up. I mean, at first I was thrilled he'd asked me, but later I figured out he only asked because his girlfriend was sick and I was the only girl available on short notice, like you said. And you know what? He *should* have asked me because he wanted to go with me. And after tomorrow night he *will* ask me out, I bet, and *then* I'm going to tell him to take a hike."

"Well, *that's* very grown-up." He scrubbed a hand over his face.

"Yeah, but it sure will be a hoot to watch his face when he finds out I knew his strategy all along."

Women. "Okay. Whatever. I'll see you when I get home."

"I love you, Daddy."

"I love you too, baby." Jordan hung up the phone with considerable ease, then rammed the point of his pencil through the blotter on his desk, left it quivering there, and buried his face in his hands, defeated. "I hate it when she does that."

Chapter Three

❧

"Hey, Susan!" Ali greeted her with open arms. "How's it going?"

"Terrible. I can't get this hairstyle down. You think you could help me? Show me how you twisted my hair up?"

"Sure. Come on in the back and we'll practice."

They spent an hour in front of the mirror with Ali showing Susan step-by-step how to lift and clip the thick stands of hair, then left her to practice alone while she made a few phone calls and waited on a few customers.

"I think I've got it now," Susan beamed at Ali when she pulled aside the curtain to check on her progress. "How does it look?" She turned side to side to give Ali a full view.

"Very nice. See, it wasn't all that hard after all."

"Thanks, Ali." Susan jumped up from her stool in front of the vanity table to hug her around the waist. "You're a lifesaver."

"Well, I wouldn't go that far. What do your dad and mom think about the dress?"

"I don't have a mom." Her arms dropped away, covering the hurt with a brilliant smile. "It's just me and Dad. He hasn't seen it yet."

"Oh boy."

"He's kind of old-fashioned, you know? I didn't want him to have the chance to make me bring it back. Once it's on, well…" she help up defenseless hands.

"Right. Stun him into silence, then beat a trail to the door."

"That's the plan," Susan admitted, grinning impishly.

"Then I guess all that's left to do is wish you luck."

"Thanks. I better get home and start dinner or else Dad will try to cook."

"Ali," Deanna said as they passed the cash register on the way to the front door. "Telephone."

"Have a good time," Ali called after Susan, who acknowledged with a wave and a smile, then took the phone from Deanna's hand.

"Ali?" Jordan Finch's deep masculine tone sent a shiver down her spine.

"Well, well. I was beginning to think that stay-on lipstick faded after all. I was going to return it and demand my money back."

"I didn't realize this was your work number."

"I don't give out my home number to just anybody, even gorgeous developers."

"Look, uh, about tomorrow night—"

"Change your mind, Finch?"

"No. It's just that my daughter has a date tomorrow night and I need to see her off first."

"You have a daughter? I knew you didn't tell me everything."

"You asked for faults, not dependents."

"True. No problem. Would it be better if I picked you up?" Oh, that one really threw him. He was probably reaching for the Tums. "What's the matter, Finch? Never had a woman pick you up for a date before?"

"Uh, actually, no."

"Try it. You might like it. Besides, it'll save time. I promise to have you home before midnight. How old is your daughter?"

"Fifteen going on twenty-five."

"I remember fifteen. I hated that age."

"So do I. Okay, I guess we can meet here. Eight o'clock sound fine?"

"Eight it is." She scribbled down the address as he rattled it off, noting it was in a better part of town.

"I'm sorry, I'll only have time for dinner," he apologized. "We can make it another night if you'd rather. I forgot all about this prom business when I suggested Friday."

"Her first prom?" Ali asked.

"That's the one. She's driving me crazy with wanting to change her hair, and if I tell you this kid's name she's going out with you probably won't believe me."

"Try me, anyway."

"Randy Peters."

Ali burst out laughing. The images that must leap into his head.

"Why did I know you'd think that was hilarious?" he asked tightly.

"Because it is. I mean…*Randy Peters*. Lord, my mother would be in a swoon. You probably aren't far from one yourself, are you, Finch?" She could hear him clearing his throat to cover the resulting silence. "Are you absolutely sure you want to chance an evening with me, Finch?"

"No. But my daughter informed me just this afternoon there's nothing worse than being a wallflower at the prom. If she can take on a guy who asked her out on the rebound, I think I can get through an evening with you in one piece."

"We'll see."

He said nothing. She said nothing. They endured the silent pause, neither wanting to sever the connection.

"I just thought of something, Finch."

"What's that?"

"I might get lost on the way to your place. Maybe you should give me your number in case I make a wrong turn."

He seemed a little hesitant to give her his home number when all he had was her business phone. But after a moment he capitulated. "Well, I'll see you tomorrow night, then."

"You certainly will, Finch. And don't give your daughter too hard a time about her hair or her makeup or *Randy Peters*. Let her enjoy the moment."

"Good bye, Ali."

"Good bye, Finch."

* * * * *

Jordan paced the foyer, taking in deep breaths, letting them out, clenching his hands, unclenching them. Susan had forbidden him even so much as a peek at the dress she had bought for tonight's prom. He told himself she was a sensible girl. She wouldn't come down those stairs dressed in a short sequined little number that left her long, coltish legs exposed to the lascivious gaze of Randy Peters. Who did the little snot-nosed bastard think he was anyway, asking Susan out on the rebound?

He started up the stairs to tell her to forget about the whole thing, faltered, and sat down on the bottom step. This was her first prom. Her first big night out in eveningwear and she was so excited she could barely eat dinner. She'd been upstairs primping and powdering and running the hot water heater down to empty for the last two hours. She and her friends had spent every night this week up in her room doing each other's faces, trying out shoes, combs and clips in their hair, tromping down the steps to get his unbiased male opinion, which he had wisely kept vague and unopinionated.

There was no Gloria to guide her through the preparation, give her the girl-to-girl talk all mothers give their daughters before a night of temptation. Boys would be boys, they would no doubt sneak in the white liquors with which to spike the punch, maybe even take a nip or two straight from the bottle before exiting the car. He'd feel much better about tonight if Randy had rented a limo instead of driving.

Randy would try to put his hand on Susan's thigh, run it up her dress, and if she was lucky the prick would pull a condom out of his pocket very discreetly.

"Oh God," he groaned, letting his forehead bump the wall. *Please just let her come home safe and intact.*

Car lights winking through the side panes of the front door caught his attention. Randy was early. It was only seven-thirty. He wasn't supposed to pick Susan up for another fifteen minutes. He had to will himself to rise from the step and answer the door, when what he really wanted to do was turn out all the lights in the house and pretend no one was home.

"Ali."

"Hiya, Finch."

"You're…early."

"Well, I thought it might take me longer to get across town than it did. On the bright side, I didn't get lost." She was wearing a low cut stretchy lavender lace dress with matching jacket that hugged her curves. The lace would have been see-through except for the lavender-colored lining. Her golden hair was up in a French twist, with lazy wisps kissing her cheekbones and nape.

"Are you going to invite me in or make me stand out on the stoop?"

"What? Oh, of course. Come in." Jordan stepped back to let her pass, getting a whiff of soft perfume as she walked by.

"Daddy, are you ready?" Susan called from the top of the stairs.

He slammed the door when he didn't mean to. "Jesus," he muttered. "Sure honey, come on down. I'm ready."

Susan began slowly descending the stairs, trailing one hand along the rich walnut railing. His breath caught in his throat when he saw the black evening gown that made her look just like she'd wanted, all grown-up. Her hair was a riot of curls pinned up in the back. Black pumps peeped from beneath the hem of the gown as she took each step.

He felt like someone had just hit him in the chest with an iron mallet, aware Ali was watching his face, taking in his expression. Then she turned to look at Susan and both broke into bright smiles.

"Ali!"

"Susan!"

Susan scurried the rest of the way down the stairs. Ali met her halfway. They joined hands. What the hell?

"Turn around, let me see!"

"What are you doing here? How did you know where I lived?"

"I've got a hot date with your dad. He said he had a daughter who was going to her first prom tonight, but I had no idea it was you. Oh my God, you're stunning. Isn't she beautiful, Finch?"

It took Ali's direct question to jump-start his heart. "Wait just a damn minute, here. Is this some kind of joke? You two know each other?"

"Ali is the woman who sold me the dress."

"And I'll have a few things to say on that subject, later." He glared at Ali, who quickly stepped back, but was still smiling as she floated toward the door to look out the sidelight.

"Don't you like it?" Susan asked, her bottom lip beginning to tremble.

What the hell was he supposed to say? *No, I hate it. Take it off! It makes you look like a woman and not my little girl. Men will stare. They'll want to do nasty, wicked things to your body.* "Susan…"

"Of course he likes it, honey," Ali said over her shoulder. "He's just a little shocked to discover you grew up when he wasn't looking."

"Really? Daddy?"

Susan looked up at him with his own hazel eyes and what could he do? "All the guys will be gnashing their teeth." He took Susan's face in his hands, mindful of her makeup, which, he had to admit, was lightly applied. "You can't know how utterly exquisite you look and how it breaks my heart to admit it."

"Oh, Daddy, don't. You'll make me cry and I'll ruin my makeup."

"Heads up." Ali had to whisk a tear from her own eye at the intimate family moment. "Here comes the stud. Wow, Suz," she fanned herself, "he's bitchin'."

The doorbell rang before Jordan could call Ali on her language in front of Susan. Susan tittered nervously by the foot of the steps. "Daddy, answer the door."

"Do I have to?"

"Yes!" Both females insisted at the same time.

"Mr. Finch. Hey. I'm Randy Peters." The boy stuck out his hand, pumping Jordan's firmly.

Jordan wanted to growl but settled for saying hello instead.

"Susan?" Randy wasn't unaffected as he stared at the young lady across the foyer. "Is that you in that dress?"

Jordan was left to cope with his railing emotions while Randy pinned a corsage on Susan's breast, with Ali's helpful instructions, of course.

All too soon Susan tiptoed to kiss him on the cheek. "What do you think? One a.m.?"

"I think eleven. I'm willing to negotiate to twelve. On the dot," he called after the departing couple. "No drinking and driving."

"No offense, Finch, but I think the whole neighborhood will think twice before getting behind the wheel intoxicated tonight."

Jordan knew a small moment of satisfaction when she jumped as he slammed the door and rounded on her. "How could you sell her a dress like that...that piece of clingy material?"

"It covers her from head to toe, practically. She could have done much worse."

"She's just a child! She's too young to be wearing something so alluring."

"She's not a child, Finch. She's a young woman approaching adulthood. I only suggested the gown when she told me what she was looking for. I didn't make her buy it."

"You could have shown her something more along the lines of what a young girl should wear."

"I could have, but that wasn't what Susan wanted. Whether you like it or not, she wants to be noticed by boys her own age. And excuse me, but wasn't that your credit card she used to pay for 'that piece of material'? Or are they giving away American Express to fifteen-year-olds these days?"

"I trusted her."

"You're angry with her for buying the dress, but you're blaming me for selling it to her. If she hadn't bought it from me, she would have bought it from another store."

"So you said whatever it took to make a sale."

"I'm honest with my customers. If something doesn't look good on them, I tell them. That gown looks damn good on Susan. If you were so worried about what kind of dress she was going to buy, you should have been there with her to pick it out." She held up a hand, took a breath, and started for the door. "I think I'd better go before I give in to the urge to tell you what a complete ass you are."

He moved to block her exit. "Oh please do. You haven't bothered to curb your tongue yet."

"You know what amazes me about parents like you, Finch? You think just because you don't want your daughter to grow up, she won't. Well, I'll give you a piece of unsolicited advice. Susan is on the verge of discovery, about herself, boys, sex, everything. If you try to put up walls and forbid her to peek over them she's going to dive in headfirst, with or without your permission."

"Like you?" He squeezed his eyes shut. "I'm sorry. That was uncalled for."

"Yes, it was," she agreed in an even voice. "But I kind of feel sorry for you, so I'm going to give you a break. You and my mother should compare notes some time. Maybe between the two of you, you can come up with some kind of time warp device that keeps teenage daughters from feeling, thinking, growing up, or developing breasts."

He almost smiled, then rubbed a hand across the back of his neck. "She did look good, didn't she?"

"It isn't my place to tell you how to raise your daughter. But from what I can see you're doing a fine job. Susan's a wonderful girl. Do you have any idea how much it meant to her when you told her she looked exquisite?"

He rubbed the center of his chest. "I know how it made me feel. Like I was giving her permission to fornicate."

Ali was wise enough to let that remark pass. "Tell me, Finch, how does Susan get around town?"

"She takes the bus."

"You trust her to roam around the city of Chicago with the crime rate like it is, and use your credit card, but you don't trust her to handle herself with a high school boy? Doesn't say much about your faith in her does it?" She snapped open her purse to extract a roll of antacids. "I told you it was a bad idea to ask me out. Tums?"

"You purposely arrived early so you could watch me suffer."

"And they say men aren't aware of the undercurrents around them unless it involves sex. I thought there for a minute you were going to throw her in the closet and lock the door."

"I was thinking about it," he muttered.

"There's just one tiny detail you forgot, Daddy." She angled her chin to the pecan entry table where his Nikon camera sat.

"Great. I forgot all about getting their picture."

"I would have said you were speechless with horror, but you covered for it nicely toward the end. Don't worry, they'll fleece you on the price of the portraits taken at the dance. Should I go home and eat a bowl of Frosted Flakes, or are we still on for dinner?"

"Only if you don't tell the waiter the food is bitchin'."

"Cross my heart." She performed the motion.

Jordan elected to drive and take his car. He wasn't comfortable with letting a woman chauffer him around. He held the passenger door for her 'til she was tucked into the seat and got another whiff of perfume for his trouble. The first red light they came to she glanced at him slyly from beneath her lashes, as if she expected him to spit out the window. It became sort of a silent game between them, she looking straight ahead or at the console until they came to the next light. Then she'd slide him a sidelong glance. He would look at the window, back to her, then shake his head and laugh when the light turned green.

When they reached the restaurant he rounded the front end of the Lincoln and opened the door for her. She didn't seem to mind that his fingers stayed in direct contact with the small of her back as he ushered her through the doors of the restaurant. At the cozy table for two he held her chair and then seated himself, nodding his approval when the waiter suggested a wine menu.

When the waiter had poured the wine and retreated to give them time to peruse the menu he said, "You're right. I should have been there with Susan to pick out the dress. We should have made the time after work hours."

"Mmm." She toyed with the rim of her wine glass. "You work a lot, don't you?"

"That's what Gloria always told me," he said before he realized what he'd done.

"Uh, if I'm sticking my nose in where it doesn't belong, just say so. But Susan said she didn't have a mother. I take it your ex-wife isn't a part of her life since the divorce?"

"Gloria's touring Europe."

"Ah."

The waiter reappeared, took their order, then melted away to fulfill their every wish. Jordan didn't want to get into the logistics of his divorce with this woman on the first date. Neither did he want to admit he felt like a failure for neglecting his wife—as Gloria had put it—to the point she not only dumped him, but decided he could play mommy for a while and see how he liked being a single parent. He'd wanted to kill her for doing such an insensitive thing to their only child, yet he loved having his daughter all to himself. If Gloria could just pack up and leave that way, without a thought to Susan's well-being, she could damn well stay in Europe. He had already filed for sole custody on the grounds of desertion. And he was pretty sure Susan wanted to stay with him permanently. Her remark to Ali about not having a mother proved as much, didn't it?

He decided to change the subject to something that didn't include his personal life. "So, how do like being in business for yourself?"

"Quarterly taxes make me crazy. Otherwise, I love it. Franny keeps telling me to get an accountant, but I have nightmares about financing some bean counter's vacation for the rest of my life."

"Franny told me your shop is quite a success. Your parents must be very proud."

"Please, you wound me. Boutique. My father's dead. Died when I was three. My mother's never set foot in the place so I wouldn't have any idea if she's proud or not."

"She lives out of town?"

"Just across town," she corrected.

"I don't understand."

She flashed him a brilliant smile and said, "Finch, darling, don't you know a woman like myself could never achieve success of this kind without the backing of a benevolent protector?" Perhaps he didn't answer fast enough because she went on to say, "Which translates to: party girl has got herself a horny old bastard in the wings." But the edges of her smile held the briefest glimpse of bitterness.

"She doesn't really think that," he said with certainty.

"Doesn't she?" she murmured, turning to smile at the waiter as he set their food in front of him.

Jordan enjoyed a thick steak with steamed vegetables while Ali had grilled lemon-pepper chicken and asparagus tips smothered in butter sauce. Over dinner she told him how Franny and she had met at college and became fast friends, talked about the Dematos like they were her family instead of the mother she said lived across town, rambled on more about her boutique and that she was considering a catalogue, and expanding and hiring a part-time worker for the summer. He told her about his latest project downtown. How the developer he'd bought out had recommended him to all his former clients and now he had more work than he could handle. And how easily Susan seemed to have acclimated since the move from Charleston.

They lingered over chocolate mousse and coffee afterward, neither in a hurry to call an end to the evening. Although Jordan kept a check on his watch as the hours passed just to be sure he wasn't enjoying himself too much. If Ali noticed, she didn't torture him with it by accusing him of being an anxious father.

"What do you think Susan and her date are doing about now?" he asked.

"I wouldn't have the vaguest idea." She snapped open her purse. "I've never been to a prom."

"Never?"

"Never."

He heard a familiar pop. A whirring sound made his heartbeat accelerate, and he thought, *she wouldn't.*

When her hands appeared above the tabletop once more, a thin string of floss was stretched tightly between her fingertips, at the ready. "Oh, lighten up, Finch. It was a joke. But you should see your face."

He took in a calming breath while she lit a cigarette instead, mahogany eyes twinkling merrily at his reaction. His heart hadn't beaten so hard in the last two years as it had in the last two hours. Part of that was Susan's fault, naturally. But the rest…

"Very funny." In contrast to the terror of floss the cigarette smoke didn't bother him at all.

"What do you think?" she asked, holding the slim taper over her plate, finger poised to tap the ashes into the remaining butter sauce. "Should I go for it?"

"Be wild. Use the ashtray."

She grinned, flipping the ashes into the heavy squared glass he nudged toward her. "You're catching on, Finch."

He propped folded arms on the table and leaned forward. "Do you think you could call me Jordan every once in a while?"

She settled back in her chair, dragged on the cigarette, blew a stream of smoke upward. "I think I like Finch better."

"Why?"

"It's sort of stuffy and correct, like you."

"And is your real name Ali, or is that a nickname?"

"Technically, it's Allison. But if you call me that I'll have to rip your throat out."

"Oooh, sore spot. Talk about stuffy."

"By God, I think you might just be able to keep up with me after all, Finch."

"Mrs. Robbins, my second grade teacher, told me I was a quick learner and an overachiever."

"You knew what overachiever meant in the second grade, huh?"

He shrugged sheepishly. "I looked it up in the dictionary when I got home."

"You must have been looking for a long time. That word wasn't in the dictionary way back when. Heck, it's not in the dictionary now."

"Okay, so I looked it up in two parts. Same thing."

"You rascal."

Jordan couldn't remember when he'd last enjoyed a woman's company so much. He and Gloria had never just sat across the table from each other tossing witty banter or making jokes or simply…talking. Granted, Ali had given him a few scary moments with the floss and the ashtray, but all in all it was a heart-stopping evening. When they reached his house he opened the car door for her and walked her to her bronze-colored Park Avenue, checking his watch once again.

"Do you want me to stay and hold your hand 'til she gets home?" Ali asked.

Yes. "My college diploma says I'm an adult and can handle it. I'm sure you have an early morning."

"I do, but you really are nervous. I mean, who knows what kind of tricks *Randy Peters* has up his tuxedo pants leg."

He couldn't help but cringe when she purred the boy's name that way. Knee-jerk reaction. They were standing less than a foot apart, she with her back to the driver's door of her car. He moved closer, slipping his arm about her lacy waist to bring her closer and lowered his mouth to hers. "I hope it's nothing like this."

She tasted like wine, butter sauce, and chocolate. He could still smell her perfume drifting up from strategic points along her slim throat. She couldn't be a heavy smoker because she neither tasted of nor carried the odor associated with a heavier habit. Her body was warm and lusciously curved into his chest, her lips soft and inviting. He kept his hands firmly on her waist, tamping down hard on the urge to deepen the kiss, use his tongue, draw hers into his mouth.

When he drew back her lashes fluttered upward. She simply stared at him for the space of a half dozen heartbeats while he let himself appreciate the feel of her, the turn of her jaw, the slightly tipped nose and deep-set brown eyes fanned with thick lashes. Such a wide, generous mouth, made for kissing. A mouth that made a man ache with want.

And that's what made him drop his hands, take a step back. The want he felt stirring in his groin. He wasn't at all sure Ali MacPherson was the kind of woman he should get involved with. His twelve- to sixteen-hour days were filled with endless accounting projections, architecture drafts, scale models, construction meetings, and deadlines. Then there was Susan, so impressionable at the tender age of fifteen. He needed to spend what free time he had with his daughter.

"Well," she blew out a breath, bumping backward against the smooth lacquer finish of the car. "I hope, for your sake, that's all Randy Peters has in mind."

"Do you have a comeback for everything?"

"No, but I do have a question. What kind of cologne is that you're wearing?"

"I have no idea. I just grabbed it off the shelf."

"Okay. Well, I guess I'd better scoot. You probably won't want witnesses if Susan arrives home with a hair out of place. Please tell her I hope she had a wonderful time."

"I will." He held the door for her after she'd unlocked it, cradling his wrists over the top while she slid into the seat, adjusted the skirt of her dress higher up on her thighs and stabbed the key into the ignition.

"Finch?" She turned to look up at him. "Would I pass muster at a dinner party in Charleston?"

He sighed heavily, unsure how to answer the unspoken question buried beneath sarcasm. "Cherries Jubilee couldn't hold a candle to you." He closed the door, careful to first check and see that her hands were clear of the jamb. She smiled, waved, then backed out of the drive, leaving him to watch until her break lights turned the corner at the end of the street.

Chapter Four

ဢာ

Randy Peters' car pulled up to the curb beneath the giant oak at precisely 11:55 p.m. Jordan saw the headlights go dark through the window, where he'd been standing in anticipation, for the last fifteen minutes — that is, when he wasn't pacing the thick Oriental carpet in front of the fireplace. The oak's thickly twined limbs, ripe with spring leaves, blocked the thin rays of light from the street lamp anchored in a neighbor's yard from infiltrating the interior of the darkened Honda Civic Randy drove.

The minutes passed like years as he waited for Susan to exit the car. He liked to think Randy was asking Susan out, as she'd predicted, and even now she was telling the little horny toad to bug off. But as the years stretched into eons he found that particular fantasy harder and harder to maintain.

It was never like this before, when Susan went out with a group of her friends or to mixed parties. She'd never had what one might refer to as a steady boyfriend. Did kids go steady anymore?

Five minutes passed. He could feel gray hair starting to take root on his skull.

Just yesterday he'd been pacing the waiting room at the hospital in Charleston, feeling this same way. Then suddenly she was clutching at his pants leg to pull herself up at eight months. Running on stubby legs to greet him at the door when she was two. Stubby legs that had grown into the long legs of a colt. He remembered the time she'd thrown squash in his face while learning to eat with a spoon. How she'd cried the first day of school, *Daddy, I don't wanna.*

Ten minutes, and his chest started to ache.

Chicken pox at eight. *Mommy says not to scratch, honey. Mommy don't itch like I do.*

School pictures with her front teeth missing. *I hope the tooth fairy has lots of money, 'cause some of the other kids at school lost their teeth, too.*

Dance lessons and recitals.

Discovering there wasn't really a Santa Claus. Tears in her hazel eyes as she'd wailed, *And don't tell me there's not an Easter Bunny, either!*

Gloria claimed he was never there, yet the memories invaded his mind so clearly.

The first time Susan had worn lipstick. *Kiss me, Daddy, and see what I taste like.*

Fifteen slow, agonizing minutes, and it hurt to breathe.

Fifteen years old, with her mother's curls and his eyes. Mannerisms she'd inherited from both him and Gloria. And what was she doing with those lips they'd bestowed on her in the womb? Kissing Randy Peters in the front seat of his Honda.

On an intellectual level he had to consider that perhaps Ali was right, he didn't want to see his that little girl was growing up. On the brink of discovery, she'd said.

More like Randy Peters on the brink of discovering *Susan couldn't possibly have worn a bra beneath that dress.*

His brain sizzling, Jordan strode into the foyer. His fingers attacked the porch light switch, ruthlessly flipping the helpless knob several times. Something Gloria's parents had done a time or two when they stood in the driveway too long or lingered in his Chevy.

"Susan!" he roared off the front steps at the same time the passenger door of the Honda swung open.

"For heaven's sake, Daddy." She lifted the hem of her dress and hurried across the lawn. "Are you trying to wake the whole neighborhood?"

"It doesn't take twenty minutes to tell a boy you never want to see him again."

"Oh, Daddy, really." She skipped past him into the house, a glow in her eyes that hadn't been there before she'd left.

Jordan tried to act normal, closing the front door, shoving his hands into his trouser pockets. "What does that mean, 'oh, Daddy, really'?" He hated himself for checking out her chest area to determine if any sweaty paw prints had been left behind.

"Aren't you even going to ask me how the dance was?"

"How was the dance?"

"Amazing!" She twirled in a circle, arms flung out. "Five different guys asked me to slow dance and Randy told them to beat it, I was his date. Can you believe it?"

Five. Five Randy Peters' manhandling his daughter. *Get a grip, Finch.* "Did he ask you out again?"

"Better than that," she informed him dreamily, climbing the stairs in a dazed state.

"Yes or no will do just fine," he said, following her up the steps.

"He's breaking up with his girlfriend. You know, the one who has mono."

"Yeah, yeah, mono girl. Did he ask you out?"

"He said tonight he realized she was tying him down. Keeping him from exploring all his options."

"Options. What options? Susan, did he or didn't he ask you out again?"

"He hinted around about it. Said he'd call and we could maybe get together."

The horny little bastard would too, just to spite him. "Guys always say that." He followed her down the hall, into her room—a frilly girl's room with posters of teen heartthrobs, needlepoint pillows thrown across the lavender and pale green paisley bedspread. He tripped over a sandal left in the middle of the floor. "They always say they'll call, then they don't. It's a standard line. You told him to bug off, right? That you knew all along he was using you—"

"Well, I could hardly tell him to bug off when he didn't really come out and ask me for a date, could I? Besides, you just said boys never call when they say they will. Can I get undressed now?"

"And that's another thing." He pointed a finger at her even though her back was to him as she sat on the far side of the double bed, slipping off her shoes. "You didn't wear a bra beneath that dress, did you?"

"Daddy!" She crossed her arms over her chest, making him feel like a pervert. "That's so gross of you to check out my breasts!"

"I wasn't checking out your breasts," he snapped, pinning his gaze on the dressing table to his left, the marble top of which was cluttered with brushes and hair ribbons and makeup and colorful glass bottles. "It doesn't take a college degree to notice the dip in that dress doesn't allow for..."

He should be sitting in the living room of their Victorian-style house in Charleston, reading the paper while Gloria had this conversation with Susan, in private, where he could hear no evil. "I'm just saying a dress like that gives young boys ideas."

She turned to give him a sulky look over her shoulder. "Did you tell Ali her dress gave men ideas?"

"Ali is a grown woman, and we're not discussing Ali's dress, we're discussing yours."

Susan slung her shoes into the closet, rucking up her dress to stomp into the bathroom.

"Susan!"

The door slammed in his face. "I'm changing."

"We're not through talking about this. Hiding in the bathroom won't help."

"You said I looked exquisite," came the plaintive reply through the door.

Jesus. "And I meant it. But when I gave you my credit card I trusted you to pick out something suitable for your age. I know you're in a hurry to grow up, but believe me, honey, adulthood isn't all its cracked up to be. The way you dress now will determine the kind of reputation you acquire. Do you really want the boys at your school asking you out because of how you look and not because you're a bright, intelligent young woman with goals?"

"Yeah, well I didn't notice anybody beating a path to our door to ask out your brainy daughter." The door swung open and she strode past him in her gown, reaching for the padded hanger on the back of her desk chair. "Ali explained it all to me. How I was wearing the wrong type of clothes for my build."

"What's wrong with your build?"

"Nothing. That's the point. But you have to wear clothes that accent your body lines rather than what everyone else is wearing. I have a long torso and skinny legs. That means I shouldn't be wearing oversized shirts and sweaters or baggy jeans or sack dresses. I should be wearing tailored clothes with darts and tucks and fitted seams."

"Is that another way of saying you need a whole new wardrobe now that Ali MacPherson has so graciously enlightened you?"

She carefully draped the jeweled straps of the gown over the padding and hung it in her closet. A closet, he noted wryly, crammed full of the latest fashions. Or so he'd thought.

"I should be wearing clothes that fit. I don't have any lumps to hide or hips to downsize like some of the bigger girls. You should see Ali's shop, Dad. It's so awesome. Everything is so, I don't know, chic."

"From the look of the gown she sold you, I'd wager Ali's boutique is geared toward women, not teenagers."

Pivoting, she eyeballed him from beneath thick tawny eyebrows. "Do you know how many stores I scoured before finding a dress I liked that fit me? Six. Six, Daddy. The major department stores only sell what's trendy at the moment. All the gowns I tried on looked like crap."

"Be that as it may, there will be no more wardrobe changes unless I'm there to approve them."

"What?" The word fairly whooshed out of her mouth. "But that's so babyfied! I can pick out my own clothes!"

"I was speaking of formal wear."

"Oh, this is so unfair!"

"How fair was it of you to hide that gown from me until it was too late to make you take it back? If you were so sure I would approve, why didn't you show it to me as soon as you bought it?"

She sunk down on the end of the bed, slumping, wedging her hands between her knees. "I wanted to surprise you."

"You did. In spades." He crossed the room, dropping down beside her to put his arm around her. "I know it's hard not having Mom here to help you with these things."

She jerked a shoulder. "I don't need her."

"Don't say that, Susan. She's still your mother. She loves you."

"If she loves us so much, why'd she divorce us and run off to Europe?"

"Baby." He hugged her close. "Mom didn't divorce you, she divorced me. I thought you didn't mind so much, being stuck with just me for a while."

"I'm not going back to Charleston," she said heatedly. "I like it here. I heard her tell you she'd die before moving away from all her friends and her luncheon parties and society meetings. She thinks more of them than she does of us. Don't make me go back there, Daddy, please."

"Shhh, it's okay, don't cry." Jordan pulled her close, stroking her hair, which she'd taken down from its clips while in the bathroom. "I guess now's the time to tell you I petitioned the court for custody. But—" he added quickly when she leaned back to look at him with hope in her eyes, "you'll still have to spend time with your mom on occasion. Please don't ever think Mom doesn't love you as much as I do. She's just…going through something right now and needs some time to work it out."

The phrase "shock therapy" came to mind.

"Then I can stay with you? Live with you?"

"That's for a judge to decide, but I'll do my darnedest to see it happens. Of course, if any judge in Charleston got a load of that sexy-as-hell dress I let you traipse out of the house in tonight, he might have second thoughts." How low could a father stoop? Using emotional blackmail on his child.

"Did I really look sexy as hell?"

"Watch the mouth." He boffed her shoulder with his, sending her sideways into a spasm of giggling. "Go wash your face and get to bed. It's late."

"It's Friday. No school tomorrow."

"Oh." He'd forgotten the weekend was on them, mainly because he spent most of his Saturdays at the office trying to keep abreast of new developments, solving problems before they got out of hand.

* * * * *

"Spangles. Can I help you?"

"Ali? It's Susan."

"Susan! How was the big night out?"

"Oh God, Ali, it was unreal. Randy didn't let go of my arm the whole night. He was really knocked out over that dress."

Bingo. "It wasn't just the dress, it was the girl wearing the dress. So, I guess I won't be making a refund any time soon, huh? I almost had to give your dad oxygen after you left."

"Yeah, I got the lecture last night about wearing sexy-as-hell clothes and getting a rep. He thinks guys should ask me out because I carry a three-point-eight average. As if."

"Well, dads are like that, I guess. I'm so glad you had a good time."

"I wouldn't have if it weren't for you," Susan insisted.

"You give me too much credit, sweetie. It wasn't me Randy was staring at when the door opened. I hope he had agonizing wet dreams all night long, thinking about what he's been missing not noticing you before now."

"I couldn't believe it when I came down the stairs and there you were. How did you meet my dad?"

That was a story best edited for content. "My best friend, Franny, is his secretary. We met at a party she dragged me to last week."

"Franny's nice. She's such a cutup."

"Tell me about it."

"Hey, Dad," Susan called out, "I have Ali on the phone. Wanna talk to her?"

Nice move, Suz, don't give him a chance to say no.

"Hello, Ali."

"I wouldn't have expected a busy man like you to be at home in the middle of such a perfectly good working Saturday, Finch."

"I was just getting ready to head into the office to catch up on some paperwork. Are you at work?"

"Yes, doing the same, actually. Susan called to tell me about her big night. She's really psyched." Ali didn't want him under the impression she had called there hoping to talk to him.

"Yes, we're all waiting with baited breath for you-know-who to call. When Susan comes down from her cloud she'll realize boys habitually lie like dogs."

"Listen, I, um…" She tapped a nail against the smoked glass top of her desk. "Well, I just wanted to say I really enjoyed the evening." She wondered what he would say if she told him she'd wanted to strip him naked right there in his driveway.

"Yeah, about last night. Ali…"

She knew immediately what he was fumbling to say. For half the space of a second her heart paused in its beating, trembled, then lunged into rhythm again, this time at a faster pace. As always, when trying to cover insecurity or uncertainty, her tone instinctively brightened.

"Finch, darling, you don't have to make excuses for not jumping in to ask me out again. It was just dinner, no cause for alarm. You won't wake up at two a.m. to find me on your doorstep with crazed eyes."

"Ali, it isn't—"

"I'm sorry if Susan put you on the spot. I really have to go, I have customers waiting."

"Ali—"

She replaced the receiver. There were no customers in the shop waiting for her assistance. Ali sat at her desk, oblivious to the invoices and order forms and catalogue strewn about the desktop. Instead, she stared into space, uncomfortable with herself for the first time in a long while. It was true, she had enjoyed last night. More than she should have. And because she'd thought Jordan Finch—stuffy, correct, Southern-bred Jordan Finch—didn't have a chance of sneaking past her natural defenses—defenses that had been in place long before he came on the scene—she'd let down her guard.

She was unprepared for the jolt of disappointment she felt at his hesitation to return the sentiment. It was only natural that he would hold back, considering the differences between them. He was a loving father with a teenage daughter and a high-profile job in the community. A woman like her didn't fit into the norm of "family." Hell, she couldn't even keep it together with her own mother. Not that she hadn't tried, she reminded herself a little too quickly. She had, and was shunned for her efforts.

Obviously she had read too much into the kiss they'd shared. He wasn't attracted to her past the point of satisfying his curiosity. The kiss had been chaste, if indeed there was such a thing among consenting adults this day in time. No hands caressing intimate places. No tongue invading her mouth in haste.

Ali let out a sigh that was more of a shudder, trying to think up a thousand excuses of her own as to why she shouldn't have been so affected by Jordan Finch. The way his mouth had moved over hers. Not only that but the way he had observed the niceties as if they were second nature. Opening her door. Asking the waiter at the restaurant for a table in the smoking section. His fingertips resting on the curve of her spine as he guided her to their corner table. Holding her chair. The easy conversation. He hadn't jumped in feetfirst to apprise her of his own noteworthy assets, but encouraged her to talk about herself, her business.

Bracing her elbows on the scattered papers, she ground the heels of her palms into her forehead. "Stupid, stupid, stupid Ali," she reprimanded herself. "What did you expect, after the way you led him to believe you were some kind of half wild Jane of the jungle?"

She was near to feeling sorry for herself when the bell over the shop door rang. Thank God. Someone with a fashion emergency to take her mind off wholesome-as-apple-pie Jordan Finch.

"Hi, welcome to Spangles," she greeted the two women cheerfully. "Can I help you find anything in particular this afternoon?"

"How about a man who isn't married, divorced, or gorgeous-as-hell gay?" the blonde half of the duo remarked casually, lingering over one of the eye-catching floor displays. She was perhaps twenty-five, tall for a woman, standing a full head above the older brunette who, Ali surmised at closer study—noting the similarity in features—was most likely her mother.

"Sorry." Ali genuinely smiled. "I'm fresh out of gorgeous-as-hell, but I do have what I like to call a 'To Hell With Men' section toward the back."

"Bah!" The older woman batted the air in disgust, jerking her chin at the blonde. "Always so picky. This one's too short, that one's too fat, another is too old. What does it matter than Vinnie Liatucci owns his own grocery chain and goes to church every Sunday?"

The blonde rolled her eyes. "Mother, I'm sure this nice lady doesn't care anything about hearing you laud Vinnie Liatucci or his produce." She turned pleading blue eyes on Ali. "Show me that section. Please."

"Right this way." Ali led the way toward the rack of clothes near the back wall, designed specifically to lift a woman's spirits in that mindless way only silk, satin, lace, and leather could do. The blouses were low cut, made of soft materials that clung to a woman's breasts, made her feel feminine. The stretch and leather skirts and pants embraced most any size hips under forty inches—no problem there. Jeans from this rack fit like a second skin. Casual pants tapered sharply from hip to ankle. Short Lycra dresses were backless, sporting daring thigh slits. Jackets were cinched at the waist and, if the woman in question was bold or depressed enough, could be worn blouseless when buttoned.

"Oh goodness!" The blonde's brows rose in alarm when Ali held up a pair of black leather pants and a silk blouse fashioned with flowing pirate sleeves that cuffed snugly at the wrist. "I could never wear something like that."

"How do you know?" Ali challenged. "You haven't tried them on. You have lovely long legs. Don't be afraid to show them off."

"And just where would she wear an outfit so wild?" the mother asked pointedly.

"You don't have to wear it anywhere." Ali winked at the grown daughter. "But I guarantee once you see it on, you'll want to walk every square inch of Chicago before taking it off."

"Hmmph."

"What the heck."

"'Atta girl." Ali showed her the dressing rooms. While the daughter changed, Ali expertly maneuvered the mother toward a more matronly section on the right side of the store, set back in its own alcove because older women didn't care to be ogled by browsing customers.

Mother was short, Italian, and no doubt preferred subtle colors, concealing drapes, and durable fabrics, if the conservative, serviceable dress she was wearing was anything to judge by.

"I didn't come here to buy anything," Mother said firmly, trying to act disinterested in the whole affair.

"Doesn't cost anything to look," Ali assured her. "Now this..." she chose a soft olive toned pantsuit with a tunic-style top and held it up for inspection, "is you. See how the sides of the top are cut high on the hip? Won't hem you in when you walk or bend or sit. And the waist of the pants is elastic, no zippers or hooks to fool with." Even the brass buttons lining the front of the tunic were big enough so that fingers with arthritis would have no trouble slipping them into place. "Buttons down the front," she continued, "which means no mussing that new hairdo or lipstick trying to get it on over your head. I don't know about you, but I simply hate having to get dressed before my hair and face are fixed. *And*, best of all, this suit is wrinkle-free. Just pull it out of the washer and hang to dry. No ironing, no rushing to the dryer to get it out before the creases set in, no shrinking or fading. A little softener in the rinse cycle and you don't have to worry about the material feeling stiff or scratchy.

"Now *my* mother," *Forgive me, Gladys*, "of course, is quite a bit older and not nearly as petite as you, bless her heart. Anyway, she finally broke down and tried on a suit like this. Mostly just to shut me up. But you should have seen her. Took ten years off her age just like that. Well, I'd better go check on your daughter. You just feel free to browse."

Gina Bertinelli waited until she was sure she was alone in the little alcove, glancing cautiously over her shoulder before reaching out to finger the pantsuit the perky saleswoman had left hanging sideways over the round rack. Ten years off her age. How ridiculous! She was married these forty years with a grown daughter and son. What business did she have with wanting to look younger than her sixty-two years? And she preferred to iron her clothes, thank you. Her Sal never left the house without perfectly straight creases in his trousers and shirtsleeves. All this business about wash-and-wear was just pure laziness, if you asked her. What little bit of effort did it take to spray pre-wash on a collar smudged with face powder? Fifteen seconds, that's how long.

And didn't she intentionally search out and buy dresses with back zips just so she could step into them without having to bunch and wrestle them over her hair? Of course, if Sal wasn't around or she didn't catch him before he left for work at the plant, she had a hard time reaching behind to work the zipper. Sometimes her arthritic fingers didn't want to cooperate. But that was neither here not there. She had no business throwing away a lifetime of strictly observed habits drilled into her by her own blessed mother. A woman should wear dresses, particularly when she left the house for an evening out. The world was in the shape it was now because women had taken it upon themselves to wear pants.

Gina turned her back on the pantsuit to gaze out the large plate glass window at the front of the store. Her daughter wearing leather pants, of all things. Bah! Theresa could do worse than a grocer for a husband. It was the future security Vinnie could give her that counted, not whether he had thinning hair and a paunch. Just then Gina noticed a dark-haired man dressed in a suit and tie, briefcase in hand, pass by the window. He glanced sideways into the shop offhandedly, faltered, did a double take, then stopped dead in his tracks, cupping a hand over his eyes to block the glare of the sun as he stepped closer to the window.

Gina wondered what it was that had caught the man's attention so abruptly. Surely he wasn't staring at the display in the front window. No, he seemed to be squinting to look farther into the shadows of the store. Gina stepped out of the alcove, following the direction of his rapt gaze. One hand went to her breast in shock, the other reached out to grasp the cold steel of yet another rack of clothing for support as Theresa's tall form came into view.

Theresa was preening in front of a three-sided mirror, admiring the mile of legs encased in black leather, unaware the man in the window was staring at her with hungry eyes. The same way Sal used to look at her when she was thirty years younger and still curvaceous. *Ah, Theresa, forgive an old woman for her foolishness. Of course you would want a husband as tall and handsome as your father. One who will always make your heart flutter just a little bit faster when he looks at you as though you're the only woman in existence.*

Gina couldn't help but smile as the man edged his way toward the door, whatever appointment he'd been in such a hurry to keep forgotten now. The bell above the door tinkled, announcing his entrance. Gina took herself back into the alcove where the olive green pantsuit still waited, and snatched it from the rack. That uppity salesgirl better be right, she thought as she briskly made her way into the adjoining dressing area. If this suit didn't take ten years off her age she wouldn't buy it and that's all there was to it.

Chapter Five

ᏕᏗ

Five o'clock came and Ali decided to close the store early. She was the owner—she could do what she wanted. And what she wanted was to go home and lounge in her underwear with a glass of wine and a good book. Gina Bertinelli had left satisfied with the olive pantsuit, and her daughter, Theresa, even more satisfied after being approached by the sharply dressed businessman who was hard-pressed to keep his eyes off her legs and on her face while making small talk that eventually led to an exchange of phone numbers.

Smiling and winking, Theresa had said, "I thought you said you were fresh out of gorgeous-as-hell?"

"New shipments arrive everyday." Ali had smiled back at her. "Now, Mrs. Bertinelli, don't you go flirting with every man who looks at you in that new pantsuit. I don't want a rabid husband on my back."

"Oh, go on." Gina Bertinelli compressed her lips into a thin line of exasperation.

Ali opened the door and twisted the OPEN sign to CLOSED, searching her pockets for the keys. The phone rang. Nuts, she'd left her keys on the counter. Something she never did. Retracing her steps to the counter, she answered the phone while rummaging through the pile of accessories she'd just finished showing to the last customer. Behind her the bell tinkled, announcing that the intruder couldn't read.

Her fingers closed over the heavy silver ring. She pocketed the keys while answering questions fired at her by the frantic woman on the other end of the phone who had mistakenly washed a silk blouse she'd purchased just three days ago at Ali's boutique without first remembering to check the collar tag for washing instructions. The woman was sure the blouse was ruined, but hadn't the courage to lift the washer lid to find out. Ali asked the woman to describe the blouse and the maker, then, because she knew the care instructions on almost every type of garment in the shop, assured the frantic woman the blouse she had purchased was washable silk and she had nothing to worry about — unless she'd done so in hot water instead of cold.

The woman thanked Ali profusely for waylaying her concerns. And no, she had not washed the blouse in hot water. For heaven's sake, did they even manufacture clothes nowadays that could be washed in hot water?

"Nothing you'd want to wear," Ali told her before hanging up.

Okay, one more customer, then she was out of here. She could lock the door now and — "Jordan!"

He stood in the doorway, hands at his sides. Late afternoon shadows cast by the door's canvas awning, combined with slanting bars of shade from saplings dotting the grassy easement lining the sidewalk, silhouetted his impressive frame.

Don't get excited, Ali, he's probably just here to ream you out again for selling his virtuous daughter a gown that could transform an inanimate mannequin into a sex goddess. "Anyone who can look up a compound word in two parts should be able to understand the antonym of open."

He approached the counter, placing his palms flat against the glass so that his broad shoulders hunkered toward her in warning. "I dislike being cut short, particularly before I've said everything I want to say."

"Well, we all have little quirks, don't we?" she replied sarcastically.

"If you had let me get a word in edgewise, I might have been able to say you weren't the only one who enjoyed last night."

"But?"

"But I work a lot of long hours. Nights, weekends. That doesn't leave a lot of quality time to spend with Susan, much less for dating. My work schedule is what ruined my marriage, or so my ex-wife says. I just wanted you to know up front how it would be if we continued seeing each other."

"I see." Her pulse did a cartwheel.

"And there's something else." He sighed, rubbing three fingers across his lower lip, as if trying to decide how to proceed. "I've filed for sole custody of Susan. She doesn't want to go back to Charleston, she wants to stay here with me. Eventually, Gloria's lawyer will catch up to her and notify her of the petition. She isn't going to like it. That means every aspect of my life, and Susan's, will most likely come under scrutiny. If I know my ex-wife, she'll hire a private investigator."

"So what you're saying is that being seen with me might be construed as immoral behavior in the eyes of a court."

"No, I'm just saying I'll need to keep a low profile for a while. No nightclubbing or bar-hopping or keeping late hours or leaving Susan alone for long periods of time. She's alone enough as it is while I'm at work."

Miffed he would think her so insensitive, she lifted a haughty eyebrow. "And you didn't think a woman like me could understand that?"

"I wasn't sure you'd want to be bothered with the inconvenience. I need to spend as much time as I can with Susan right now. She resents Gloria for packing up and leaving like she did. I don't want her distancing herself from Gloria that way. Whatever Gloria's reasons were for divorcing me, she's still Susan's mother and they'll be spending time together no matter what the court decides."

"But you have a good chance, right? I mean, Susan's old enough now where a judge would take her wishes into consideration."

He shrugged. "Possibly. But if it appears I'm trying to pit Susan against her mother, it will hardly help my case. Gloria was a good mother."

Ali wondered if he realized he'd referred to Gloria's skills as a loving mother in the past tense. "Oh, Finch, Susan's a bright girl, she's just hurting right now. Divorce is almost always hard on kids. It takes time for them to adjust to shuttling between parents."

"Before the divorce Susan would never have been tempted to buy the kind of gown you showed her, then hide it from me."

"Are you absolutely certain of that?" she asked softly. "I've never been married and I don't have any kids, but it seems to me like your divorce just sort of coincided with that time in a girl's life when she's starting to get interested in the whole boy-girl thing. Heck, you're lucky she waited this long to notice boys. Girls nowadays start putting out the signals at eleven and twelve."

"What signals?" He blinked, his forehead marred by a series of fine wrinkles.

"You know, like...flipping their hair, tossing their heads, gazing at the cute guys in sort of a dreamy daze, thrusting their chests out... Sorry," she muttered when his eyes closed against the visions her words invoked. "Maybe that last one wasn't such a good example. Listen, maybe it would be a good idea to warn Susan against mentioning anything to Franny about our, um, date. Susan asked how we met when she called to tell me about the prom, and I told her Franny was my best friend."

He frowned. "What does Franny have to do with anything?"

"What Franny doesn't know she can't tell a judge if she's called to testify as a character witness on your behalf. We'd only just met and she told you I had a navel ring. Need I say more?"

"I hadn't thought of that." He shoved his hands into his trouser pockets, pursed his lips, and nodded. "Susan does tend to pop into my office after school sometimes. And she usually talks to Franny while she's waiting."

"You're one of those people who rides around on a guilty conscience, aren't you, Finch?"

"Why do you say that?"

"Because if you didn't feel guilty about the divorce you wouldn't be letting the possibility of what Gloria will do when she finds out you filed for custody dictate your every move. She might have divorced you, but I get the impression she just up and dumped Susan in your lap. Did her job take her to Europe? Require that she spend too long a time there to take Susan with her? Does she call? Write? Keep in touch with Susan on a regular basis to assure her things haven't changed between them?"

The corners of his mouth hardened. "She hasn't called since leaving six months ago. Not that I know of anyway, but I think Susan would have told me if she had."

"Then the simple fact is, Finch darling, Gloria, for all intents and purposes, abandoned her daughter. Susan has every right to resent that. Trying to convince her otherwise will only make her more resentful."

"Gloria is still her mother, Ali."

"So what! Her technical status as a mother doesn't automatically entitle her to love and respect. You don't turn your back on a child just because it's convenient or because they didn't turn out exactly the way you wanted."

Her outburst had them staring across the counter at each other. One with the bitterness of a lifetime showing in her eyes, the other forced to admit that his heretofore perfect society wife—ex-wife—had, without any outward sign of remorse he could fathom, suddenly, and ever so coldly, cut their only child out of her life.

If Ali was tempted to apologize for maligning Jordan's ex-wife, she quickly strangled the urge. The little girl inside her hurt for Susan. It had touched her deeply to watch the two of them together before Susan left for the prom with Randy Peters.

Susan still called Jordan "daddy". Still looked at him with adoring eyes when other girls considered themselves too mature to act in so unrestrained a manner toward a parent. And it was easy to see that Jordan doted on his daughter, as well. How could he question his qualifications as a worthy parent, a deserving father, when you had only to look at the two of them together, father and daughter, to see the love?

"Well, this has been very productive," she remarked dryly. "Now you've discovered I can snarl like a wild dog."

He shook his head, stepping away from the counter to peruse the floor display behind him. "I shouldn't have dumped on you like that."

"I happen to like Susan very much," she told him as she rounded the corner of the counter to lock the front door. "Anything I can do to help, just say so. Would it help if she spent her after school hours here instead of at home, alone? She could get her homework done and, if she wants, help me around the store. I'd pay her, of course. I've been thinking about hiring a part-timer anyway."

He seemed baffled for a moment. "I couldn't ask you to do that."

"I don't recall that you asked, I recall that I offered." She sent the bolt home on the door and pulled the striped shade. "Sometimes men are so dense," she murmured quietly to herself. When she turned around he was there.

"I'm six months out of a failed marriage, Ali. It may take me a while to get things under control and running smoothly, but I'm not out for sympathy."

"Me either, Finch, darling. I'm just in it for the totally hot sex."

"We haven't had hot sex. And would you please stop calling me Finch darling?"

"Please. In my perfect fantasy, I strip naked and dance on the dinner table and you choke on your steak. Naturally, I have

to give you mouth to mouth to resuscitate your shocked heart."
Oh, Ali, why do you have to say such outrageous things?

"Naturally."

It was there between them, the kiss they'd shared the night before, in his driveway. As palatable as the air curling electrically around them while each recalled what the other had tasted like. For Ali it had been a mixture of textures and scents and hard, planed muscle. Had his heart kicked up a fuss as hers had done—was doing now—just remembering the way his lips had moved so persuasively over hers?

How would he feel naked, pressed against her? Was the rest of him he as solid and firm as his chest? Did his features soften when he slept? He looked rugged enough in a polo shirt that stretched across his broad shoulders. There was no "approaching middle age" paunch, which meant he watched his diet and exercised regularly, but clothes could hide so many little faults, like a sagging butt and—

"Do I survive?" he asked.

"What?" She ripped her gaze from his chest.

"In your fantasy. Does my heart survive the shock?"

"I don't know. I never get to finish the dream."

"Maybe I choke to death instead," he suggested.

"Didn't your mother ever teach you it's rude to cough up meat at the dinner table?"

"Yes, but in her defense I feel obliged to point out that we weren't allowed to watch naked women dancing on the dining room table she so dearly cherished."

She placed five fingertips to his chest and pushed until there was enough room for her to squeeze around him. "Poor you."

Behind the counter once again, she reached beneath the cash register for the ever-present bottle of Windex, sprayed a generous amount on the glass where he'd left palm and fingerprints moments earlier, and swiped. The last to leave the boutique, whether it was she or Deanna, always made sure the glass countertops were wiped clean and all accessories returned to their velvet-lined enclosures. Signs were straightened, dressing rooms checked for forgotten garments. A reputable, bonded cleaning service came in once a week, after hours, to vacuum, dust, empty trash bins, wash the plate glass windows and in general tidy up.

The first week they had come to work in the boutique she had been a wreck, thinking how easy it would be for the workers to steal her blind if they so wished, bonded or not. She'd taken inventory the day before and rechecked it the day after for almost four months before breathing a sigh of relief, not to mention the sleep she'd given up to obtain peace of mind. This boutique was her life. It represented what she had accomplished on her own, without the support of her mother or some horny old bastard's tip money. Though she enjoyed plenty of free time, Ali couldn't bring herself to hand over any major part of running her business to strangers.

She started in on a circular rack next, rearranging the clothes according to size, smallest to largest. "If you change your mind about Susan hanging out here after school, just let me know."

"You're sure it wouldn't be a bother?" he asked from the other side.

"I'm sure. Do you want me to wear a sign around my neck that says I like your daughter or will you take my word for it?"

"I guess I'm not used to women shrugging off the intrusion a teenage daughter represents."

"Then you're dating the wrong kind of women."

"I've only had two dates since the divorce, and one of them was you."

"Jeez, no wonder your face froze up like Erie when I pulled out that floss."

"Took me two weeks to learn how to floss with my eyes closed," he admitted.

"Now, that's a gift."

He let out a long-suffering sigh. "You'd think by now I'd have learned not to give you an opening."

"Stick around, Finch, I'll teach you how to look up the word fun in the dictionary."

"I know what fun is," he muttered.

"Really? What do you do for fun, Finch?"

"I golf."

"What else?" When he didn't answer immediately, she rolled her eyes. "Well hell, don't hurt yourself thinking up something."

"Dinner with you was fun," he said at last. "We have decided we'll keep seeing each other, haven't we?"

"Are you kidding? What's a little inconvenience like Susan when I get to sit across the table from a snooty guy from Charleston, who has table manners coming out his ears. I think I'm getting the better end of the bargain, Finch. I really do."

* * * * *

Jordan knew as soon as he walked into the kitchen, saw the way Susan was lazing in the oak bar chair one minute, curling her legs around its side the next, who she was talking to on the phone. When she wasn't toying with her hair or coiling the telephone cord around her finger, she was staring dreamy-eyed into space.

He did his damnedest to eavesdrop while making himself a sandwich he wasn't really hungry for. But Susan lowered her voice or moved off in another direction, stretching the long cord to its limit several times. Well, he could be just as stubborn as she. He'd show her, and eat the sandwich.

Finally, she sighed into the receiver and said, "I have to go. My dad's home. I'll talk to you later, okay?"

"Who was that?" Jordan bit into the ham and cheese, playing dumb.

"Randy." She opened the fridge and stood studying the contents.

"Uh-huh. And did you tell him to bug off this time?"

"Dad, really. He hasn't actually asked me out yet. We were just talking."

Dad? What was with the *Dad* business all of a sudden? "Talking about what?"

She shrugged, reaching for a soda. "Stuff." Popping the top, she took a swig. "So what's up with you and Ali?"

"That's something we need to talk about. Get me a soda, too, will you, honey?"

Susan opened the refrigerator and pulled out a Pepsi, popping the top for him before setting it on the table. "So, is there like a problem or something?"

He took a drink of soda to wash down his food before answering. "Not a problem, *per se*, more like avoiding future problems. Like I told you last night, I filed for custody so you could stay with me. You said you were agreeable, no problem there. But your mother isn't going to take the news well. She naturally assumes you'll live with her when she gets back, but—"

Her expression turned mutinous. "I don't want to live with her, I want to live with you."

"First, let's get something straight. There's no guarantee a judge will see things our way if it gets that far. Secondly, even if you do end up living with me, you'll be spending vacations and holidays with your mother, so don't get the idea this is a one-sided thing. I know you're upset with her right now, but Susan, she's your mother and the precedent you set with her on her return will determine how amiable she is with this arrangement."

"She dumped us, Dad. I don't understand why you keep taking up for her. She hasn't called. She hasn't written. We don't need her. We do fine on our own."

Jordan set his sandwich down, ran his tongue around his teeth. "I'm not taking up for her, honey. I'm just trying to keep things from getting blown out of proportion. She might have been the one to file for the divorce, but it wasn't any easier on her than it has been on us." Probably.

"Yeah, right. I didn't notice her having a rough time trying to decide what clothes to take on her little trip. She hummed the whole time she was packing."

"People handle stress in different ways. She always hums when she's nervous." Why *was* he making excuses? He was mad as hell at Gloria, too—he just didn't show it. He tried hard not to let his anger spill over onto Susan. She had enough to deal with, what with moving from Charleston to Chicago, and switching schools, and having to make new friends, learn her way around a new city. As far as he was concerned she'd had to make too damn many adjustments in the last six months.

"She can hum herself all over Europe for all I care," Susan said, taking another sip of her soda.

He was no good at this, he knew. He came from a prominent family, as did Gloria, where parents and elders were respected no matter the circumstances. Yes, they might be whispered about behind closed doors—this one drank like a fish on the sly, that one cheated on his wife, another was cold and bitter to the point of rudeness over love lost and a money-based marriage. But they were treated with respect nonetheless, having earned their positions in society through family ties.

Jordan and Gloria hadn't exactly married for money reasons. Their families had known each other for years and, because it was more or less expected, had gravitated toward one another. Perhaps Gloria hadn't been given to overt displays of affection, but he just couldn't bring himself to accept the fact that Susan wanted no kind of relationship with her mother.

"Well, look, that wasn't what I wanted to discuss with you. You asked about Ali. She said she told you Franny and she are friends. But for the time being, I think—actually, Ali and I agree on this—it might not be a good idea to mention anything about us seeing each other to Franny."

"How come?" A worried look came into her eyes.

"Because if push comes to shove Franny could be called as a character witness and I wouldn't want a judge getting the wrong impression about...certain things."

Susan grinned knowingly, wiggling her eyebrows. "You mean like sex stuff?"

"No, I do not mean like sex stuff. I'm talking about perfectly normal situations that could be construed as...inappropriate."

"Oh, you mean something like Ali coming over to watch a movie and you two smooching on the couch while I'm asleep upstairs, innocently unaware."

He wasn't going to ask what she knew about smooching on couches. "I mean like you having friends in the house without supervision while I'm gone, or staying out past curfew, or taking up with the wrong kind of kids. Those things can, and will, reflect badly on both of us. A judge might say I was spending too much time away from home. That I let you run wild. Or he might view my spending time with Ali as neglect. Now, I'm going to try to do as much work as I can at home, but you're going to have to help me out and be extra responsible."

"Dad, I am responsible," she insisted.

"Buying that gown at Ali's shop when you knew I would object wasn't responsible. It's that kind of thing that a judge will take into consideration when making a decision, Susan. He's going to look at how you were raised, how things were before the divorce, and how the situation has developed since. Your mother's going to claim I worked all the time and was never there, and she's right, I did work more than my share of normal hours. That's going to be a plus for her, because she can claim you'll be without adult supervision now more often than not— something she can supply on a day-to-day basis."

"Oh, that's a load of crap." Susan pushed off the counter, slumping into the chair she'd been sitting in when he came in. "She was always dragging me to some charity meeting or the country club or a card party where I got shoved off into another room with the other charity cases whose moms were on the same committees. She didn't have any idea I was out behind the golf cart shack, playing doctor with Bobby Summerfield or that Becky Larkin and me used to switch people's drinks when they weren't looking. She was too busy playing hostess to a bunch of blue hairs in the tea room, and I always made sure I was back where I was supposed to be before it was time to leave."

He rubbed the edge of his forehead. Bobby Summerfield had always struck him as being shifty-eyed. He wasn't altogether sure he wanted to know the details concerning who was the doctor and who was the patient during those illicit meetings out behind the cart house. On second thought, he was positive he didn't want to know, so pretended he hadn't heard that part.

"Switching people's drinks is strictly off-limits from here on out. And while we're on the subject, so is staying home alone after school. Ali said you could come by the shop and hang out with her. Said she'd even let you work part-time for her if you wanted to earn some extra cash. I can pick you up on the way home from work."

She cocked her head, studying him with shrewdly narrowed eyes, as if trying to discern if he had some ulterior motive for suggesting the arrangement. He did, but he wasn't about let on that the thought of Randy Peters sweet-talking her over the phone while he was at work had anything to do with it.

If it was a choice between Randy Peters and Ali MacPherson, he'd take his chances with Ali. Besides, it gave him an excuse to see her. Like he'd told her this afternoon, his schedule didn't allow him much free time and he needed to spend as much of that time as he could with Susan.

"That's cool, I guess," Susan decided. "I like Ali. She isn't snobby and doesn't treat me like a child who should be seen and not heard. Dad, you didn't run over there and nag her about selling me that dress, did you?"

"I can't imagine anyone getting the chance to nag Ali. She doesn't shut up long enough to let you nag her."

"Ali is sooo totally awesome. I mean, she dresses sharp and she's witty and funny and sophisticated. And so easy to talk to. And when I told her she didn't have to go to all the trouble of helping me learn to fix my hair she said oh yes, she really did, because she was me once, only skinnier. She even made a bet with me. I told her you don't usually notice how I dress and she said if your eyeballs didn't pop out of your head when you saw me in that dress, she'd take the dress back and give me a refund."

It seemed Ali MacPherson had made quite an impression on Susan. "Just remember what I said about buying clothes that are too old for you."

"Okay, okay. You don't have to keep telling me. I get it."

"I took the rest of the day off. How 'bout taking in a movie?"

"Can't," she said, rolling to her sock-shod feet. "Bonnie's coming over. We're going to listen to CDs and study for a math test Monday."

"Math. Right. Of course, that's more important than a movie. I could drill you both on it later if you want."

"Dad, we're not babies." She kissed him on the cheek then flitted off toward her room.

Oddly enough, he felt rejected. He'd always been the one to drill her on subjects like math and science, because they were his strong points. Now some girl named Bonnie had taken over in that area.

"Hey, Susan?"

"Yeah?" She paused at the kitchen door to look at him over her shoulder.

"Listen, I'm sorry I forgot to get your picture the other night before you left for the prom. I had the camera out and everything."

She graced him with a forgiving smile. "That's okay. They took portraits at the dance. I can get them through school."

He no more wanted the leering image of Randy Peters clogging up his desk at work or the credenza in the family room than he wanted a case of athlete's foot. He'd wanted a picture of his little girl dressed up in her finery, standing at the foot of the stairs smiling at him.

"Stuff", she'd said casually when he'd asked what she and Randy were talking about on the phone. Not to mention she was using a technicality to postpone telling Peters to take a hike. Big deal, Peters hadn't actually asked Susan out on a date. He'd taken her to the prom, hadn't he? Kept her out in the car for what had amounted to ten years of Jordan's life, doing God only knew what. He was calling the house, wasn't he?

It was the same damn thing as sparking her — as his grandfather would say — if you asked him.

Except nobody had bothered to ask him. Least of all Susan.

Chapter Six

છ

How Susan and Bonnie thought they could retain two plus two with some hoarse-sounding guy yelling that he wanted to push someone around was beyond Jordan. He certainly couldn't concentrate on the projections he was working with while the walls of his study, which was situated directly beneath Susan's room, were vibrating. The raspy singer should have contracted laryngitis by now. They played the same songs over and over until Jordan found himself anticipating the words, at which point he gave up and wandered into the kitchen for a beer.

Ali's card was stuck beneath a piggy magnet on the front of the refrigerator. He removed it from beneath the magnet, flipped it over, saw her home number scrawled on the back, and thought about how she'd expertly maneuvered him out the shop's back door this afternoon without giving him a chance to ask for her home number. For a woman who claimed she was a party animal with a tattoo on her butt, and liked to have fun, she didn't once try to kiss him or brush against him or any of the flirty things women did when coming on to a man.

Oh, she teased and flirted with words, wore sexy clothes, but she hadn't exactly encouraged him to, well, try anything like kissing her again.

He checked his watch. Eight-thirty on a Saturday night. She probably wasn't at home, anyway. Probably out on the town with a date or some friends, having a high time. Women like Ali never lacked for invitations. She was outgoing, outspoken, unreserved. Combine all that with honeyed hair, mahogany eyes, and long, slim legs and the results were as powerful as any aphrodisiac. She had a tiny waist and just the right amount of hip to make a man's mouth water. Cleavage enough to make his throat go dry. She was flat damn gorgeous.

So, if she wasn't at home he could leave a message that Susan might be dropping by her boutique after school on Monday.

* * * * *

Ali played the message back three times just so she could hear his voice. She'd spent the evening at the Dematos'. Gladys called at the last minute and talked her and Franny into dinner. Since neither woman had plans for the evening they stayed afterward to play cards. She hated being Franny's partner in the game of spades. No matter how many times she'd told Franny not to lead with the king in a suit, Franny did anyway. It usually ended up costing them a trick, or point, which would set them back because Franny refused to bid conservatively.

Ten-thirty, she noted by the clock on the mantel. Was Jordan one of those fuddy-duddies who went to bed early and rose at the crack of dawn? God, she hoped not, because if so he was going to be rudely awakened as soon as she shed her blouse and jeans and snagged a Coke from the fridge.

Jordan didn't sound like he'd been asleep when he answered the phone. "Hiya, Finch. Got your message."

"Oh, yeah, my message. You're sure—"

"If you ask me that just one more time I'm going to drive over to your house at midnight and TP your trees."

"Ali, are you going to let me be a working part of this conversation? Or should I save my breath and let you talk for both of us?"

"Mmm, that could be dangerous." She set her drink down long enough to shift the phone onto her shoulder while working one arm through the sleeve of her robe. "When it's my turn to be you, I might say something totally inappropriate."

"Listen, um, I know it's short notice, but if you're not doing anything tomorrow, maybe we could play a round of golf."

83

"I don't know how to play golf."

"Susan and I can teach you."

"Susan plays golf?" Poor kid.

"Occasionally."

She'd rather be tied to a truck and driven down Main Street. Naked. "Sounds like fun. Except, darn it all, I don't have any clubs."

"No problem, we can rent a set."

She switched ears to slide on the other sleeve, shrugging the robe the rest of the way over her shoulders. "I have to warn you, I'm not very athletic."

He wasn't taking the hint. "The course is near my house. Why don't we meet here at seven, then we can drive over together. The place is always crowded on weekends, not much parking."

"Seven," she repeated, swallowing hard. "In the morning?" Sundays were her only days to sleep in and she usually took full advantage. Only a natural disaster could roll her out of bed before noon, and if Mother Nature didn't see fit to rain that disaster down directly on her condo's square footage, not even then.

"If you'd rather not…"

"Seven's fine. So, Finch, how long did it take you to figure out my home number was on the back of the card I gave Susan?"

"About as long as it took you to figure out I didn't really call just to leave a message about Susan coming by the boutique."

"What made you change your mind?" she asked, flopping down in the stuffed chair by her bedroom window to take another sip of soda.

"About?"

"About Susan spending time at the boutique after school."

"Stuff."

"Stuff? You lost me, Finch."

"Good, that makes two of us. Susan was talking to you-know-who on the phone when I got home. When I asked her what they were talking about, she said 'stuff'."

Poor thing. He couldn't even say the boy's name out loud. "Ahhh."

"Please don't say ahhh like that. It makes me think you know what 'stuff' is and I don't."

"Finch."

"What?"

"You know how we were talking and laughing the other night over dinner?"

"Yeah," he replied cautiously.

"That's 'stuff'. And locking her up in my boutique every afternoon isn't going to solve your dilemma with Randy Peters. That's something Susan has to do herself. Give her a chance. Oops, there I go again, giving unsolicited advice. Forget it. You should do what you think is best."

"Will you inform me if he starts hanging around the boutique?"

"Absolutely not," she told him in no uncertain terms. "If the only reason you want her to sit at my boutique every afternoon is so I'll squeal on her, forget it. We're friends. She trusts me. I'm not going to carry tales to you over every boy she looks at."

"I just meant—"

"I know what you meant," she cut him off, her temper starting to rise. "And I'm not her mother, Finch. I'm her friend. That means I'll give her the best advice I can when she asks for my opinion, but what I will not do is be your undercover spy. You didn't say two words to that boy when he came to pick up Susan. He could be a nice kid for all you know. But you can't get past his name and the images it stimulates in your brain. Hell, you can't even *say* his name. Has poor Randy Peters done anything to be persecuted for besides ask your daughter out on a date?"

"He gave his girlfriend mono, for starters. And he only asked Susan to the prom because he didn't have a date!"

"Stop yelling at me!"

"Quit pushing my buttons then!" He let out a frustrated breath. "Jesus, Ali, I don't want you to spy on Susan, I'd just like to be informed if things start to get out of hand."

"Apparently, you think I'm the kind of person who would let two teenage kids suck face in the back room of my business without blinking an eye. A jaded businesswoman who gets a kick out of letting teenage boys hang around her shop to sniff the merchandise as it walks by."

"You don't have the first clue what I think about you. Forget I mentioned it," he said tightly. "Let's just drop it."

"Why don't you come out and say what you think of me, and save yourself the trouble of teaching me to smack a little white ball around a bunch of trees and bushes?"

"Christ, a person doesn't need to bother riding an exercise bike for an hour to get their heart rate up around you."

"I'll take that as a compliment, if you don't mind. See you at seven, then."

"Ali—"

"I have to go, Finch. I'm getting one of my urges."

"What kind of urge?"

"I'm wearing my robe and nothing else. You have a college diploma, figure it out." She heard his breath hitch, squeezed her eyes against the zing of shivers that shot straight down her spine, one vertebra at a time. "Good night, Finch. Pleasant dreams."

* * * * *

Jordan didn't have pleasant dreams that night. He had dark, thrilling, sexual dreams. And woke up with a hard-on that had nothing whatsoever to do with urinary tract urges.

Now, leaning over Ali, her backside snuggled into his front as he showed her how to grip the driver correctly, he was forced to admit that teaching her to golf might not have been such a good idea. Susan was standing off to the side watching, hiding an amused grin behind the head of her Big Bertha.

Ali had shown up on his doorstep at seven sharp, wearing a little nothing of a tennis skirt and spiffy tennis shoes. Maybe he should have suggested tennis instead. Then she'd be across court from him and he wouldn't be tempted to put his hands on her.

Wrapping his fingers around hers, he positioned her hands along the wrapped shaft. For a split second he imagined those hands touching *his* shaft. "Fold your pinky between your index and middle fingers. That's it. Keep your eye on the ball at all times. Feet squared beneath your shoulders." He used his foot to shove at hers until it scooted into alignment. "Now, watch Susan. Okay, Susan, show her."

"Yeah, yeah, yeah. I've got it." Ali shifted from foot to foot, trying to get comfortable with the stance, sending a hard slice of need through his system. "Now where am I aiming again?" she asked over her shoulder.

Her perfume was scrambling his brains. Lifting an arm, he pointed. "That flag straight down the fairway."

She tipped her sunglass down to peer over the rims. "All the way down there?"

"This is a par three hole," he explained, hoping his voice sounded normal. Susan wasn't more than six feet away from them, still watching. He stepped clear of Ali as she eyeballed the distance. "You don't have to hit the ball that far on the first swing."

"And par is...?"

"How many strokes it should take you to get the ball to the green and in the cup. Okay," he nodded when he judged the distance was safe.

"How many strokes does it take you to get there?"

When Jordan looked over at her, saw the wicked light dancing in her eyes, he was almost sure the question had nothing to do with golf. Ali flashed him a smile, drew back, completely forgot to keep her eye on the ball, and swung.

"Wow, look at that sucker go, would ya!" The ball arced, hooked to the left, and landed with a plop into the lake. "Better give me another ball, Finch. That watering hole ate mine."

Behind him, Jordan heard Susan giggle. He teed up another ball for Ali, wondering if he'd just set a precedent for the next seventeen holes, quickly deciding nine was more than enough to strain his patience.

Seven strokes and two sand traps later, she managed to sink the ball in the cup on a five-inch putt.

"Eight for Ali," he murmured, marking down her score. "Two for me. Four for Susan."

"Wait just a minute, pal." Ali darted past Susan to cast a furtive glance down at the scorecard in his hand. "What do you mean eight? I counted seven."

"The ball you hit off the tee into the water counts."

"Like hell it does! It isn't my fault somebody had the bad sense to put a frigging lake in the middle of a golf course."

"You have to play around the natural hazards, Ali. Every stroke, no matter how bad or where it lands, counts."

"Oh, I get it." She folded her arms, accusingly. "You're going to make up the rules as we go along."

Susan backed off and busied herself returning her putter to her bag, leaving him to explain the finer points of golf to Ali. He had the feeling his daughter was snickering under her breath.

"Maybe someone ought to point out to you that sand dunes aren't indigenous to the Chicago area, Finch. So, technically, those two sand pits—"

"Sand traps."

"Whatever." She waived a negligent hand. "Technically, they shouldn't exist, so they can hardly be called natural hazards, now can they?"

"Daddy, come on. It's Ali's first time. Give her a break."

"Finally," Ali muttered, "someone who understands reason."

At this point he was ready to give in just so they could move on. "Fine. Seven."

"Minus two unnatural hazards makes five," she argued.

Behind them was a foursome waiting to tee off so Jordan slashed through the seven, which was crunched in next to the slashed eight, and made it five just to shut them both up. "Five. Happy now?"

"Very." She smiled up at him like a Cheshire, striding off to perch herself behind the wheel of the cart he'd rented for her and Susan, preferring, for the sake of propriety, to walk.

When he caught up with them at the second hole Susan was telling Ali she could tee off from the women's marker. Ali was all for anything that took a few yards off her score. They looked like the best of friends, chattering away, laughing, joking. All of which ceased immediately when he drew near enough to overhear the conversation.

By the third hole Jordan thought he had Ali's system of scoring down pat. Basically, anything outside the fairway didn't count. Nor did hazards situated within its boundaries.

Ahead of them about one hundred yards out on the fourth hole was a maintenance man who was working on the sprinkler system. "You can go ahead," he told Ali, "just be sure to call out 'fore' before you swing, so anyone in the general vicinity knows you're teeing off." Forewarned was forearmed, in Ali's case.

"Why can't I just yell 'heads up'?"

"Because on the golf course, it's 'fore'." If he didn't know better he would think Ali was purposely trying to get his goat.

She bent to place her ball on the orange tee at her feet, mumbling, "Okay, okay, you don't have to get so snotty about it."

"Daddy," Susan hissed, elbowing him in the ribs. "It's just a game. Don't be so hard on her. She won't want to come with us next time."

Teaching Susan to golf hadn't been near this frustrating. Or exhilarating. When he played a round or two with business associates he didn't have to argue over whether sand traps were indigenous to the immediate geographical area, much less fight against the constant distraction of their bare legs. Against his will, Jordan caught himself wondering which cheek Ali's professed tattoo rested on as she wiggled her hips into position and swung.

"Comin' through!" She swung at the ball as if it were a detestable pest about to bite her. It sliced to the right, heading straight for the maintenance man. The guy glanced up just in time to catch sight of the small round missile plowing toward him and scrambled to take cover in a surrounding copse of trees.

"Little bastard," she muttered. "Toss me another ball, Suz. I'll get the hang of this, yet." She caught the ball in her right hand, and teed up, going through all the motions of perfecting her stance.

The foursome that had been trailing them caught up. Not an unusual occurrence when you considered Ali made an average of three attempts per tee before counting her strokes. Two men, two college boys, fathers and sons most likely, all content to stand in a huddle watching Ali, occasionally bending their heads toward each other to make a comment. The set of their faces told Jordan they weren't discussing her general ineptness with a golf club. He'd much rather the testosterone quartet went ahead of them. Besides, it was just good golf etiquette to let them play through.

"Hold up, Ali," he told her, motioning for her to join him before addressing the foursome. "Go ahead, guys. We're in no hurry."

"Nice swing," the tall blond youth of perhaps twenty said to Ali with a grin, choosing a titanium driver from his bag. She leaned just the slightest bit toward the younger man and whispered something that had his cheeks flushing. After that, the guy hurried to set up his ball, eyes glued to the turf beneath his feet.

"What did you say to him?" Jordan demanded as she sidled up next to him, resting folded hands on the hilt of her club.

"You don't want to know."

"Yeah, I really do want to know," he said low as Susan moved off toward a nearby drinking fountain to wet down her hand towel.

"Just enough to put his mind back on the game instead of the pointy little bulge under his zipper."

He *would* breathe, he ordered himself. Nevertheless, the boy quickly sent his ball down the fairway, gathered his clubs without so much as a peek in Ali's direction, and moved off a fair distance to wait for his *compadres*.

"Stop glaring at me, Jordan," she said without looking at him. "He was referring to my ass and everyone here knows it. I doubt he'll make the mistake of approaching Susan in the same manner."

True to Ali's prediction the college kid had gravitated toward the drinking fountain where Susan was still standing, swiping at the back of her neck. Joe Smooth wet his own hand towel and used it to cool the heat in his cheeks. Whatever Ali had said to the kid had cooled his ardor considerably, Jordan noted, because he no longer wore a cocky expression on his face.

Leaning down so that his mouth was on the level with her ear he said, "I thought you weren't going to carry tales?"

She opened her mouth to speak, closed it again, patted him affectionately on the cheek. "I'll let you have that one."

"I thought you would," he said, straightening, letting his gaze wander to his daughter once again.

"So, do I?" she asked a moment later, as they waited for the third man in the passing group to tee off.

Pulling his attention away from the pair chatting casually at the water fountain, he looked down at her. "Do you what?"

"Have a nice swing."

More like a battering ram, he thought to himself. But he had to admit the way Ali lined up in stance would raise Lazarus from the dead. "No comment."

Though he was just as guilty as that college kid of staring at her ass, he was wise enough to keep his lecherous thoughts to himself. Not for the first time today was he sorry Susan had accompanied them, which made him selfish, he supposed, and had him feeling more than a little guilty. Susan had never been so excited about spending a day on the golf course. He'd had only to mention Ali would be joining them and the girl fairly dove from beneath her bedcovers to stumble to the closet, still half asleep, in search of something chic to wear.

* * * * *

Susan stood by the water fountain studying her father and Ali in conversation. They made a nice couple, she thought, noting how Ali's darker hair contrasted with her father's golden bronze. If Dad played his cards right, she could end up with a really cool stepmom.

She hadn't worried about the possibility of her dad marrying again until recently, when he'd started to date. It was kind of weird the way women were always staring at him or licking their lips when he accompanied her to the mall, or out here on the golf course, or to a movie, or when he came to a special event at school. She'd never stopped to think about her dad in that way. The same way she thought of Randy Peters.

Compared to the four bozos playing through, Jordan Finch was a hunk. If you noticed things like that about your father.

Susan wondered if Ali thought her father was a hunk. She also worried that if things went sour between her dad and Ali, or Dad started seeing other women, how she could end up with an old-fashioned cutthroat battle-ax with visions of playing surrogate mommy, or another version of her own "not now, honey, I'm busy" biological mother. Ali was never too busy to talk to her. They'd been talking and laughing most all afternoon about boys and music and clothes. Susan had already told Bonnie all about Ali and how she'd helped her pick out her prom gown, and fix her hair just the right way, and told her what kind of shoes to wear and jewelry and makeup best set off her features.

And by golly, it had worked. Randy Peters had noticed her, hadn't he? He'd held her hand while they sat out in the car, kissed her for the longest time, too. Now he was calling her on the phone. Didn't that mean he was interested in her as more than a substitute date? Because now that they were talking he would learn more about her as a person.

Had Dad kissed Ali the same way Randy had kissed her on prom night? She'd have to remember to ask Bonnie about it. Bonnie's mom and dad were divorced, too, and Bonnie's dad went out on dates all the time.

* * * * *

The foursome played through, never to be seen again. When they hit the ninth hole, while waiting to tee off Jordan said, "Want to cut the round short and finish up with nine?"

Susan, not wanting the day to end so swiftly, was quick to say, "I'm game for another nine. How about you, Ali?"

Boiling in hot oil sounded more appealing, but Ali put on her best killer smile and said brightly, "Heck I'm just getting warmed up. But your dad looks pretty whooped. What's the matter, Finch? Stay up past your bedtime last night?"

"In your dreams, MacPherson."

"Yes, well…" She chose the driver with the biggest head she could find from the rented bag. "We've already established my dreams are pretty much the kind to keep a person up nights. But you don't hear me crying uncle."

"Have it your way. We'll play eighteen. But I don't want to hear either one of you whining when your arms feel like they've fallen off."

Her arms fell off long before they reached the eighteenth hole. The Scots must have been damned bored to invent a game where you spent all your energy smacking around a little white ball with a very thin, unwieldy stick. What kind of masochist thought fun was keeping track of how many times you whacked a ball through brush and woods and around lakes and sandy dugouts into a little cup with a flag?

Probably the same guy who invented high heels, Ali mused, careful only to massage the muscles lining her waist when Jordan wasn't looking. All this twisting and rotating was the exact reason she avoided aerobics classes. It had better be worth it when Finch's iron-fisted control finally snapped and he kissed her like a man on the prowl should.

How many of his buttons was she going to have to push before he made a move? It was killing her, this wanting that had reared its head during their first meeting only to grow stronger every day until she was ready to scream. The longer he held off, the more she discovered she liked about him, and she didn't want to like him, she just wanted to go to bed with him, dammit. Once that happened this ridiculous fascination would be over and she could move on.

Not for a moment did she fool herself into thinking there could ever be anything serious between them. Jordan Finch was a phase. A detour on the road of life. Getting emotionally tangled up with him just wouldn't be smart. She was who she was, and she couldn't—wouldn't—pretend to be anything else. Men didn't fall in love with women like her—the non-conformists, women who shunned smothering ties and scoffed at the rules that bound. Rules made by mothers who preached that fun and men were interconnected evils leading to ultimate ruin. No, women like her fell into lust. It was safer.

She would no sooner pretend to be an empty-headed bimbo to catch a sugar daddy than she would pretend to be mother material to impress a potential husband. She wasn't either. She just wanted to spend time with someone who shared her passion for life instead of trying to control it. Someone who wouldn't heap their expectations on her head, but would let her be herself—understand her need to be appreciated, yet gave her space to grow within.

Her own mother couldn't love her for who she was. Why would she expect Jordan Finch to be any different?

"Ali." Jordan's hand came down on her arm before she'd perfected her stance. "That's enough," he said softly. "You're tired. Let's call it a day."

"I can make it," she insisted. "There are only six more holes to go."

"No. I shouldn't have let you talk me into continuing. A full eighteen's too much the first time."

"And let you show me up? Forget it." But he was already prying the club from her cramping fingers. *Thank you, Jesus.*

Susan, slumped into the passenger seat of the cart looking like a wilted flower, blew out a long breath. "I hate to admit it, Ali, but I'm pooped, too."

"Well, there's a fine how-do-you-do." Ali stomped over to the cart and plopped down in the driver's seat, while Jordan returned her club to the golf bag strapped on the rack behind them. "Playing possum just so I'll give in gracefully."

"Yeah, but it gets me a cold Pepsi and a few minutes in the video arcade up at the clubhouse. Guess what else they have."

"What?"

"Saunas and whirlpools and massage tables."

"Take me to your leader."

"Scoot," Jordan ordered, bumping her hip with his until she moved to the center of the cart, where she was forced to sit sandwiched between him and Susan for the ride to the clubhouse.

Her body overheated at shoulder-to-thigh contact with his. She could detect hard muscle beneath his pleated pants, felt the curve of his hip pressing into hers. He shifted, laying his arm along the back of the seats, which only served to throw her off balance where she was perched between the seats, drawing her more fully into the dip of his shoulder. Susan, the little hussy, didn't seem inclined to move even an inch toward the edge of her seat to make more room.

Ali had nothing to hold onto as they rolled down the paved cart path that twisted and turned with the course. The first sharp turn had her digging her nails into Jordan's thigh to keep from falling fully against him, deciding it was her imagination that Susan had snickered.

The combination of wind rushing past their ears and the whining buzz of the cart's battery-powered engine kept a humming Susan from hearing the question he murmured in her ear. "Are you trying to hurt me or turn me on?"

"Are you flirting with me, Finch?"

"Maybe."

"Well, for God's sake, wait until Susan's out of sight so you can do it right."

Chapter Seven

ॐ

Susan was off like a shot the moment the cart pulled to a stop outside the rental building, heading straight for the clubhouse. Ali would have followed suit, but Finch had hold of her wrist to keep her from doing just that.

"We'll meet you out at the car in half an hour," he called after Susan, dropping the key to the cart into the attendant's palm. She waved a hand in acknowledgment. The second Susan was out of sight around the corner of the low-slung brick building, Jordan swerved off in the opposite direction, tugging her behind him along a gravel path that wound around and through a rose arbor, then past and around a two-tiered bubbling fountain.

"Finch, where are we going?"

"Some place private where I can put my hands on you. If you have any objections, voice them now. And I swear, Ali, you call me Finch one more time, you won't be able to sit for a week."

Down a second narrow path, around what looked like a gardening shed, he hung a hard right, and swung her around until her back was pressed against the back of the shed.

"It's—"

"Shut up, Ali," he growled just seconds before his mouth captured hers, his warm tongue snaking past her parted lips in a shock of heated lust. One hand tunneled through her hair, loosening the ribbon holding the thick mass just below the nape while the other closed around her hip. His fingers lightly massaged the back of her neck. What breath she had left in her lungs was stolen by his greedy mouth. He took his time, kissing her thoroughly, tasting, nipping, worrying her lower lip with the edge of his teeth.

The edges of her mind began to cloud. The kiss turned slower, deeper, drugging her senses, dulling her reflexes. She was helpless to do anything but moan when he cupped her buttocks to haul her more fully against him. Not that she wanted to do much about it. She felt the hard core of his cock, and rubbed against it to ease the ache between her own thighs.

One minute her back was against the wall, the next they had switched places, with her sprawled against his chest. His hands wandered her back, her hips. She attacked his throat, breathing in the aroma of his cologne, a purely male scent that thrilled her, left her without the willpower to protest any invasion he wanted to attempt. She wanted his hands on her. Wanted him like she hadn't wanted anything or anyone in a very long time.

"Christ, I can't remember when I've sunk to seducing a woman out behind a garden shed," he said thickly. "Or any kind of shed, for that matter."

"And you're doing a bloody fabulous job of it," she murmured, tugging at his earlobe with her teeth. "I knew there was a horny, middle-aged bastard in this fit, trim body somewhere."

"Thirty-seven is hardly middle-aged." He kissed her again, long and slow, rubbing his thumb across the sensitive nipple already straining to break free of the sheer lace and cotton that prevented flesh-to-flesh contact.

"You're telling me. Do it, Finch," she whispered hotly against his mouth. "Right here. Right now."

"Ali..."

She hung from his neck, arms wrapped tightly around corded muscle and sinew, arched into him invitingly, pleased when his breathing turned more ragged and uneven. He wanted to, she could see it in his eyes, knew by the urgency of his hands he was only a step away from saying to hell with it and ripping her clothes off.

"You'll hate yourself later if you don't," she warned.

"I'll hate myself later if I do," he said huskily, burying his face in her throat. "This isn't the way…anyone could come along…"

"That's half the thrill, darling. You want to."

"Yes, I want to. God knows, I want…"

"What?" She was mindless to know what was going on in that very proper head of his. "What is it you want, Jordan? Tell me."

"Jesus," he muttered, letting his head bang back against the wood planking. "I can't believe I'm saying this, but I want to see that tattoo on your ass so bad I can't see straight."

She leaned back to gaze into his hazel eyes, which were glowing with a sexual light he couldn't hide. "Why, Jordan Finch," she cooed silkily. "Is that why you were pretending not to stare at my ass all day?"

"Never mind."

She took his hand in hers and pressed his palm down to the exact location on the backside of her hip. "There."

His chest swelled against her breasts as he took in a breath. "There?" His fingers flexed.

"Mmm, hmm. Now you're trying to decide if it's something appallingly vulgar."

"Sorry. I've never dated a woman with a tattoo before."

"You need to get out more." She disengaged herself from his hold and stepped back, righting her shirt where it was twisted about her waist, restoring her hair to what would have to pass as a mussed ponytail.

He grabbed for her wrist when she turned to leave. "Now you're pissed."

"On the contrary," she shot him a sultry look over her shoulder. "I think maybe you need a little more time to stew over it. Time's up, loverboy. You should have jumped my bones while you had the chance."

He glanced at his watch, cursed beneath his breath, and ran his hands around his waist to tuck the wrinkled tail of his polo shirt under his belt. When he was satisfied he was presentable he made a sweeping gesture, indicating she should precede him down the gravel path. "After you, Allison, darling."

"You'll pay for that, Finch. See if you don't," she warned, taking the lead.

* * * * *

"Okay, what's the theme for tonight?" Franny asked, dropping onto the carpet, Indian-style, to set up the Scrabble board.

"Sexually repressed, anal-retentive men." Ali poured two glasses of wine, flipping her silk robe out behind her before plopping down across from Franny, who was also wearing nothing but her underwear and favorite cotton terry robe.

Franny took a sip of her wine. "Are we skipping the dictionary rule tonight?"

"Yes." It didn't take a genius to figure out they cheated on a regular basis, making up rules as they went. To start, they divvied up all the letters. Each would have to work with what they had until they could make no more words. Whoever was left with the least amount of letters won.

"Cool. Okay, let's see what I've got." Franny tapped a nail against her teeth, studying the letters she'd drawn. "Ah!" With a catty smile she spelled out p-e-c-k-e-r-s-w-e-a-t.

"Peckersweat?" Ali lifted her own glass to her lips.

Franny shrugged. "I figure a guy who doesn't screw on a regular basis has to at least think about it, right? You think men sweat everywhere but their peckers?"

Shaking her head, Ali spelled out s-m-o-l-d-e-r-i-n-g.

"Well hell, don't get creative on me or anything." Franny whipped out her cigarettes and lit two, passing one across the board. "What's the matter with you tonight? You've been jumping around here like you need your cork popped."

Ali puffed manically to keep from spilling her guts to her best friend about how crazy Jordan Finch could make her. "Nothing's the matter with me." She waved Franny's concern away. "Spell or take a pass."

"Pass."

Shit. "Cost you five points." Cigarette dangling from her mouth she shoved the letters h-u-n-g-r-y onto the board.

"I knew it!" Franny pointed an accusing finger at her. "You're seeing somebody and you don't want me to know!"

"Take another pass and it'll cost ten."

"Bitch." Franny scrambled to build another word with what she had. "I hate when you keep secrets from me."

"Then you shouldn't tell every bloody thing you know."

"I don't know anything," Franny reiterated, rearranging her letters with a series of irritated clicks.

"There you go."

"What's so special about this guy that you can't tell me who he is?"

"There is no guy."

Her denial only served to send Franny into second gear. "Save yourself public humiliation later and tell me now. I'll find out, Ali. You know I will. Oh my God!" she clapped a hand over her mouth. "He's married!"

"He's not married," Ali answered automatically, then cursed herself for falling into the trap.

Franny's lips peeled back shrewdly. "The guy you're not seeing isn't married. How interesting. You were never very good at lying to me, I don't know why you bother to try. Hmmm. Sexually repressed. Anal-retentive. Hungry. Smoldering. Add hot lips and a killer ass and you could be describing my boss,

Jordan Finch. By the way, did I mention I was thinking about raping him in the copy room?"

"No, but thanks for sharing."

"He would look sooo good handcuffed to my bed."

She loved Franny. She really did. But if she hadn't gotten to her feet just then she might have scratched the poor girl's eyes out. Pouring another glass of wine, she paused by the window. She simply had talk to someone about Jordan Finch and the way he made her feel, even if she were forced to stick with vague generalities.

"Ali, I'm serious now." Franny began to gather up the game pieces. "I teach you to smoke your first cigarette, throw up your first beer, and this is the thanks I get. What gives?"

"Okay, I am seeing someone, but…"

"Yeah, yeah, you're seeing someone. I need more detail than that."

"Well, he's…not what you'd call my type."

"What's wrong with him?" Franny dumped a handful of letters into the box and started gathering more.

"Nothing. Everything."

"Which is it, honeybun, nothing or everything?"

"Both. He's like old money. Refined, courteous, impeccable manners. He pulls out my chair, holds the door, restrains himself admirably from pawing at me like a wolf."

Another handful of wooden letters clattered into the game box. "Then he must die. Is he cute?"

"I get wet just looking at him."

"Oh." Franny sat back on her heels, reaching for her wine glass. "Bad kisser, huh? BO?"

"Not a chance," she sighed, taking a sip.

"Lousy in bed, then."

"I don't know. We haven't been to bed yet."

"What?" Franny's green eyes grew wide. "Why not?"

"Because we've only been out a few times and I spent each time testing his mettle, waiting for him to be shocked or appalled or run screaming into the night. He's like fine wine and I'm...beer. Sooner or later he'll come to his senses and realize we can never have a serious relationship. But until then he just keeps taking everything I say and do in stride."

"The bastard. Beer. You think you're...beer." Ali knew that tone, wasn't surprised by the irate light in Franny's eyes as she stood, bracing for a tirade. "In other words, he's too good for you, so you might as well run him off now and save yourself the trouble later. I swear to God, I hope that bitter old pruned-faced witch rots in hell!"

They both knew Franny was referring to her mother and the resulting self-pitying lapses she sometimes fell into. "Franny, don't start."

Franny stalked across the room and grabbed her by the shoulders in a firm grip. "You are a beautiful, intelligent, caring woman with normal sexual urges, who likes to have a little fun. That is not a sin, goddammit! I know you, Ali. You don't sleep around. You're selective, probably more so than I am. But you have this ridiculously aggravating habit of seeing yourself as less. Twelve years I've spent, drumming into your head the fact that your mother is wrong for the way she puts you down. Why do you let her get to you like this? Why don't you drive over there and have it out with her once and for all?"

"This isn't about my mother," she said through clenched teeth.

"Oh, yes it is," Franny argued. "Sure, you have months and years where you can ignore the cruel things she says to you, but then you start feeling guilty and wondering if they're true. I remember how you used to come back to school with puffy eyes after you'd been home for a visit. And how you'd mope around for days, withdraw into that little shell Allison MacPherson built around herself. My God, the day you told me she called you a whore I wanted to kill her myself. Do you think I'm a whore, Ali?"

"No!"

"Do you think every woman who comes into your boutique looking for that perfect something to catch a man's eyes is a whore on the make? Is every man a fine wine and every woman who gives in to the urge to be held and cherished by him just another can of beer to be tossed aside after guzzling?"

Ali jerked away, busied herself folding the Scrabble board and placing the lid on the box. "I didn't tell you about him so you could lecture me."

"Why did you, then?" Franny demanded, hands on hips. "So I would agree this bozo's too good for the likes of my best friend? He sounds like an idiot if you ask me. Snooty and pretentious and stuck on himself. Big deal he doesn't suck spaghetti off his plate, that doesn't give him the right to make you feel like a slut for wanting to go to bed with him."

"He doesn't make me feel like a slut. He just... It won't work, that's all."

"It won't if you don't want it to, that's for sure. I've never seen a guy yet who stuck around when you decided it was time for him to hit the road. That's all fine and well. But don't use the lame excuse that you *think* he's too good for you so you can back off and slink away with your tail between your legs." Stripping off her robe, Franny snatched up her jeans and shirt and jerked them on. "My mom and dad happen to be excellent judges of character and they think the world of you. How dare you insult me or them with this 'my mother says I'm a whore so it must be true' shit."

"Franny, don't leave mad."

Franny bundled up her robe and snapped up her purse, not bothering with tying the strings on the tennis shoes she'd shoved her feet into. "Sometimes you really piss me off, Ali. You worked like a dog all through college, saved up to open your own boutique. You're successful. You *have* a family—me and mine. But none of that is good enough for you. After all these years you're still trying to earn your mother's approval instead of accepting she'll never give it because she hates the fact you learned to stand on your own without her."

Still hot under the collar, Franny stomped to the door, pausing with her hand on the knob. "Well, you know what? She had her chance to be supportive. She had her chance to stand behind you and be proud of you. To be a part of your life. And instead she took vindictive pleasure in ripping your self-esteem to shreds. I guess it's the rest of us who are fucked up in the head for believing in you. Good fucking night!"

Chapter Eight

ဢ

"Mendez file." Franny slapped the folder down rudely on his desk, sending papers scattering. "Anything else?"

Jordan leaned back in his swivel chair, clicking the pen in his right hand. He had been going to ask for another cup of coffee, but thought better of it after glimpsing the dangerous light in Franny's eyes. "Rough weekend?" he ventured.

"Not if you don't count the fact it was ruined by a woman I *thought* was my friend. Do I look like the kind of person who would—oh, never mind."

Relief flooded through him. He liked Franny well enough, she was an excellent assistant, but he didn't make a habit of getting personally involved with his employees' personal lives. What Franny did on her own time was her own business, as was his. And that's the way he liked it. "Yes, well, if Mendez—"

"She actually expected me to feel sorry for her, if you can imagine," she blurted out, slapping a palm on the desk.

"She. The woman you thought was your friend."

"Yeah. Well, you met her at Dale's party, remember? Ali. The one in the kitchen."

Now he was interested. "Ali. Sure."

"She's dating some jerk-off she says smells like old money."

"Smells like old money?" He felt his spine stiffen at the insult. Unless, of course, Franny was referring to another of Ali's conquests. He imagined a woman like her would have quite a few men on a stringer.

"Yeah, you know the type," she went on, pacing back and forth in front of his desk. "Charming, smooth, thinks he's God's gift to women. Treats Ali like she's some kind of…of…golddigger. Like she should be grateful he noticed her. I mean, she has a marketing degree, owns her own business, lives in a swanky condo, drives a to-die-for car. And let's face it, the woman's a knockout. She doesn't need to take that shit from some two-faced, uptight mongrel who doesn't have the sense to know when he has a good thing going."

"So, er, why doesn't she break it off with him?"

"Who the hell knows?" Franny threw up her hands in disgust. "Men are pigs. It's perfectly okay for them to jump into bed with anything in a skirt, but when a woman gives in to those same natural urges, well…she's just plain slutty. If I ever find out who this asshole is, you can bet I'll track him down and set him straight on a few things." She stopped pacing, scooped his coffee cup up, asking in the same derisive tone, "You want more coffee?"

"Only if you think a pig like me deserves a second cup."

"You're not a pig."

"You just said all men are pigs," he reminded her.

She set the cup down and leaned both hands on his desk. "Jordan, you met Ali. What did you think of her?"

"Um…" he struggled to base his answer on what should have been his and Ali's only meeting. "Well, she's forthright. Witty. Strikes me as the kind of woman who knows what she wants and goes after it."

"Exactly. So why does she want to let some sexually repressed dildo treat her like she's not good enough for him?"

"Maybe that's something you should ask her," he mumbled, clenching his fist beneath the chair. *He* certainly intended to. The least she could have done was be honest with him about her intentions to date other men. Here he'd been holding back, trying to act like a gentleman, to give her time to get to know him, and him her before jumping in the sack.

"I'm sorry." Franny straightened, calming herself. "I shouldn't have dumped on you like that. It's just that she's my best friend and I hate to see her wasting her time with a guy who's not worthy of a second look from her. I don't care if he does make her wet just looking at him. I'll get that coffee now."

His stomach clenched. A slow burning started just beneath his breastbone, working its way up the back of his throat.

Franny paused at the door, suddenly remembering he'd been about to tell her something about the Mendez file. "What was it you were going to say about Mendez?"

"Tell him I'm working on the projections and I'll get back to him in a day or two."

"Got it. Hey, Susie Q. What's shakin'?"

Jordan looked up to see Susan standing in the door, her eyes lit up like a Christmas tree. "You aced the math test, huh?" he asked as she skipped over to him and flopped down on his lap, planting a kiss on his cheek.

"How can you doubt it? Look!" She dug beneath her blouse and pulled out a class ring suspended on the gold chain he'd given her for Christmas last year. "Can you believe it? Randy broke up with his girlfriend and gave me his class ring!"

Oh, God. This couldn't be happening. "Susan—"

"And look what else." She dumped the pictures onto his desk, spreading them out so he could see each and every pose. "We got the pictures back. Randy slipped the guy some extra cash and he put a rush on them. Aren't they fabulous? Daddy?"

Suddenly his tie felt as though it were choking him. He ran a finger around his collar, but the tightness in his throat refused to be eased. "Look, Susan, don't you think you're moving a little fast with this Randy guy? I mean, if he two-timed his other girlfriend, what makes you think he won't do the same to you?"

"He didn't two-time her," Susan objected hotly. "She's the one who got mono from some other guy. She two-timed him first."

"Okay, but that still makes you the rebound girl. You don't break up with one girl and turn around and give another girl your ring the next day. And I know what I'm talking about,

Susan. He couldn't have cared for his girlfriend much if he can slide into another relationship so easily."

"Oh, so now I'm not good enough for him to be interested in."

"I didn't say that."

"You most certainly did!" she shouted. "First, you think I'm trying to act older than I am by buying that dress, now I'm so stupid I can't see anything but stars. You're making judgments about Randy and you don't even know him!"

"I don't have to know him. I know his kind."

"And what kind is that?" she snorted, tossing her head.

"The kind who always thinks the grass is greener on the other side of the fence. *He's* not worthy of *you*, Susan. The first time another girl wags her fingers at him, he'll be breaking up with you and taking up with her. And besides, you're too young to be going steady with any boy."

She looked at him as if he'd just slapped her. "Are you…are you saying you won't let me see him?"

"Susan is on the verge of discovery, about herself, boys, sex, everything. If you try to put up walls and forbid her to peek over them she's going to dive in headfirst, with or without your permission."

Jordan took in a cleansing breath, forced himself to slow down, moderate his tone. "No, that's not what I'm saying. It's just that when you really like someone, you tend to overlook certain…tendencies, certain qualities of a person's character that might seem harmless and even endearing at the time. But later, when weighed against good judgment, those same qualities take on a different tone, a different meaning altogether. Understand?"

"Could you say that again in English?"

He rubbed his eyes, forced himself to continue when what he really wanted to do was drag her home by the hair and lock her in the closet until she was thirty. "Okay. You say I'm making judgments about Randy when I don't really know him. And you're right—" he held up a hand before she could crow, "to an extent. It angers me that he didn't notice you before the prom, only after he saw you in that gown. It's what's underneath that counts, and I don't mean that literally. Frankly, you're guilty of the same thing. You only wanted to go out with him because he's the school hunk."

"That's not true!"

"Really? What's his grade point average? Do you know? Do you know what his goals are in life? Whether or not he intends to go to college? What are his parents like? What do they do for a living?"

"Well," she shifted defensively. "We haven't gotten around to discussing all that yet."

"Exactly." He pointed a finger at the vee of her blouse. "Yet you're wearing his ring around your neck like it's some kind of trophy. You had plenty of time to discuss that stuff in the six hours you were gone on prom night, more time while you were sitting out front in his car. So far the only thing you can tell me about Randy Peters is that he's hunky and his last girlfriend has mono. Sorry, but those aren't quite the recommendations a father hopes to hear about the boy his daughter is gaga over."

"I *knew* you wouldn't understand," her tone took on a sulky quality.

"What I don't understand is why a bright girl like you doesn't want to spend time with a boy who is equally as challenging to her brain as he is to her hormones."

She began to gather up the glossy photos, shoving them into the envelope she'd pulled them from. "I didn't notice your hormones under lock and key yesterday."

He slapped a hand down on hers, trapping it on top of the eight by ten shot of her and Randy smiling out at the camera from beneath an arbor of silk flowers. "What's that supposed to mean?"

"It means I saw you staring at Ali's butt when you thought I wasn't looking. Real smooth, Dad, since it's her brains you should be interested in. Can I have my pictures, please? If you don't want to buy them I'll use my own money."

Embarrassment had him clearing his throat, brushing her hand away so he could take a closer look at the pictures. "I didn't say I wasn't going to buy them," he muttered gruffly.

"Daddy, can't you just give Randy a chance? If you don't like him, at least trust me to know my own mind. You think I want to get hooked up with some doofus football jock who can't add two and two?"

"It appears you're already hooked." He cast a derisive glance at the ring nestled between her breasts.

"Yeah? Well I can cut Randy loose just as quickly as I hooked him if he tries to pull any crap over on me."

"Nice to know I'm buying two hundred dollars' worth of pictures in hopes you don't take the scissors to them in about a month." He sighed heavily, tossing the eight by ten onto the pile. "Pick out the ones you want and leave the forms on my desk in the study. I'll write out a check tonight."

"Thanks, Daddy." She came around the desk and bent to hug his neck, pressing another kiss to his cheek. "I love you even if you are grouchy."

"You're such a suck-up. Go on, I have to get back to work."

"I'm on my way to Ali's. She's dying to see the pictures. See you there."

Chapter Nine

🔊

Ali looked up when the bell tinkled. She and Susan had worked out a system to avoid any mishaps should Franny come to her senses and rush in to apologize for her obnoxious behavior over Scrabble, wherein Susan would keep to the back of the shop, slip out the side door on cue, and watch for Franny to leave.

"I guess you heard the big news," Jordan said flatly, stopping in front of the cash register.

"I did," Ali nodded. "Must be hell having to share your desk with Randy Peters' pretty mug. Tums?"

"Whiskey, straight up."

"Yeah, that usually does it for me, too. But it's really hard to worry whether or not the IRS will haul you in for filling out quarterly tax returns wrong when your head's stuck in the toilet."

He reached across the counter, snagged her notepad, tore off a piece, and shoved it at her. "Write down your address."

"My, my," she remarked, reaching for the pen tucked behind her ear. "We are in a snit today, aren't we? Thinking of sending me flowers, Finch?" She thought she heard him grinding his teeth as she wrote out her address. He all but snatched the paper from beneath her fingers when she was done, shoving it into his pocket.

"Susan!" he barked, bringing the girl out from behind the curtained-off break area. "Let's go."

"Be right there. Gotta get my books."

Ali propped an elbow on the register. "You'd better go home and loosen that silk tie, Finch, before you choke on it. It's just a high school infatuation. She'll get over it."

"Ready." Susan cruised up the aisle to stand beside Jordan, announcing with a smile, "Ali's buying one of my prom pictures."

"Is that so?" He shot Ali a sideways glance, arching a brow.

There was something she didn't quite like glowing in the depths of his hazel eyes. Animosity? Amazement? Then it was gone as he turned back to Susan. "Meet me at the car. I need to talk to Ali a minute."

"Sure. See ya, Ali."

"Later, kiddo."

"Are you free Saturday evening?" he asked somewhat curtly.

She studied him a moment, and decided she didn't like the way he'd asked. "Finch, is there something stuck in your craw besides Randy Peters?"

"I take it you aren't."

Several browsing customers were stopping to stare. Ali gestured to Deanna to approach the customers and distract them. She rounded the counter and took Jordan's arm, leading him to the break area behind the curtain. "I'm sorry if you had a bad day, what with the pictures and Susan's little bombshell about the ring, but do you think you could manage a civil tone with me?"

He ran a hand around the back of his neck. "Sorry. It was rather a trying day. Franny was out of sorts. There was a moment when I thought she was going to throw hot coffee on me. Then Susan came dancing in with her news. Next thing I know I'm out two hundred bucks for prom pictures and promising to hold off smashing in Randy Peters' face."

What would it have been like, she wondered, to have a parent who wanted to protect her from the cruelties of life, yet swallowed those parental objections so she might test her wings, make her own mistakes, learn from them? She might not be so headstrong now if she'd had those small chances.

"Oh, Jordan." She placed a hand to his cheek, felt her heart melt a little at his obvious misery. And Franny Demato in a snit wasn't a pretty sight. "I know it was hard, giving in that way. But isn't it better than Susan sneaking around behind your back to see him? At least this way things are out in the open."

He covered her hand with his large one, lowered it to his chest, holding it there, caressing the inside of her wrist. "It was hard," he admitted. "Ali…" His eyes searched hers. "That night at the party, why did you agree to go out with me?"

"Wow," she breathed, "you really did have a rough day."

"I need an answer." His fingers tightened around her wrist, keeping her from moving away. "Why?"

She lifted a shoulder, but couldn't bring herself to meet his intense gaze. "I-I don't know, exactly. I was intrigued, I suppose. Besides, I really wasn't sure you'd call. You know how it goes when you exchange phone numbers with someone you've just met."

"Actually, I don't. I didn't do a lot of swapping phone numbers during the fourteen years I was married. I usually concentrate on one woman at a time. Do we have that in common, you think?"

"Concentrating on women? No, I'd say you're all by yourself in that department. I'm strictly heterosexual."

"Christ," he bit off an oath. "Could you be serious for one damn minute?"

"I could if I knew what it was you were talking about." She pried his fingers from around her wrist. "At any rate, this isn't the time to discuss whatever *it* is. Susan's waiting out in the car for you and I have customers."

He nodded curtly, afraid he would actually speak the words if he remained a minute longer. "I'll call you later."

Ali watched from inside the curtain as he strode down the main aisle and out the door. It was the first time she'd seen him in a suit and tie. A very expensive suit and tie that screamed understated elegance. He wasn't only handsome in the most classic of ways, with his tawny hair and strong, square jaw and deliciously defined mouth, but successful, and extremely well-proportioned. He walked with an air of confidence, oblivious as to how potently he affected those around him, particularly women. Several of the customers stopped browsing altogether just to watch him pass by. One woman used the Oriental fan she'd been examining to briskly cool her heated cheeks. Another actually licked her lips and sighed.

Jordan Finch was a mixture of quiet strength and leashed power in subtle shades of gold. God help her if he ever discovered just how easily he could make her forget they stood at opposite ends of the spectrum. How she was slowly coming to crave that lazy smile, to appreciate his shy, cautious ways. She should end it before one of them got hurt. Before she let herself wade too deeply into the waters of his life.

One of them would drown. And she was obviously so much better at navigating the shark-infested waters of physically satisfying relationships than the recently beached Jordan Finch. Jordan wasn't the type to have a casual affair. A man didn't dedicate himself to fourteen years of marriage, his job, relocate his daughter and himself to a strange town and worry over an ex-wife's reaction to his filing a custody suit, then, without a second thought as to how it would affect his future, turn around and indulge in meaningless sex.

Unfortunately, that's all she could allow it to be when they finally came together. Just sex. And they would collide in bed, she knew, because she was bound to do something stupid like jump his bones the next time she had him alone for more than ten minutes. What if he was right? What if Gloria Finch had set private detectives on him? Had everyone he consorted with investigated? What if one of those detectives had followed them to the golf course? Taken pictures of them behind the shed, groping and kissing like a pair of hounds in heat. What better evidence could be submitted to prove that he was an unfit father than him dallying with a...a promiscuous woman like herself, when his innocent daughter was inside the clubhouse having a soda and playing video games?

Ali closed the boutique that evening with a heavy heart, her steps dragging as she made her way to the car, unlocked it, and slid behind the wheel. She inserted the key into the ignition but didn't start the engine. Just sat there, staring out the windshield, not really seeing the children's park across the street where swings hung empty, teeter-totters slanted at a forty-five-degree angle, their painted wooden seats fading and peeling from years of exposure to harsh sunlight. How could she continue seeing Jordan when to do so would put him at risk, simply because she couldn't control these God-awful urges that came on her like mad fits descended on the insane?

She had known him less than two weeks, yet already she knew he was a good father, and a dedicated businessman who took his responsibilities seriously. He had worked so damn hard to make a living and provide for his family that it had cost him that family in the end. Worked so hard he didn't notice he played golf like he did everything else, with complete concentration and precise movements. She hacked at the ball haphazardly, disregarding any rule she didn't like, just as she continued replacing ball after ball after ball on the tee until one of the little buggers soared in the general direction she wanted it to go. Jordan played like a professional, carefully studying each shot, examining every angle, playing by every rule, and never once reached for a second, third or fourth ball.

Jesus! She let her forehead thump against the steering wheel. That was her, all right, hacking her way through life, discarding what didn't suit her, ignoring the rules in favor of making up her own as she went. Don't follow the rules. Be different. Get noticed. Well, he'd noticed, and would likely get a peck of trouble in the bargain. Jordan had already studied his shot for obtaining full custody of Susan, examined every angle, and was willing—more than willing—to follow the rules he'd laid out to her about late nights, barhopping, spending more time with Susan. And what had she done to help him fall off that wagon but slide up next to him behind the rose garden, dangling the fated apple women the world over, since time began, have used to bring men around to their way of thinking. *Do it, Finch. Right here. Right now.*

Well, by God, she might not be able to do anything about the tattoo on her ass, aside from laser surgery that would leave worse scars, but she could do something about the gold ring in her navel. She could take the damn thing out and flush it.

Well, maybe not flush it, but put it away somewhere for the time being.

"Right, Ali," she muttered to herself, firing the car to life. "Like that's going to rank real high on the pro side of a judge's list once he gets a gander at eight by ten glossy photos of Jordan's hands on your tits."

Her mood had worsened by the time she got home. Sexy underwear and silk robes were out of the question. Baggy jean shorts, a raggedy T-shirt, braless and barefoot, her face washed clean of makeup, she sat down at the parlor table huddled in the breakfast nook of her fitted-out kitchen with a simple peanut butter and jelly sandwich, accompanied by only a glass of milk. Needing to feel wholesome, which she wasn't. No pretenses. No slick barriers of smartly chic clothes and expertly applied makeup to protect her against the outside world. Or perfectly prepared antipasto by candlelight to soothe her. No wine to relax her tense shoulders or relieve the dull ache in her chest.

No Franny to bitch to about the injustice of life.

No mother with a sneer plastered on lips thinned with disproval.

Just Allison Macpherson, an all-American PB&J sandwich, and a glass of cold milk.

When the doorbell rang unexpectedly, she almost choked on the clot of peanut butter that plastered itself to the roof of her mouth. Hurriedly swallowing a gulp of milk to wash down the lump, Ali glanced at the clock above the sink, wondering who would come knocking at her door at a quarter past eight. It wouldn't be Franny—the woman held a grudge with the best of them once her Irish was lit. Franny had been known to go deaf, dumb, and blind until she deemed the sinner who'd held the match that had fired her temper had had enough time to ruminate on repentance. Preferably in the form of a surprise gift. Failing that, crawling on hands and knees would suffice.

"Jordan!" Ali fell back a step in surprise, grinding her knuckles against her chest where the lump of peanut butter she'd forced down her throat seemed to be stuck. "Wh-what are doing here?"

He'd changed out of his suit into, what, for Jordan, seemed like a personal dress code outside the office—a polo shirt and trousers.

"Susan had play practice tonight. She nabbed a part in the production they're putting on this year. *Oklahoma!* The tinker's daughter."

"I—" The man's timing sucked. She must look like a mess. Self-consciously she swiped at her mouth with nervous fingers, praying she didn't have a milk mustache, or worse, peanut butter globbed at the corners. "You said you were going to call—"

"May I come in?"

No! It's not safe here. Go away! "Should you really be here? I mean, how would it look if..." she trailed off, kneading the pad of her ring finger uncertainly. He took the decision out of her hands and crossed the threshold, reaching behind to close the door.

"This is," his gaze swept over her attire, "an unexpected surprise. I figured you for silk lounging pajamas or form-fitting denim and lace."

Her toes curled under at being caught looking like Allison MacPherson instead of her sophisticated counterpart. She all but jumped out of his reach when his hand came up to thumb a smudge from the edge of her cheek.

"I think it's jelly," he said, dropping his hand to lean closer.

She ran the heel of her hand down the left side of her face and came away with a smear of strawberry jam streaked across her palm. He chuckled, reaching into his pocket for a handkerchief. "Be still," he ordered, clamping a hand on her shoulder before she could react, dabbing gently at her cheek. "There," he wadded the cloth and stuffed it back into his pocket. "Should I ask what you were doing with the Smucker's?"

She felt utterly ridiculous standing in front of him like a wayward child who needed her face washed. Gone were not only her much-needed barriers, but also, it seemed, her normally glib tongue. His hand was still on her right shoulder. The T-shirt she was wearing was no deterrent against the heat from his fingers. Her tongue felt thick, glued to the roof of her mouth as his thumb moved lazily over her collarbone.

"You shouldn't be here," she finally managed. Visions of crazed photographers with cameras at the ready, hiding in the bushes outside her door, leaped into her head.

"Why, does the complex haves rules against male visitors after eight?"

"For Christ's sake, Jordan. Anyone could have seen you come in here!"

"Like a jealous lover, maybe?"

"What?"

Jordan's fingers tightened on the curve of her shoulder, then released. He had stewed over it all right. It was eating him alive inside wondering if what Franny had said about Ali's current lover was true. "Are you seeing someone else?"

"You mean, seeing someone else as in dating around?"

"That's not an answer. That's a question. I thought we agreed to be honest with each other up front. If you are, I think I have a right to know." He advanced on her. She backed through the archway leading to the living room.

"Where did you get an idea like that?"

"It's a very simple question, Allison. Yes or no?" The edge of the couch brought her to a dead stop. He blocked her evasive sidestep in one swift, stealthy move, caging her in with an arm on either side, his hands anchored to the curved lip of the couch.

"Don't call me that," she said tightly.

"I can't stop you from seeing other men, but you could at least do me the consideration of being truthful about it. Yes or no?"

She pushed at his chest, temper sparking in her dark eyes. "Just who do you think you are barging into my house issuing questions and demanding answers?"

Jordan refused to be moved. He was pretty sure he had it figured out now. The reason Ali hadn't wanted Franny to know about them wasn't to protect Susan, but because Ali hadn't wanted her best friend—who just happened to work for one of the men she was currently juggling—to carry tales about who she was doing on what day of the week.

And damn it to hell he couldn't get that tattoo on her ass out of his head. He couldn't get anything about the little minx out of his head. They way she tasted. The way she smelled. The saucy way she titillated his imagination.

"I'm the guy who had his hands all over you behind the golf course garden shed. Not to be confused with the guy who smells like old money."

"Smells like old—" Recognition came into her eyes. She broke off, covering her lips with three manicured fingers.

He leaned into her, forcing her to strain backward over the hip-high back of the couch to avoid full-body contact, and said, "Trust me when I say now isn't a good time to start giggling. And don't hand me that guff about 'I told you not to ask me out'. I don't like to be led around by the nose."

It hit Ali, then, how he'd gotten his wires crossed. Franny had evidently used Jordan as a sounding board. It was the only explanation for his reference to old money. Trust Franny to hear only what she'd wanted to hear and not the facts.

"Then you shouldn't follow trails laid out by maniacal redheads and jump to conclusions," she shot back. "Franny and I had an argument. She thinks I'm seeing someone on the sly, trying to keep it from her. Left mad when I wouldn't give her a name or any juicy details. So if Franny knows about us now you can blame yourself, not me—"

"I didn't tell her a damn thing."

"And I did *not* say 'he smelled like old money', I said 'he *was* like old money', rhetorically speaking."

"Then you admit you're seeing other men," he rammed home his point, fingers digging into the sofa.

"You're not listening to me, Finch. I gave her generalities and vague observations to satisfy her curiosity so she wouldn't try to play Sherlock Holmes."

"Funny, I thought her description of the jerk-off, two-faced mongrel asshole who thinks he's God's gift to women was quite explicit. Imagine me, riveted to my chair while she force-fed me her thoughts on the subject."

"This conversation is beyond ridiculous. I didn't say any such thing. Franny gets…melodramatic sometimes."

"She was upset because she cares about you, Ali. She doesn't want to see you get hurt."

"She's pissed because I didn't give her the lowdown on the nitty-gritty details," she corrected waspishly. "Would you rather I had told her that her esteemed boss and best friend played doctor out behind the clubhouse over the weekend? You want to imagine something, imagine being riveted to your chair while she force-feeds the judge hearing your custody case her thoughts on that little scenario."

Confusion clouded his eyes. He straightened, dropped his hands to his sides. "I thought…"

"Spare me." Ali sidestepped him and headed for the kitchen. "I know what you thought."

He followed, hovering at the kitchen door. She felt his eyes on her, watching silently while she cleared the table, dumped the remains of her peanut butter and jelly sandwich in the garbage then rinsed her glass and put it in the dishwasher. It shouldn't have hurt that he assumed she passed out sexual favors like party hats. But it did.

"How far did I stick my foot in it?" he asked quietly, hands jammed in his pockets.

"Pretty damned far." Squeezing out the dishrag that had been draped over the divided stainless steel sink, she wiped down the table, replacing the woven bamboo placemats and dried flower centerpiece.

"Ali—"

"Look, Jordan," she whirled to face him, "this just isn't a good idea—us seeing each other. We're...not compatible. And I don't want to ruin your chances of obtaining custody of Susan."

He looked away, offsetting his jaw. A faint line appeared between his brows as he considered her words, his hesitation to assure her otherwise lending even more credence to the fact that she was in no way comparable to his ex-society-wife, in pedigree or character. Her heart was clubbing in her chest by the time he glanced back at her.

"When Susan came into my office today, all giddy and excited over Randy Peters giving her his high school ring, I came very close to forbidding her to have anything further to do with him."

"But you didn't," she said stiffly.

"No. I didn't. Because a very smart lady warned me that if I put up barriers at this stage of the game and forbade her to peek over them, she would dive over headfirst anyway. Susan accused me of making rash judgments about Randy when I hadn't taken the time to get to know him, informing me that she would drop him like a hot potato if he so much as tried to pull the dumb jock routine on her. Then she accused me of ogling your ass when I thought she wasn't looking."

"You *were* ogling my ass."

"Yeah, but I really thought she wasn't looking. I've learned more about my daughter in the last two weeks than in the prior six months. Care to take a guess as to why?"

"You opened your eyes and listened?"

"No," he shook his head slowly. "A woman I met at a party I didn't want to attend wrote down her number on a paper towel in red lipstick, then pretty much dared me to call her. I made the same rash judgments about her as I did about Randy Peters, and now I'm not so sure she'll give me the chance to make it up to her."

It was Ali's turn to look away. "Maybe some of those rash assumptions weren't entirely off base."

"Maybe I don't care anymore," he replied huskily.

"You should care." She still couldn't look at him, transferring her attention from the cabinets to the dishrag in her hand. "For Susan's sake. I've been thinking about what you said about Gloria possibly hiring a private detective. My past isn't what you'd call unblemished. I've accomplished plenty I'm proud of, but there's just as much I'm not so proud of."

"Have you done jail time?"

She gave a short laugh that was more of a grunt. "Not yet."

"Well, you haven't lived until you've done time in Sheriff Bradshaw's jail for drag-racing past the courthouse at high noon."

She did look at him then. Stared, actually. "You're making that up."

"That's just what I tried to convince my daddy Sheriff Bradshaw did, but he didn't go for it. Maybe if I hadn't had a wad of cash bulging out of my pocket from taking bets, he might have believed me. 'Course I told Ellen Ginsworth I'd call her again, and I didn't."

"Who's Ellen Ginsworth?"

"She was my steady for two whole days in ninth grade. She wrote 'Jordan Finch is a lyin' son of a bitch' on the girls' bathroom wall."

"What did your daddy do after he busted you out of jail?"

"Made me take driving lessons for six months." He walked toward her, took the dishrag from her and tossed it into the sink.

"What about Ellen Ginsworth?" she asked, delighted to discover a rebel of sorts inside the stand-up Jordan Finch.

He linked their fingers and gave her reluctant hand a tug to bring her closer. "Married my brother Arlan, and moved to Savannah. She still calls me a lyin' son of a bitch, only with affection now. So, how about it, party girl?" he bent to ask softly. "You gonna give a drag-racing jailbird from Charleston another chance?"

"Gloria might not like—"

"Gloria can go to hell. Susan learned how to play doctor with some shifty-eyed kid on her watch." He touched his fingers to her face, traced her temple, the outline of her mouth. "You don't have shifty eyes. And I must confess, Miss MacPherson, I have a case of the hots for these lips."

He touched his mouth to hers. Nothing more, really, than a whisper of breath at first, softly entreating her to accept his apology. When his arm came around her waist to draw her closer, her arm rose to lock around his neck. Tongues lingered, entwined. Tasting, parting, returning to mate through shallow sighs that soon turned to small gasps and throaty groans.

Lifting her against his chest, he buried his face against the side of her neck to catch his breath, inhaling the soft scent that lingered there. She tilted her jaw to give him full access. His tongue swirled lower, lower, leaving a wet trail as he worked his way down the front of her soft cotton shirt to close over a straining nipple.

Ali let her head fall back, groaned as the first hot flash of need drove straight to where she lived. He suckled, laving the material until it clung wetly to her skin, then released the object of his affection to blow across its peak gently. Chills chased the scorching heat down her spine, rolling, tumbling over each vertebra until she wasn't sure which caused the quivering shiver that left her clinging weakly to his shoulders.

Then she was against the long oak cabinet lining one side of the ovens, supported by one hand beneath her buttocks, braced by his weight. Kisses stretched deeper now, almost desperate. His free hand slipped beneath the loose shirt to skim her ribs, the concave of her abdomen. And she knew, before he did, what he had found just above the low-rise waistband of her jeans shorts that made him go as still as stone.

"What is this?" he rasped, fingering the object he couldn't see. His released it long enough to find the edge of her shirt and draw it up. "Jesus!" he breathed, stunned. For long, tense moments he simply stared at the small gold navel ring, his expression one of blended horror and fascination. "I thought she was kidding."

The hope that burgeoned in her breast when he'd admitted to wilder days himself died a quick death. Clearly, he was having trouble comprehending what would make a person do such a thing.

Her tone hollow, she said, "I-I was going to remove it." But inside she was thinking, *Look at me, Jordan. Say it doesn't matter.* Yet, she knew it did matter.

His chest puffed out as he drew in a halting breath, held it, then exhaled with deliberate languor. "Bed," he said in a strangled voice.

"Wh-what?"

"Bed," he said more forcefully. "Point me in the direction of a goddamn bed or we're going to do it like two rutting pigs, right here against the cabinet."

Chapter Ten

ഔ

They fell on the mattress, blindly clutching at each other, at their clothing, then shoving coverlets and pillows aside. Later, Jordan would notice how the blonde wood of the four-poster bed complemented the bronzed iron and gauzy drapes drawn back at the corners. But for now his vision was hazy, even with his glasses still in place. He could see nothing but her dusky skin beneath his tanned hands as they explored every inch of her from neck to thigh, and every valley and slope in between. He heard nothing but her throaty moans, her harsh breathing and his own as he tasted his way across her breasts and the dip of her stomach.

Arousal, hot and dark, pounded through his veins. The tattoo he'd fantasized about was forgotten for the moment in favor of fondling the small ring at her navel, tonguing it.

When he would have removed his glasses she reached out to stay his hand. "Leave them."

"I don't need them to see what I'm doing to you."

"I don't care if you need them or not," she panted, "the damn things turn me on."

It was the first time a woman had ever asked, no, demanded that he wear his glasses when making love. It was much simpler to do what he'd planned to do if he laid them aside, but the smoldering in her dark almond eyes left no room for argument. Then her hands were on him, stroking, testing the muscles of his shoulders and those lining his pecs. His shirt was gone, and greedy, deft fingers tore at his belt, shoving his trousers over his hips. He kicked them aside, pushing her back against the sheets to continue where he'd left off.

Before his brain shut completely down he managed to ask, "Birth control?"

"Absolutely."

"Do we need to have the other conversation?"

"What other — oh, that. No, we're safe."

She arched upward as his tongue found and celebrated the change of terrain and texture, driving her hands through his hair to breathe his name.

The tigress beneath him was writhing, twisting, clawing at the sheets as he bathed the swollen flesh between her thighs, willing aside his own sharp need, which coiled tighter and thicker with each passing second. Her fists began pounding at his shoulders in frustration, but he refused to relinquish his grip on her hips. He wanted her mindless when he entered her, as dizzyingly mindless with lust as he, and would accept nothing less than complete surrender. She could taunt him and tease him however she chose once he had gorged himself on the pearled cream of release that had her bucking under his restraint.

His tongue slid deeper inside her, coaxing the flow of wetness to erupt, taking savage pleasure in lapping drop after precious drop throughout her strangled cry of gratification realized. Afterward, he soothed the sensitive area with soft, wet kisses until she calmed, then moved over her to take her in his arms, and brush his lips against the pulse at the base of her throat.

"Touch me," he demanded, voice gravelly from holding back the hunger clawing at his gut.

He sucked in air when her hand found him, closed around him. This time he couldn't fight back the wave of lust that coursed through him, so indulged in the feel of her soft fingers flexing around his rigid shaft, giving her back the taste of herself from his lips. Urging her with a thrust of his tongue to drink deeper, to fondle him as a woman does a man she'll soon take inside her body. She dragged hot, wet kisses across his chest, flicking a nipple with the tip of her tongue. His hands filled themselves with her silky hair, the turn of her jaw, trailing his fingertips down her flushed chest to trace circles around the distended areola.

He needed this intimacy before joining their bodies. His bed had been lonely and cold for too long. He craved the feel of her generous mouth on his heated skin. The open way she explored his maleness, cataloguing the bunch of muscles, the pelt of golden hair covering his chest, the taut skin over his ribs. And oh, God, how he loved the way her hands moved so sensuously through his hair, fingernails scraping lightly along his scalp. It was this touching, he realized, that he'd accustomed himself to doing without through fourteen years of marriage.

Charleston did not rear its society darlings to marry for the privilege of long, lush moments spent caressing and being caressed. Only a woman who craved the same emotional closeness could touch him with such reverence, move so that she could watch his expressions change with each new emotion her hands and mouth evoked. He burned to be inside her, a part of her, to make her a part of him.

As if knowing what he wanted, what he so desperately needed, her thighs parted in invitation. He rolled to position himself between her legs, the tip of his engorged shaft straining like a wolf on a chain.

"Now," she whispered into his mouth.

Released from hell, he drove into her, pausing for the barest instant to clamp down on the rush of sensation that threatened climax before its time, giving her a moment to adjust to the length and thickness of him. Finding purchase against the mattress with his knees, he began to move, overwhelmed with the perverse desire to finger the gold ring at her navel between slick strokes.

"I'll take it out if it offends you," she offered, covering his hand with hers.

"Jesus Christ, Ali, does it look like I'm offended?" he choked out, raking her hand away so he could view both the ring and damp sable curls nestled below.

"You were repulsed," she insisted.

"I was fucking fascinated," he growled throatily, bending to drag his mouth across hers in an open-mouthed kiss.

She folded her legs around his torso, lifted, arching to enfold him completely, wholly, crying out when another wave of bliss rolled over her. Jordan watched her tremble, saw her eyes glaze over, and the sheen of perspiration dew on her skin. Felt her thighs lock against his sides as she rode it out, and he with her, harder and faster. Skin slapped against skin. A red haze blurred his vision as release built, stronger and hotter, scalding him from the inside out. He pumped into her again. Again. Straining to the limits of body and mind to have more, fingering the gold ring one last time before baring his teeth to the violent shudder that racked his body.

She drew his head to rest on her breast as they both lay panting, absently stroking his hair. Jordan closed his eyes, lost in the afterglow of lovemaking, content, replete.

"What time do you have to pick Susan up?" she asked at length.

"Eleven. What time is it now?"

"Nine-thirty. Want to doze for a while? I'll wake you in time to get dressed."

"Mmmm." He nuzzled against her full breast, brushing his knuckles along her thigh.

In less than thirty seconds he was asleep. Ali gently removed his glasses and set them on the nightstand, then used her foot to snag the sheet, drawing it to their waists. She studied his features, relaxed now in slumber, and felt her eyes tear up.

How could she have thought having him then giving him up when it was over would be easy? Undoubtedly, they would have a run of passion-filled encounters that bordered on addiction. But she had spoken the truth when she told him they were incompatible. Though it had been their differences that brought them together, it would be those same differences that forced them apart when the novelty of the gold ring in her navel and the tattoo on her butt, which he still hadn't seen, had worn thin.

And he liked being touched, not just in a sexual way, for even in sleep he shifted closer, draping one arm across her middle, nudging against the hand that played lightly through his hair.

She had a blessedly peaceful half hour before he woke at ten, wherein she had given in to the fantasy of imagining what it would be like to have him spend an entire night with her, making love, talking, listening to more of his childhood stories.

"Plotting my downfall?" he asked, voice still husky from sleep.

"My own, most likely."

"Ali?"

"Hmmm?"

"I know this is hypocritical as hell, but do me a favor and don't show Susan your belly ring."

"Afraid she might decide she can't live without one?" she teased.

He blew out a breath, rolling to his back to throw a sinewy forearm across his eyes. "Why do I find it erotically stimulating on you, but thinking about her having one sends cold chills down my spine?"

"Because you're her father and you don't want her abusing her body with malice of forethought."

He lifted his arm to look at her. "You say that like that's the reason you have one."

"It is."

"Want to talk about it?"

"Not particularly."

"How long have you had it?"

"Three years."

He propped himself on his side, using his elbow to support his head. "Tell me," he coaxed, running the edge of his knuckles down her arm.

"Nothing much to tell. Had a fight with my mother, gave in to the insane urge to spite her. And presto, belly ring. We haven't spoken since or God knows what would have been next."

"Come here." He rose and pulled her down to lie half beneath him, brushing his lips against her temple. "Has she seen it?"

"Who?"

"Your mother."

"No."

"Well, I guess you showed her."

Anger, fierce and hot, shot through her. He was intimating she'd done nothing more than spite herself by retaliating with what could be construed by some to be a form of self-mutilation. She surged up, but he was quicker, having anticipated the move. He used his greater weight to pin her to the mattress, wrists shackled above her head.

"If you want to vent, I'll listen. But don't blame me for feeling guilty about running out to do something your mother wouldn't approve of."

"Let go," she said through clenched teeth.

"I like it, Ali." His free hand smoothed over her stomach to hover over her navel. "I can understand why your mother wouldn't, but neither one of those things is really the issue. You didn't have this ring put through your navel because you thought it would be sexy. You did it for the wrong reasons and now you feel guilty."

"Like hell I do."

"Then why did it make a difference if I was repulsed or overjoyed? Did you need a lay that badly?"

She tried to kick him but he clamped a hard thigh around her legs, trapping them. "Fuck you. I don't give a damn if you like it or not."

"Yes, you do. You give a damn about a lot of things, you just don't want anyone to know it."

"Don't." She jerked her head sideways as he bent to kiss her. "Get your...hands off me."

"Will you spite me the same way for trespasses I'll never know about?" he asked, kissing her exposed neck instead. "You like to be touched, Ali, the same as I do. By someone who cares. Someone who wants to touch more than just your body."

"It doesn't make any fucking difference how you touch me, it's just sex." Oh, God, she was losing it. The filth spewing from her mouth should have him recoiling in disgust. Instead his hand continued to lovingly stroke the curls nesting in the apex of her trapped thighs. He caressed her hip, the underside of her breast, placed small kisses over her face no matter which way she turned to avoid them.

Why wasn't she fighting for release instead of breath? Why couldn't he leave off prodding at the wound she had spent the last twelve years treating with attitude and outrageous behavior and trophies brought home after a binge of insanity?

"You're so beautiful," he whispered. "So soft."

The short skirts. The high heels. Dyeing her hair. It had all started off so innocently.

Whore.

The bouts of rage and depression after she and her mother had fought like Satan and the avenging angel.

Whore.

The late nights and rounds of parties until she was sick of them, sick of herself.

The tattoo. The navel ring.

Franny understood. The Dematos loved her.

A tear escaped to slide hotly down her cheek. "It's not wrong to have fun," she whispered raggedly. "It's not."

He kissed the tear away, cupped her cheek to thumb her quivering lips. "No, baby, it's not wrong."

"To her it is. It's wrong and it's evil to want a boy to hold your hand out on the porch. It's wrong to want a dress that doesn't cover every inch of skin from neck to knee. To go to parties or flirt or stay out late or fix your hair differently, or fucking breathe because people might notice you have breasts!"

"I'm sorry." He gathered her tightly against his chest, soothing a hand over her hair. "I'm so sorry she hurt you that way."

"Don't you let Gloria have another chance to hurt Susan. Don't do that, Jordan."

"I won't."

"Swear it," she sniffed, pulling back to look into his eyes. "Swear you'll do whatever it takes to keep Susan with you. To make her feel loved and accepted."

"After what Susan told me about Gloria ignoring her more often than not, I'm not kindly disposed toward my ex-wife at the moment. But no judge is going to bar Gloria from seeing her own daughter through visitation. That's something Susan will have to accept and make the best of."

"Well, then...I guess you'd better go. It's ten-thirty. Susan isn't waiting by herself after play practice, is she?"

"No." He sat up, swinging to his feet to search for his discarded clothes. "The teachers who are helping produce the play wait until all the kids have left before packing it in."

"Oh. Good."

"Hey. Guess what I did on the way over here," he said, snagging his underwear and pants from the floor to put on.

She enjoyed sitting in the middle of her bed, watching him dress. "What?"

"Spit out the window."

Coining a phrase from Ellen Ginsworth, she gasped, "You lyin' son of a bitch. You did not." She found his shirt on the corner of the bed and threw it at him.

He caught it and pulled the stretch knit over his head, grinning lazily as he tucked the tail in at the waist and tightened his belt. "Swear to God."

"Here, put your glasses on so you don't kill yourself walking down the stairs."

"Get up here."

Kneeling on the bed in front of him, she twined her arms around his neck and kissed him.

"Please say you're not going to run to the bathroom the minute I'm gone and rip out this belly ring."

"You really like it?"

"I really like it." He slapped the cheek of her butt playfully and left.

Ali fell back on the bed, her emotions whirling like a dervish, but she was happy. For the first time in a long time she was completely, utterly, giddy with delight.

"Now if I can only manage to stay sane long enough not to fall in love with him."

* * * * *

The next day Ali swung by the body and bath store in the mall and picked out a basket packed with lotions, scented body oils and soaps, and a perfume spritzer that would have Franny foaming at the mouth. She was happy. She wanted everyone else to be happy, too. And that included the champion grudge holder herself, Franny-good-fucking-night-Demato.

"Hiya, doll." Ali stopped directly in front of Franny's desk upon arrival at the office. "I'm here to take you to lunch."

Franny looked up, blinked once, and said in a voice as dry as fall leaves, "I'm sorry, do I know you?"

"Ah, Franny, you're such a hardhead, but I love you anyway. I got you a present."

"I don't want your present. And I'm too busy for lunch. Some of us punch a clock." She returned her attention to the papers on her desk.

"Franny, don't make me get rough."

"Franny—" Jordan came to a halt just outside his office door, clearly surprised to see her standing in his outer office. The flash of uncertainty in his eyes told Ali he wasn't sure how he was expected to react. "I'm sorry, did I...interrupt something?" He glanced at Ali, then Franny, then scratched his head.

"Mr. Finch, right?" Ali glided toward him, offering her hand. "We met at a party several weeks ago."

"Right." He picked up the tempo and went with it. "Ali."

"Listen, you wouldn't mind if I stole Franny here for a while and took her to lunch, would you?" She batted her lashes at him for good measure, amused when his hazel eyes widened for the merest instant.

"Er, no—"

"Yes, he most certainly would!" Franny cut him off, rising to her feet. "We're very busy. We have contracts going left and right. He can't possibly do without me this afternoon."

Franny really was leaving her without much choice. And besides, she owed the redheaded rat. "Darling, are you going to come along peacefully, or do you want me to tell Mr. Finch that you hope to get a pinch on the ass for Secretary's Day?"

Two red flags appeared across Jordan's cheekbones. Franny's mouth flopped open in embarrassment. Ali's smile sweetened. "Oh, I'm sorry. Was that supposed to be a secret?"

Red-faced, Franny jerked the bottom drawer of her desk open, grabbed her purse and slung it over her shoulder like a warrior readying for battle. When they were halfway down the hall leading to the elevator she hissed, "What the hell is wrong with you?"

"Please." Ali rolled her eyes. "You taught me everything I know about public humiliation."

"What was I thinking?"

"You weren't thinking." Ali punched the elevator button and was rewarded with the swishing of doors almost immediately. "You were just trying to save me from living the rest of my life in misery and I never really thanked you for it."

"Done feeling sorry for yourself, are you?"

"Yes. For the most part, anyway."

Franny took out her compact and flipped it open to check her makeup. "Bearing in mind you have serious groveling to do, where are we going?"

"On a picnic. I packed a hamper with all your favorites."

"German chocolate cake?"

"Yep."

Franny snapped her compact shut. "I'm willing to be wooed."

They didn't have far to go, just across the street from Jordan's offices, actually. Ali stepped off the curb and unlocked the car's trunk, retrieving a picnic hamper and blanket, then they made their way through traffic to the park across the street.

"Why don't men ever think of romantic things like this?" Franny wondered aloud as Ali spread the blanket, opened the hamper, and took out linen napkins and utensils.

"Haven't you heard? They're from Mars." Unpacking two wine glasses, she opened the first petite champagne bottle and poured.

Franny accepted the glass gratefully, sighing, "If you were a man, I'd marry you."

"Slut." Ali grinned affectionately, pouring herself a glass, then reaching for the sandwiches. "Salami and Swiss with brown mustard on rye for you. Chicken salad for me."

"Mmmm. Would you consider having a sex change?"

"Speaking of sex." Ali bit into her sandwich.

"Were we?"

"Maybe I should start over. Franny, listen, you know I love you like a sister. You're right, you and Mr. and Mrs. D are my family. You've always been there for me, through thick and thin, always supported me. If I could have picked from any family in the world, I couldn't have picked better."

"By the way, I told my father you were mean to me."

"Shit, Franny. Now I have to make up with them, too."

Franny shrugged, unconcerned. "Stab me in the heart, stab my family."

"Okay, okay. I'll suck up to them later." She paused to take a swallow of champagne. "Where was I?"

"I'm the greatest. My family is practically royalty…"

"Right. And I appreciate your concern. I have been seeing someone, but this time, Franny I don't need vocal support, I need silent understanding. We're trying to keep a very low profile right now. He's going through a very difficult…"

Franny stopped chewing. "Divorce?"

"No," she said slowly. "A custody battle."

"This guy has kids?" Franny's face showed her surprise.

"One. Anyway—"

"Who is he? Where did you meet him?"

"That's just it. I'd really rather not say just yet. It has nothing to do with trusting you, it's just that…well, there's a possibility his ex-wife will try to cause trouble, make him look like an unfit father. He's not. I've seen with my own eyes what a good parent he is. And whether this thing between us develops into more or not—which is up in the air at this point—I don't want to do or say anything to draw attention to myself or my past."

"So you have a past." Franny held out her glass for a refill. "Big deal. Who doesn't?"

"Come on, Franny, you know how easily innocent situations can be made to look bad."

"Ali, what is it you're really afraid of?" Franny queried softly.

"My past comes complete with a mother who might be persuaded to make her point about my 'loose lifestyle' in a courtroom," Ali said quietly, almost desperately. "Franny, I just can't take that chance. I'd never forgive myself if…"

"Ali, you're so damned stupid. Why didn't you explain this to me the other night? I thought you were having misgivings about being good enough for this guy because he was la-de-da rich or something."

"He does come from a prominent family. That's exactly why his dating me could be taken out of context. Face it, tattoos and navel rings don't go over well in high society circles."

"Your mother doesn't know about your tattoo or the ring. Does Romeo?"

"Yes."

"And?" Franny leaned forward slightly, hanging on every word.

"He's okay with it. Actually…I think he has a secret fascination with the belly ring."

"Speaking of sex." Franny grinned solicitously.

"Were we?"

"We were about to. How is it? Oh, shoot, I forgot. You said you haven't been to bed with him yet."

"That situation has been remedied. It's almost frightening how he…"

"What!" Franny shouted in frustration, her sandwich forgotten in the anticipation of a vicarious thrill.

"It's like he knows what's going on inside me. I can't explain it."

"Try," she demanded flatly.

"I think I might be falling in love with him," Ali admitted miserably.

"You better pass me that cake, now. I feel a wave of jealousy coming on."

Ali dug out the carefully wrapped slices of German chocolate cake. "I need to ask you one more favor."

"This present you got me better be good," Franny said between bites.

"It is," Ali assured her.

"What's the favor?"

"Well, could you call before coming over for the time being? We don't really get to spend a lot of time alone, and obviously not at his house."

"Gotcha. Now, where's my prize for being the best friend you ever had?"

Chapter Eleven

🔊

They played another round of golf the next Sunday. A foursome this time, including Randy Peters, who shared a cart with Susan, while Ali rode with Jordan. Jordan did his best to strike up a conversation with Randy, but he needn't have worried because Ali, though the little witch would never admit to it, kept an eagle eye on the boy, cleverly drawing out tidbits about his family, his interests, hobbies. His grade point average.

She wore a pair of summer slacks with a matching knit shirt. Very respectable. Nothing about her attire was intended to be provocative. No gentle swell of cleavage above the vee of her blouse. No shapely legs drawing the attention of other players on the course.

Jordan wanted to strip her naked and kiss every inch of skin from nose to navel, and then some.

Susan talked Ali's ear off about the play, her part—the tinker's daughter—how she loved doing theater. By the time they had finished dinner in the clubhouse, dropped Randy Peters at his house—not altogether an unlikable boy as it turned out—and returned home, it became obvious that the only moment he and Ali would have alone would be when he walked her out to her car.

Unfortunately, it was still daylight. Neighbors were out mowing their lawns, walking dogs, barbecuing, enjoying lounging about their yards and making the most of the warm spring evening. A friend of Susan's had come over earlier, a girl who lived one street over and shared several classes with her at school. They were upstairs doing what teenage girls do. Whatever that was.

Jordan wanted to put his hands on Ali, pull her into his arms and kiss her. Instead they stood apart to say their goodbyes. "Ali…" His hand found hers.

She squeezed hard, once, then let go. "Jordan, we agreed. No touching in public."

"This is ridiculous." He blew out a breath. "I'm standing in my own goddamn driveway, four states away from Gloria, yet I have to watch every move I make."

"Better safe than sorry." But he saw in her eyes that she wanted the same thing he did. To touch.

His throat felt tight at the thought, his mouth dry. "Susan has play practice every night next week before the show. She wants you to come and see the play."

"I don't think it would be a good idea."

"There's nothing inappropriate about you accompanying me to a school play," he argued, shoving his hands into the pockets of his trousers so he wouldn't be tempted to haul her against him.

"It's a school function, which in itself lends the connotation of me being intimately involved."

"You are intimately involved," he said quietly. "With me."

"Which isn't the impression we should be giving this early in the game. It could be months before you get a date for the custody hearing."

"I'll talk to my lawyer. See if we can speed things up. But Susan's going to be very disappointed. I did talk to her about how appearances might be misconstrued, that we should play it cool until after it's settled. She understands for the most part, but she thinks more of you than she does of her own mother."

She swallowed, looked away. Her voice was strained when she spoke. "Shit. That's not fair."

He shifted, scanned the freshly mowed lawn across the street. "It's not fair that I have to stand three feet apart from you pretending I'd rather be in my own bed tonight instead of yours."

She dug into her purse for her keys. "What is this, some kind of tag-team set up? Susan didn't say a word this afternoon about wanting me to come to her play."

He moved to get the door for her at the same time that she reached for the handle. Their hands met for a brief second before she pulled back, eyes locked with his. A spark of need bolted through him. "She thought it would be better if I asked you."

"I guess I could drive separately and sit in the back."

"No." The denial came out in one harsh word.

"Jordan, you're not being sensible."

"You're Susan's invited guest, the woman she works for part-time after school. I won't have you sitting in the back like some second-class citizen." God, how he hated this. Gloria was free to roam Europe at will, doing who knew what with God knew whom, while he was forced under the bridle. "I want you next to me. That's as good an excuse as any for your presence."

"You're not fooling me for a minute, Finch. You just want to hold my hand and play footsie beneath the chairs."

Her off-the-wall comment broke the tension. He smiled, opened the car door and motioned her inside. "Get out of here before I say to hell with it and French you in front of the neighbors."

He waved her off then turned up the walk leading to the porch. Susan fell on him the second he entered the house, eyes glowing excitedly. "So? So? Did she say yes?"

"She's not comfortable with it, but she agreed. I had to do some fancy arm-twisting."

"Yes!" She made a victory fist. "Oh, Daddy, I knew you could do it." Sitting down on the second step from the bottom, she propped her chin in her hand and grinned. "You've really got a case for her, huh?"

Was he so transparent that his daughter could see right through him? "She's a very attractive, intelligent woman."

"Admit it, Dad, she's a babe. Besides," she stated airily, "Ali's good for you. She makes you laugh."

"You act as though I never laugh."

"Not much, anymore. You know," she studied the cuticles of her nails, "I can catch a ride home with Bonnie's dad after play practice. You could take us and he could pick us up. Or vice-versa."

"Susan…"

She held her palms up, rising to her feet. "It was just a suggestion. Bonnie doesn't live that far from us. It's not like it'd be out of the way or anything."

"We'll see." Chauffeuring a carload of chattering teenage girls was enough to give him the sweats. But after a week's worth of having to exchange pleasantries with Ali over the shop counter when picking Susan up after work, he was beginning to think the end very definitely justified the means.

As he stood in the master bath later that night, flossing, squeezing the toothpaste from the middle of the tube, Jordan told himself he was not obsessed with Ali MacPherson. How could he have known, when he made love to her that first time, that she would have such a profound effect on him? How suddenly, for no reason, she would interrupt his thoughts during the course of the day, linger in them at night.

Fourteen years of marriage hadn't prepared him to deal with a spontaneous, unpredictable woman like Ali. She called him "Finch darling", told him he was an ass on their first date, waltzed into his office as cool as you please to manhandle his assistant into lunch, then just as easily charmed a high school boy into spilling every detail of his suburbanite life. Of course, if Randy Peters hadn't been so bewildered over Ali's peculiar way of picking and choosing which drive or chip or putt to count, the kid might have realized he was being grilled.

He thought about the way Ali's mother had frozen her out emotionally and understood, now, why she'd spoken so vehemently against Gloria's inherent right to love and respect from Susan. Clearly, all was not as it should have been in the MacPherson house during those formative years. But then, he hadn't realized things had deteriorated to such an extent in the Finch house until Gloria had presented him with divorce papers.

So, here he was, everything in his life changed. No longer was he Jordan Finch, married to Gloria Haversheim Finch, respected by Charleston society as a man who had it all, including one loving child, a dog, and a thriving business whose pace matched that of the city he grew up in. Now, he was a single parent struggling to guide a troubled teenage daughter who despised her mother into womanhood, working in a new town where competition was fierce and feral, living in a new house filled with new furniture, including an empty bed — which hadn't seemed quite so disturbing until Ali MacPherson had dared her way into his life with a tube of red lipstick.

Dammit, he shouldn't have to feel guilty about spending time with Ali. He shouldn't have to dissect every circumstance for probable cause. He'd done his time under Gloria's reign. This was his life. Gloria had made it clear that she didn't want to be a part of it anymore. Slinking around under the guise of mutual association would only make it seem as though he had something to hide. Ali wasn't just good for *him*, she was good for Susan, too. Someone Susan could talk to about things she might feel uncomfortable discussing with a man, even if that man was her father.

But as Jordan climbed into bed, stacking his hands behind his head to stare up at the textured ceiling, he knew he would continue to do what was in Susan's best interest. His lawyer in Charleston had assured him that Gloria's flighty disappearance would indeed aid their case. There was the fact that Jordan had little — if any — say in the current living arrangements. Gloria hadn't bothered to discuss her sudden trip with him beforehand, even though she knew he was in the process of relocating. He'd had no choice but to uproot Susan in the middle of the school year. If the judge took Susan's wishes into account, given the absence of contact between mother and daughter in the last six months, there should be no problem obtaining guardianship.

Unless Gloria could prove he was an unfit father, thereby ensuring that her own callous abandonment of Susan seemed of little consequence.

Jordan made a mental note to ask his lawyer about contacting Gloria. Surely, if he made an attempt, even a failed one, on Susan's behalf, it would go a long way in convincing a judge that he was doing his best to make sure Susan's needs were being met, physically and emotionally.

When he tried to discuss the prospect with Susan the next morning, she balked. "I don't want to talk to her!" she practically shouted across the breakfast table.

"Susan, we have to at least make an effort," he explained patiently.

"Why?" she all but spat. "She hasn't made an effort to contact us."

"Exactly." He regarded her stiff form over the rim of his coffee cup.

"If they make me go back with her, I'll run away."

"Susan!" Icy fingers clutched at his gut.

"I will! I swear it!" She jumped to her feet, eyes blazing. "I hate her! She doesn't want me, or for us to be a family. She doesn't care about anyone but herself and her garden club charities and her weekly manicures and stuck-up friends. Why should I care what she wants? Why should you care after the way she made you move out of the house into an empty apartment with nothing but your clothes?"

Tears replaced the angry sparkle in her hazel eyes, and coursed down her cheeks. "Did you know she went through the house after you left and took down all the pictures of you and hid them away. She took...she took the picture of you and me on my tenth birthday out of my room."

"Jesus!" He bolted from his chair and gathered her into his arms. "Oh baby, I'm so sorry. I didn't know."

"You didn't know because she made you wait out in the car when you came to pick me up," she sobbed against his chest.

Jordan's throat was raw with emotion, his shirt soaked where Susan shoved her face against him to hide the tears. "Honey, why didn't you tell me?"

"You always looked...so sad," she sniffed. "I didn't want to. I thought she might change her mind and ask you to come back home, and then you wouldn't have to know I was a coward."

He stroked her hair. "Sweetheart, how could you believe I would think you were a coward?"

"I should have hidden the picture where she couldn't find it when she started taking down the others. I shouldn't have let her take it. She had no right. It was my picture. But you were packing up your office to move here and I was afraid if I made her mad she would...leave too, and..." she trailed off, swiping the heels of her hands down her cheeks.

And Gloria had done just as Susan had feared, dumping her off at his office only days before he was scheduled to depart Charleston.

"Don't worry, baby," he said huskily. "You're not going back." The part of him that had stubbornly continued to revere Gloria because she was once his wife, the mother of his only child, shriveled to minute proportions beneath the weight of Susan's tearful confession.

"P-promise?"

"I promise. Now go wash your face, you'll be late for school." He watched her plod from the kitchen, shoulders slumped in dejection. What dread and anxiety she must have experienced, he thought, keeping all her fears bottled up inside during the divorce. He wasn't sure which was worse—Gloria's unthinking cruelty or his obliviousness to what was happening around him at the time, to his marriage, to Susan.

Goddamn that bitch to hell! Maybe he had spent more time than he should have working, but that was no excuse for Gloria to take out her dissatisfaction with him on a blameless child.

He worked like a fiend that afternoon, hoping to dull the edge of his temper. Those who ventured into his office without invitation left with no desire to do so again in the near future. He put a call through to Jeb Kingsley, his lawyer in Charleston, and briefly discussed the pros and cons of initiating contact with Gloria, instructing Jeb to use every bit of influence he had procured over the years to get a court date as soon as possible.

"Certainly it's a good idea to try and locate Gloria," Jeb agreed. "I'll see if I can get a number where she can be reached from her lawyer. Though, you realize, he's under no obligation to give it to me. Most likely he'll agree to pass on the message and have her contact you, which defeats the purpose."

"What the fuck am I supposed to do if an emergency comes up, Jeb? Waste precious time trying to track down her lawyer at some society function so he can pass along the message?"

"You didn't let me finish, Jordan. That's exactly the bug I intend to drop in Judge Stonewall's ear when he agrees to have lunch with me tomorrow. We don't want just any judge sitting on this case. Gloria has just as many friends in high places in this town as you, and I don't want to take the chance that we'll end up with one of her daddy's golfing cronies. Stonewall's been on vacation for the last month, he only just returned to the bench. I've got a few favors owed me at the courthouse, I'll call 'em in, and see if we can get assigned to his docket."

"Fine. Do it. I want her ass flapping in the wind by the time we get to court. Am I making myself perfectly clear, Jeb?"

"As a sunny day."

Jordan hung up and leaned back in his chair, massaging his temples. This wasn't the way he'd wanted to handle the situation, but Susan's anguish this morning had completely undone him.

* * * * *

While Susan was upstairs changing for play practice the phone rang. Jordan answered, hoping it was Jeb calling to let him know how lunch with Stonewall had gone.

"Hello, Jordan." There was no mistaking the cultured, soft southern voice.

"Gloria?" Jordan immediately closed the door to the den so Susan wouldn't overhear the conversation. Then he sank down into the swivel chair behind his desk. Stunned.

"How are you?" she asked hesitantly.

"That's what you called to ask?" he said incredulously. "How I am? Is that the next step in therapy, calling your ex after six months incommunicado to make small talk?"

"I should have known you'd be difficult," she replied petulantly, always the drama queen, even over the smallest of problems.

"What do you want, Gloria?"

"I want to talk to Susan."

"Well, she doesn't want to talk to you," he snapped. "And after some of the things she's finally told me, I don't blame her. What in God's name were you thinking, taking away that picture of her and me sitting behind her tenth birthday cake? Do you know how that hurt her? Do you even fucking care?"

"I wasn't thinking straight at the time. I was having a breakdown, Jordan!"

"Because your therapist told you so? Just like he told you a divorce and a trip to Europe would miraculously cure you?"

"I needed to distance myself from you. I explained that to Susan. She said she understood."

"Well, what the hell did you expect her to say!" he exploded, straining to keep himself from shouting. "She was scared to death. You'd already kicked me out and were running around the house hiding family pictures. Can you blame her for thinking she'd be next if she crossed you? Christ, you amaze me,

Gloria. You had a husband and a child who loved you, a nice home, anything you desired, and you never had to work a day in your life. So pardon me if I don't comprehend why you thought you had it so bad."

"Maybe I wanted to work, Jordan. Maybe I was tired of living in your shadow. Of always being Mrs. Jordan Finch instead of Gloria Finch. I have a right to my own identity, you know."

"Then you should have taken your ass out and gotten a job. Nobody held you back. Maybe if you'd had to work for a living you would have appreciated what you did have instead of sitting around feeling sorry for yourself. You have a degree in Art History. You could have done something useful with it besides chairing banquets at the country club."

"How dare you talk to me this way? You were never there. Your work always came before me."

"Your analyst is going to have to come up with a new line of defense, because that tired old scenario isn't going to work on me anymore, Gloria. You have alienated Susan to the point of no return. And if you fight me on this custody case, I swear to God, I'll drag you through every court in the land until you get tired of fighting and have a real breakdown. You know where they send people who have legitimate emotional disturbances? To a hospital. You want to spend the rest of your life on a shrink's couch, go ahead, but you will not get another chance to fuck with Susan's mind."

"I can't believe you'd do this to me," she sputtered. "I don't even know you anymore."

Jordan remembered a time when he would have given his left nut for her to ask him to come home, because he, too, had recently measured the success of his life by his job and the status of his marriage and the oversized Victorian-style house on Wimple Street and his one-point-five kids and a dog. A dog Gloria hadn't allowed in the house because he might shed on her fine, expensive Aubusson carpets. Where, too, Susan hadn't been allowed to drink Kool-Aid anywhere but in the kitchen in case she spilled it.

"The trouble is," he said, resignation coloring his tone, "you never did. Getting to know me would have required that effort be spared from protecting your precious antiquities and scouring the florist shops for bouquets fit for the graves of the glorious dead."

"Oh, now we're back to that," she replied pithily. "It was quite all right for you to spend sixty hours a week kowtowing to a bunch of bulldozing beer guzzlers, but let me spend a few days a week filling my time volunteering for a few civic functions, and suddenly I'm a terrible wife and mother."

"You wanted the divorce, Gloria, not me," he pointed out. "That's water under the bridge. But you had no right to abandon Susan the way you did. To push her away because you were angry with me. She needed you, needed her mother throughout this last six months. And what were you doing? Distancing yourself in Europe. Well, as far as I'm concerned you can keep your distance. She doesn't need any more upheaval in her life, or to be uprooted again within such a short period of time. And I'm not going to have her holding her breath, waiting for your analyst to get another hair up his ass and send you off to Tibet so you can mediate with the monks. Good bye, Gloria."

He severed the connection before she could do anything more than suck in a breath, afraid of what he might say next if they had continued in the same conversational vein. Leaning back in his chair, he ran a hand along his temple, trying to calm the sick pounding in his chest. What if Gloria took him to court and won? Would Susan run? Would she run to her grandparents, to him? Or would she end up on the streets, scared and hungry and mistrusting of the judicial system that claimed to know what was best for the children of families torn apart by divorce? He realized he was shaking, not just with anger, but fear.

"Daddy?" Susan rapped at the closed door. "You in there? We're going to be late for play practice."

"Coming, honey." He took a deep breath, willed his heart to slow, and managed to school his features before opening the door.

On the ride to Bonnie's house Jordan considered telling Susan her mother had called, had wanted to speak to her, wrestled with it in his mind so much that he felt the bile rise in his throat. At a stoplight three blocks from school he rolled down the window and cleared his throat, then remembered he wasn't alone and swallowed the bitter taste. When Susan gasped in astonishment he turned to look at her across the seat. "What?"

"You were going to spit," she accused dazedly.

"I was not." The light turned green. He punched the gas pedal. The Lincoln jumped forward.

"Sure looked like it," she muttered.

"My brother does that." Bonnie interjected, scooting forward to drape her arms over the front seat. "He says it's sinuses, but I think he just likes spitting. Once he rolled down the window and hawked a big glob out before he looked and it splattered all over this guy on his bicycle who was pulling up beside us." She broke of giggling. "It was so gross."

He and Arlan had spit out the window a time or two when they were kids. They'd just made darn sure their mother wasn't in the car, nor any of their aunts — who would have gotten on the phone straightaway to say, *Lord A-mighty, Cloe, where are those boys' manners? It was like riding down the road with a bunch of hooligans, spitting and making rude noises with their hands and under their armpits.*

"I had something in the back of my throat," he mumbled, pulling the Lincoln to the curb outside the gym. "Remember, Bonnie's dad is picking the two of you up after practice," he reminded Susan as she gathered her bag and slid from the car. "I'll see you at home around eleven-thirty."

"Bye, Dad. Tell Ali hey for me."

No kiss on the cheek. No wave before she and Bonnie entered through the gym's double doors. And he hadn't said one word to her about going to Ali's tonight.

But he found himself driving there. Pulling alongside the curb in front of her condo. Cutting the engine, killing the lights, sitting there staring out the windshield at the ornamental trees lining the small, well-manicured triangle-shaped yard.

He'd meant to call first, more out of courtesy than for any other reason, so she'd be expecting him. But then she might have said she was busy, that something had come up, and he hadn't thought he'd feel so morose after talking to Gloria. Hell, he couldn't have been more stunned if someone had bashed him with a two-by-four when he'd answered the phone and heard her voice on the other end.

He told himself he hadn't come here for the sex. He wanted to hold Ali, touch her, yes, but more than that he needed to tell her about his fucked-up day, hear about hers. She would call him *Finch darling*, hand down unsolicited advice about mothers and daughters that eluded male understanding, and he'd feel better.

He smacked the steering wheel hard with the heel of his hand. He had no right to burden Ali with this bitterness and disillusionment he was feeling in the wake of Gloria's untimely call. No right to expect her to take on his problems with Susan, to get tangled up in what might turn into a full-scale custody battle and all that entailed. The time he spent with Ali shouldn't be overshadowed by his surliness or the threat of Gloria watching every move over his shoulder. Yet he couldn't make himself start the car again and leave. So he sat, brooding. Wanting. Needing. While his conscience and subconscious warred.

You came here to go to bed with her.

Not just to go to bed with her.

You want to fondle that ring in her belly button and find out what the tattoo on her ass looks like.

I'm curious.

You're horny.

Dammit, it's not just sex. I think I love her.

Oh, well then…

Chapter Twelve

ဢ

Ali watched out the window, cradling a glass of Chablis in her palm. Something was wrong. Jordan had pulled up almost fifteen minutes ago. He just sat there, in his shiny black Lincoln, staring out the window. Whatever was bothering him had him by the throat, apparently, so much so that he hesitated to leave the car. She wanted to go to him, open the passenger door of his car and slide across the seat, smooth his brow, tell him everything would work out fine. But she wasn't so sure it would be fine.

Not now. Not after the way her mother had coldly turned her away from the door not two hours ago. She'd been stupid to take Franny's advice and try one last time to make things right with her mother. Driving across town, through the old neighborhood, she had prepared herself for one of two things—a truce or one hell of a row.

She'd gotten neither. Walking up the crumbing concrete steps of the modest two-story brick she'd grown up in, Ali was careful not to put her weight on the rickety railing, wondering why her mother hadn't used the money she'd sent over the years to make a few simple repairs around the place. She had knocked on the door and waited nervously for the rattling click of the lock to be thrown, then had seen the flutter of yellowed lace curtains.

It took her sixty agonizing seconds to realize her mother was pretending not to be home.

Lost in thought, Ali started when the doorbell rang. The resounding Windsor notes echoed through the tiled foyer. She set down her glass and moved through the living room, around the couch, into the hall, taking a deep breath to calm her jagged nerves.

"Hi." He stood in the shadowy porch enclosure uncertainly, glancing down at his shoes, then up again. "I should have called first."

But she had known when he'd said Susan had play practice every night this week before the final show that he would come, so had taken care not to be caught looking as harried as she felt. "Come in."

She closed the door behind him, offered him a draught of Chablis. He declined with a shake of his head, pulling her instead into his arms, his grip on her tight as he inhaled the scent of her hair. "What's wrong?" she asked.

"Nothing," he muttered. "Bad day."

When he let her go, she scooped up her flute of champagne from the low-slung coffee table and flopped down on the couch, crossing her heels on the glass top. "Mind if I imbibe? My day was shit."

He sat down next to her, hands gripping his knees. "Want to talk about it?"

"You've got enough on your mind lately. You don't want to hear my whining."

"I'd rather hear your whining than mine." He crossed on ankle over the other knee.

"Mine would be interspersed with invectives unfit for clean ears."

"Try me." He settled back against the couch.

"I went to see my mother today, the bitch. I don't know why I let Franny talk me into it, but I went over there and knocked on her door. She wouldn't answer."

"Maybe she wasn't home."

Ali drained the flute, sat twirling it between her fingers. "She was home."

"You okay?" he asked softly, shifting to lay one arm along the back of the couch, just above her shoulders.

The flute's slender stem broke under the pressure of her fingers.

"Don't." Jordan reached over to pry the pieces from her hands, leaning forward to lay them on top of the magazines littering the center of the coffee table. Then he took her hands in his, examining her palms for cuts. Finding none, he took one captured hand to his mouth, kissing her fingertips lightly.

"I don't know why I told you that. But this time…"

"This time was worse than the others," he guessed.

"I wanted to beat down the door and call her everything but a white woman."

"Why didn't you?"

"Because I'd swallow my own tongue before giving her the satisfaction. Jordan, please don't baby me," she protested when he hauled her onto his lap. "I'm not fragile. I'm not going to break and do something stupid like slit my wrists. She's not worth it."

"You're absolutely right. She's not. And I like babying you. Somebody has to want to sit in my lap. Susan thinks she's too mature for such babyfied things."

"Well, I certainly hope Daddy's swizzle doesn't stand at attention when she does."

"Ooo," he cringed, stroking a hand over her thigh where her robe parted. "That was crude."

"No, crude would be if I called you 'Daddy' while we felt each other up. Jesus!" She pushed away, lunging to her feet to put distance between them. Whirling, she demanded, "Why do you let me do that? Why do you let me verbally slap and kick at you without fighting back?"

"Because when you care for someone, you want to be there for them. And you want them to let you be there."

Her throat constricted painfully. "No," she whispered, shaking her head in denial. "Don't. Don't say that."

"I don't know when it happened or how it snuck up on me, but—"

"No!" she practically shouted. "You don't care for me! You can't!"

He rose from the couch and started toward her. She backed away, turned to run, but he caught her sleeve and brought her around, holding her upper arms. "I do."

"No!" She thumped his chest. Hard. Her voice cracked as she struggled against the arms he locked around her torso. "It's only been... How can you say...no...don't..."

"Let me," he whispered, cradling her head beneath his chin. "Everything your mother despises about you are the things I love. You make me laugh. You made me open my eyes and be the father Susan needed at a difficult turning point in her life. Christ, I'm doing something unpredictable for the first time in my adult life, at a time when I can't afford to make mistakes, and it scares the hell out of me."

She stilled, pressing her face into his shirt. He rubbed soothing hands up and down her spine. Waiting. Waiting for her next reaction. She could hear his heart thumping in his chest, felt the rest of him stiffen as the silence stretched out.

"Say something, Ali."

"I'm not sure what you're supposed to say when a stupid man without the sense God gave a goose says he wants you in his life."

"Well, I don't either. No senseless man ever said he wanted me. But there was this woman in a short black dress at a party I went to once, who told me not to ask her out. Silly me, I did anyway. She can't play golf to save her life, has a sassy mouth, a tattoo somewhere on her ass, and damned if I'm not crazy about her."

"Maybe if you took her to bed and told her about three hundred more times, she might believe you."

He lifted her in his arms and strode up the stairs to the bedroom. "Hey, you think if I asked real nice she'd let me see her tattoo?" He set her on her feet next to the bed, tugging on the sash of her robe.

The lapels fell away from her shoulders, revealing a peach silk and lace teddy. "Jordan," she said his name, undone by the darkening of his hazel eyes as they swept over ample cleavage cuddled in lace.

His knuckles brushed over the soft rise of her breast. "You knew I would come tonight."

"I hoped."

"You knew," he repeated with certainty, running his hands down the indention of her waist, and over her ribs to the flare of a hip edged in high-cut silk. "I think I love you, Ali," he said, sealing their lips in a long, slow kiss that went on forever.

She helped him out of his clothes, let him draw her down on the bed with him, and closed her eyes to savor the rightness of it. She didn't want to think about the hurt that had ripped through her soul while standing forlornly on her mother's front porch. Didn't want him to know she hoarded the whispered words of love between caresses so she might garner the courage to give them back. She loved the Dematos, but had never actually said so. Franny was like a sister, though communication between them was tempered with sarcastic, facetious undercurrents.

And here was this man, this beautiful man whose heart had been crushed, his marriage broken, fighting to piece his world back together, and he had the fortitude to risk becoming involved with her—rebel without a cause, Ali MacPherson. He loved her with his hands, his mouth, those hazel eyes, all skimming over her flesh simultaneously. Peeling the silk away to gaze down at her cupped breasts, he nuzzled a sensitized nipple, and suckled as his fingers found and flicked the gold ring at her navel through the material spanning her stomach.

Ali gave herself up to the pleasures of the flesh, arching into his hand, marveling at the tiny frissions of desire that raced along her skin as his long fingers stroked her heated core. But always, always, he returned to be mesmerized by the gold ring, playing with it, fondling it with his tongue, drawing lazy circles over and around the loop.

"Promise me you won't take it out," he murmured gutturally against the dip of her stomach.

"Finch, darling," she ran her hand through his hair, "you're developing a very unhealthy obsession here. Are you in love with me or my navel ring, I wonder?" He paused, leaning on one elbow to remove his glasses, holding them out of reach when she grasped at his arm. "Put them on."

"Why?" he growled when she clasped his arm.

"Because…"

"Because?" He bit the corner of her bottom lip. "Because they make you hot? Or because you're obsessed with making love to a man whose vulnerability is so obvious?"

"Are you suggesting I'm a pervert?"

"Could be. I'm half of this sexual frenzy and my half gets hard just thinking about that little hoop. What does your half want?"

She shuddered visibly as he grazed the cool edge of the gold rim frames down her arm, leaving in their wake a trail of goose bumps. "I can't help it," she said in defense when he cocked a tawny brow at her.

"Anymore than I can help searching for gold…here."

The gold frames of his glasses clicked against the gold ring. An erotic wave of heat coursed through her veins. He flattened the round panes against her inner thigh, teasing the quivering flesh until she trembled, then dragged the smooth disc over her swollen female lips. She cried out as climax came, swift and hot.

"Now tell me I have an unhealthy obsession," he said into her mouth. "Do you have any idea what sex was like with a society matron? The same. Always the expected, never the unexpected. No bedroom games, no innovative positions. After a while, devoid of only the most perfunctory of touches. I can count on one hand the number of times Gloria rubbed up against me like a woman does a man she wants inside her."

"I don't want to hear—"

"There's nothing more to hear," he cut her off, nursing her lips into submission. "Except it is possible to have sex with someone without being intimate, and I won't allow that to happen with us. Talk to me, Ali. You tell me what you want. What makes you happy or sad or melancholy. Bitch, rant, rave, scream if you want, but don't try to pretend it doesn't matter when I'm inside you, because to me it does."

He tossed his glasses to the pile of clothes on the floor, rolled between her open thighs, slipped inside her and began to move. Emotions she had thought non-existent billowed up from deep within, closing off her throat so that she couldn't speak. He made their joining beautiful and intensely erotic at the same time. Tender one moment, crazed with lust the next. There were no pretenses, no embarrassing, awkward moments where one partner was afraid to touch the other in a hidden place. No fear of saying the inappropriate. Just the two of them, lost in each other, in the discovery of forgotten erogenous zones, the making of new ones. Thrilling, sweet, oh-so gratifying food for the starving soul.

It was as though he was driven to release every ounce of pain, sorrow, and hurt in her heart, soothing each eruption with slow, warm kisses, until there was nothing left but the tears of joy that leaked from her eyes when she scaled the last wall to join him in the ever after.

Once the body rush cooled to a warm glow, he fit himself against the crisscrossing of bronzed iron at the head of the bed and pulled her close, tucking her head onto the pillow of his shoulder. They lay with legs entwined, his hand curved possessively around her hip, hers splayed across the mat of tawny hair covering his broad chest.

"You know what I learned today?" he said at length.

"What?"

"That it's possible to kill love."

Ali leaned back so she could look into his face. He turned his head, met her concerned gaze with serious, tired eyes. The tiny lines fanning from the edges seemed to be etched a little deeper today. "Susan…" she started.

"Gloria." His voice was strained. "She called tonight." He went on to summarize the incident, ending with, "God, the things I said to her."

A cold finger of dread trailed down her spine. Try as she might to ignore it, the feeling grew stronger. "Do you regret giving Gloria a divorce?"

"No." His hand stroked her hip lazily. "What I regret is that fourteen years of marriage has come to this, a cold war over Susan's affections. I resented her at first, for breaking up our family, running off at the drop of her therapist's hat. Now I see that her leaving was inevitable. I tried to talk to Susan this morning about contacting her mother, talking to her. Then she told me this story about Gloria hiding all the pictures and swore she'd run away if she was forced to go back. When Gloria called and asked how I was, like we were at some goddamn Sunday social, I blew."

Ali's heart ached for him. For Susan. She reached up to smooth the lines on his forehead. "That's why you sat out in the car for so long," she said softly.

He clasped her smaller hand in his, touching her knuckles to his mouth. "Bad timing. I didn't want to drag you into the middle of it."

"Yeah, and here I am, kicking and screaming all the way. I guess now I should tell you the reason I went to my mother's this afternoon." She disengaged from his arms, sitting up cross-legged on the bed, the sheet twisted about her waist. "I went there to ask her not to talk to anyone who might come around asking questions about me…about us."

He reached out to caress her arm, his voice tender when he said her name. "Ali, you didn't have to do that."

"Yes, I did. For some stupid reason I thought—hoped—I could reach her. That somewhere inside her there might be a shred of motherly sentiment left. Enough that ,even though she might not laud my accomplishments to the world as such, neither would she maliciously libel me to strangers looking to use my promiscuously degrading past as a means to destroy other people's lives."

He leaned up on one elbow, touching his fingers to her face. "I didn't realize things were quite that bad between you and your mother."

"You don't understand, Jordan." She stared hard at him, willing him to read between the lines. "She'll do it for no other reason than to rain down righteous victory on my head. Nothing would give her more pleasure than to tell a judge I corrupted you and Susan. What the *hell* is so funny?"

"You." His grin deepened as he tugged her reluctant body beneath him. "You were going to face off with your mother for the sake of Susan's happiness, yet you can't look me in the eye and say you care. Would it be such a crime to admit it?"

It was there again. The chill in her spine. Like a warning, a foreboding she couldn't define. The words hung in her throat— thick, heavy, struggling for a way out. Until now she had always managed to avoid emotional entanglements. Did he really love her or was he merely infatuated with having her? His marriage to Gloria had been less than ideal. Was he only stretching his newfound wings of freedom, or was he looking for a serious, meaningful relationship? How could she ever be sure his resentment of Gloria hadn't driven him into her nonconforming arms?

"I guess it would," he muttered tightly, rolling off her to stride naked into the bathroom, anger vibrating from every line of his body. He slammed the door so hard she jumped.

Ali heard the water running. Then silence. Hugging the sheet to her breast she sat up, pressing four fingers to her trembling lips. *I think I love you. Why am I so scared to say it?* There was no witty comeback to hide behind this time. No clever way to say she cared that would insulate her from the backlash of heartbreak when he tired of her and moved on.

Coward! Here's your chance. He loves you. Tell him!

It's too easy.

You'll lose him if you don't.

Shut up! I can't think!

Like that ever stopped you before.

This is different. He's not a goddamn navel ring I can take out and forget.

You'll lose him.

Leave me alone!

That's exactly what you will be if he walks out that door without knowing you care. Alone.

Her head jerked up when the bathroom door opened. Without so much as glancing in her direction he strode to the other side of the bed where his clothes were piled on the floor. The mattress dipped under his weight when he sat, reaching for his underwear first, then his trousers, his back still to her, cold and unyielding.

She opened her mouth. Closed it again, rubbed at the center of her chest where a dull ache had started to build. He scooped up his shirt, turned it right side out, snapping it into submission before pulling it over his head. The pregnant silence drew out as he yanked on his socks until the roar in her ears was deafening.

Ali sucked in a panicky breath as he rose to his feet, made worse by the fact that he wouldn't look at her, as though he had already banished her from his mind. His heart. He walked across the plush carpet with measured steps, pausing halfway through the door for the space of five heartbeats, still refusing to turn and look at her. Ali's heart leaped into her throat. He would never know what it took for her not to call out to him, beg him to understand her uncertainty. But she simply wasn't capable of begging another human being for anything, least of all emotional support or solace from the pain locked deep inside.

She couldn't have conceived agony as intense as what she experienced when he left without a word or a backward glance. But she knew instinctively, somehow, that he was hurting just as much as she, if not more. He had opened himself up to her and she had hesitated a beat too long in accepting what he offered.

And what had he offered? she asked herself as she stomped to the bathroom. Love? The only thing she knew about love was that it came with strings attached. Then her gaze fell on the washrag he'd used, and she felt the dampness building in her eyes. It lay damp, but neatly folded on the marble vanity. The hand towel, too, next to it. Dammit, he'd had no right to spring this on her. They'd only known one another for a matter of weeks. But her heart cared nothing for the infinitesimal days or hours or minutes that had passed since that night he'd caught her rearranging a stranger's paper towels. He'd gotten over fourteen years of marriage quick enough. How much easier would it be to forget a woman he'd only known for a scant few weeks?

Ali picked up the washrag, still warm in the folds where it had stroked against his heated body, cursed his handsome face, then threw it against the tiled wall. She had the sudden urge to strip her bed of the sheets that smelled like him, burn the hand towel he'd touched, run downstairs to the kitchen, fling open the refrigerator and take a big whiff of something moldy to rid her nostrils of his scent. Instead, she leaned her palms against the cool marble counter, took deep breaths, then ran herself a warm bath.

* * * * *

Susan didn't come by the boutique after school the next day, or the next, or the next. Ali jumped every time the phone rang, but let Deanna answer. She busied herself rearranging racks of clothing, redressing the windows, changing the displays lining the aisles. She came in early and stayed late doing paperwork and decided to stop toying with the idea of a catalogue and do it. It was that or end up in another tattoo parlor.

Armed with bids and brochures from various graphic design firms, she pored over their suggestions, systematically weeding out those whose ideas were tired, outdated, or just plain carbon copies of current circulating catalogues. Using models would prove too expensive, yet she needed to show how the apparel would look when worn. The answer came in the form of Franny Demato.

"Hiya, doll." Franny strolled into the back room Friday afternoon, looking harried and exhausted. "Deanna let me in as she was leaving. What do you say we do the town tonight? I need to let off some steam."

"Not tonight," Ali said without enthusiasm. "I want to finish going over these design packages."

"So, you're really going to do it, huh?"

Ali chewed absently on the end of her pen. "If I can figure out how to get around hiring professional models without sacrificing the integrity of the project."

"So hit up one the talent agencies for new blood," Franny suggested. "Better yet," she flopped onto a chaise lounge, idly draping one ankle over the other, "grab yourself a couple of college girls with curves and offer them a deal they can't refuse."

Ali slumped backward in her chair, legs crossed, her foot swinging like a pendulum as she considered the idea. "You know what? It could work. Using local college girls could be just the edge needed to grab people's attention. I mean, if it were your daughter modeling the clothes, wouldn't you want to check out the catalogue?"

"Plus it gives them some experience if they're thinking of going into modeling," Franny added, getting excited about the project herself. "The possibilities are endless, Ali."

"I could start off with a biannual issue, work up to quarterly. Do a calendar, maybe, highlighting various themes like 'the power executive', or 'an evening on the town'. But it has to appeal to women of all ages. And men. You know how many men live to find a Victoria's Secret catalogue in their mailboxes?"

Franny rolled her eyes. "You know how many men come to work with them stuffed in their briefcases? Playboy hasn't got a thing on Victoria."

"An issue devoted to redheads!" she blurted out the idea before it was fully developed in her mind.

"Brunettes."

"Blondes."

"The Silver Edition!"

Frantically, Ali searched her desk for a notepad, scribbling down the brainstorm of ideas.

"Here's the catch," Franny interrupted a moment later. "You can't scrimp on the photographer. He, or she, has to be good. Fashion photography is tricky. They have to shoot in exact lighting, use all kinds of filters. I mean, hell, those high-priced models are people just like us, they have flaws, you just don't see them in the finished product."

"Oh God, Franny." Ali jumped to her feet. "I have the most bizarre idea! What if I offered the project to the photography and theater majors at the university? I'm talking backdrops, lighting, the works. It wouldn't have to be school-related — unless they wanted it to — anyone interested could form a group and they could work on it in their spare time. I don't have a deadline or a timetable or investors to cater to."

"Can you do that without going through the board of directors at the university?"

"I don't see why not. I'm footing the bill. Participation would be on a strictly voluntary basis. I'm using stock from the store, whatever equipment is needed I can probably rent or borrow, and if the first issue generates income I can pay the students. No red tape with the university, but in time, if the university is agreeable, I could offer an associated internship."

"Well, if it's a paying job I might apply." Franny kicked off her heels and sat massaging her stocking feet. "Jordan has been a bear this week. Susan—that's his daughter—has been hanging out at the office lately, after school. And I love the kid, honest I do, but Christ Almighty, she can talk a blue streak. She's dating some boy named Randy Peters, if you can imagine, and it's Randy this, Randy that. If it's not her mooning over Randy or this part she's doing in the school play, it's Jordan stomping through the office snapping and growling at everything that moves. Now get this," she snorted derisively, "Susan's tying up the phone in the conference room talking to this Randy character, and Jordan chews a hole in my ass."

Yes. The play. The show was tonight. At eight. Nonchalantly, Ali glanced at her watch. It was seven-thirty already. Jordan was probably on his way to the school by now. Susan would have had to be there early for makeup and costumes. "Then maybe you should point out to him that you can't be expected to baby-sit her and cater to him at the same time."

"Unfortunately," Franny reached for her heels, working them on, "that would mean I'd have to instigate conversation with him. Thank you, but no. Not until he gets whatever burr is up his butt extracted. Think I'll stop by Mom's on the way home and grab a bag of sympathy. I'll go out the back. Call me."

"I will." Ali followed Franny to the door, locking it after her, then went back to her desk.

Don't do it, Ali. Just get in the car and go straight home.

But the Park Avenue had other ideas, specifically that of commiserating with a certain black Lincoln Town Car.

Chapter Thirteen

Ali pulled into the main entrance leading to the school's parking lot. It was crowded with cars of every make and model jammed into every available slot, along the illegal fire lane, and around the raised curb of the flagpole. The student's lot, located around the back of the gymnasium, was the same. As was the residential street butting up next to the gates. After driving through the narrow rows of cars for ten minutes she finally found a grassy spot near the football field. The squish of mud beneath her heels had her grinding her teeth, but she was no less determined to trudge on.

When she reached pavement, she stopped and searched her purse for anything resembling a tissue. It came down to a choice between a paisley silk scarf or finger spitting. She chose the scarf. Leaning one hand against the brick wall of the gymnasium, ankle balanced across the opposite knee, she wiped the clinging mud from one alligator pump and then the other, knowing it would be the last time she'd ever lay eyes on this particular silk scarf. On her way past the big square trashcan outside the double doors she disposed of the ruined silk neck adornment.

Five minutes later she bought a ticket and slipped discreetly into the auditorium, taking a seat along the back wall. Parents and grandparents were smiling and talking at once. Siblings of the actors fidgeted in their seats, making faces at each other, tugging at their enforced finery for the occasion. Ali's eyes automatically scanned the hall, searching out Jordan. She found him three rows from the front, on the end of the aisle opposite her, wearing a dark suit and talking to the woman seated next to him. Was the attractive brunette his date?

The lights dimmed. The hum of conversation wound down as the principal, Mrs. Haley, crossed the stage with microphone in hand to thank everyone who had made tonight possible, from the students to the teachers and parents, then gave a short introduction. The music swelled. The curtains drew open. And for the next two hours Ali was immersed in the sights and sounds and songs of *Oklahoma!*, watching proudly as Susan executed her role of the tinker's daughter with zest and panache.

It was during a dance scene that Susan loitered near the corner of the stage where Jordan sat, using the moment to scan the crowd for her father. From her shadowy corner Ali caught the silent question in Susan's hazel eyes—Did Ali come? Jordan answered with a slight shake of the head. For just a second Susan's bright smile faltered, then without missing a beat, her attention snapped back to the scene in progress. Ali's chin dropped to her chest. She squeezed her eyes shut but couldn't block out the disappointment she'd glimpsed on Susan's face. Apparently, Jordan hadn't explained to Susan that they were no longer seeing each other.

When the last note had faded and the thunder of applause erupted, Ali slipped from her seat and headed for the exit. The lights came up just as she reached to push through the double doors into the lobby of the gym. Thankfully, the outer hall wasn't crowded, only a few students and those who'd ducked out early, like herself, milled about. Young men tugged uncomfortably at their ties, pretending inordinate interest in the sports trophies encased in a glass cabinet on the far wall, when sly glances over their shoulders proved they were much more interested in the girls with big hair, short skirts, and clunky heels who gathered in groups to giggle and admire each other's trendy attire.

Before she could change her mind about leaving, instead of waiting around to congratulate Susan, she hurried out the second set of double doors leading to the parking lot, where several adults who couldn't bear another minute without sustenance were engaging in a nicotine-fest. She could use a cigarette herself about now. Would, by God, when she made it to the car and could root through the glove box for the emergency pack she kept on hand.

Clumping through the soft, dewy minefield of muddy ruts once again, she paused only long enough to palm off her pumps, striding on toward the football field heedless of the muck that oozed around her stocking feet. So what if the brunette sitting beside Jordan was his date, she thought acidly, snapping open her leather bag in search of her keys as she neared the car.

Why the hell hadn't she dug out her keys in the lobby when she could see better? The state of Ohio was packed into her purse. She could hear the key ring jangling, but the keys themselves continued to elude recovery.

I love you, Ali. I usually only concentrate on one woman at a time. "Lying son of bitch," she muttered, clawing at the bottom of her leather bag.

"For the love of Pete, Jordan, why did you have to park all the way out here?"

Ali froze, glancing furtively over her shoulder. Behind her, still on the pavement, the brunette who had accompanied Jordan was regarding him with hands on her hips. The sidelight attached to the corner of the gym illuminated the paved area enough for her to make out their shadowy forms, standing close together.

"This was the only spot available," he answered.

"If you think I'm walking through that muck and ruining these shoes you're crazy."

"I said I'd pick you up at the door, sugar. You didn't have to walk all the way out here."

"Well, I'm here now, so you'll just have to carry me, big strong man."

Ali pressed against the car to avoid being seen as Jordan swung the laughing woman up into his arms. She squinted into the darkness, trying to make out where, exactly, his black

Lincoln was parked. But the shadows cast by the hulking brick structure obscured all but the cars adjacent to her on either side.

"When we get home I'm going to call your mother and tell her what a bad boy you've been," the brunette purred, linking her arms around his neck.

Please don't let them turn down this row or I'll have to kill that bitch. But fate was not often kind to those who sought its protection. He did turn down the row, and Ali's pride wouldn't let her skitter away into the surrounding darkness like a thief.

Fool.

They were nearly on her when Jordan looked up, his low laughter at something the brunette was saying cutting off as their gazes collided. "Ali."

The sight of him made her knees go weak. "Hello, Jordan."

"You see," the brunette pointed a crimson nail at the mud-encrusted pumps in Ali's hand. "That is why I didn't want to walk across this field. You poor thing, those shoes are probably ruined."

Ali's eyes never left Jordan's. "Well then, I'll just have to dump them and pick myself up a new pair, won't I? One pair of spikes seems to be as good as another."

"Jordan, honey," the brunette cooed in his ear, "I'd like to remind you I paid two hundred dollars for these shoes in Vegas, so if you're thinking about dropping me to assist the lady, it better be on a solid, dry surface."

Jordan didn't look at the brunette but continued watching Ali, his expression guarded. "Susan will be glad to know you came."

"When she comes out please tell her I thought she was wonderful."

"She's celebrating with the cast and crew this evening," he explained haltingly, seemingly wanting her to know why Susan hadn't accompanied the two of them to the car. "She looked for you."

"Jordan, why don't you take me to the car then come back and help Ms...?"

"Hold on a minute," Jordan told Ali, glancing down at her muddy feet. "I have a towel in the trunk."

I'll just bet you do. So the seats of your shiny new Lincoln don't get stained. "Don't put yourself out. A little dirt never hurt anybody." Ali turned her back on the couple and continued digging through her purse. He turned right just past the front of her bronze Park Avenue, striding through the darkness several rows across as though the woman in his arms weighed nothing. She heard their muffled voices, the thump of the Lincoln's door shutting, and frantically renewed her efforts to find her keys, pawing through the mess in her bag. She almost sobbed in relief when her fingers closed over the metal ring.

Ali punched the unlock button, tossed her muddy shoes onto the floorboard, her purse into the passenger seat, jumped in, and slammed the door. Shoving the key into the ignition, she started the engine and rammed the gearshift into reverse, spewing grassy clumps and mud beneath the undercarriage in her haste to back out of the cramped space late arrivals had wedged her into. The beam of her headlights momentarily struck Jordan, who had just rounded the car parked beside hers, towel in hand, his expression grim, jaw set. But Ali ignored him, manhandling the gearshift into drive, and stomped the gas with her slippery foot, toes curled around the edge of the pedal for purchase.

In the covered garage of her condo she stripped her hose off and used them to wipe most of the mud from her feet, and dumped them in the garbage can upon entering the kitchen. Her pumps landed on one side of the stainless steel sink to be cleaned later. Right now all she wanted was a hot shower.

But the steamy water failed to wash the vision of Jordan and the pretty brunette from her brain.

Jordan had had his hands on the woman. Was holding her gallantly in his arms, laughing with her, while she'd—the bitch—had her arms around his neck, cooing in his ear like a lover. And he'd had the temerity, the utter gall to stop and make small talk about Susan, and offer her a towel from the trunk of his car. As if she could have stood for him to touch her when she could barely stand to breathe the same air. Then he'd stood watching her maniacal retreat, motionless, trapped in the headlights of her car, with need he wouldn't voice reflecting in his eyes.

He couldn't have hurt her more if he had tried. Yet she would have given anything for one touch, one look that said, "I don't want it to be like this, let's start over."

She had punished herself the night he'd left by sleeping on sheets that smelled of him, of them, of their lovemaking. Still, though she had ripped those sheets from the bed the next morning, she sometimes imagined a hint of his cologne lingering on his pillow, the one she buried her face in to cry herself to sleep.

* * * * *

"Well, that was uncomfortable," Ellen remarked wryly on the drive home. "I thought for sure you were going to dump me in the mud and have at her."

"Leave off, Ellen," Jordan said quietly. His stomach was still in a knot. The last person he had expected to see in the crowded school lot was Ali.

"Was that by chance Ali-the-idol-of-all-that's-teenage-and-female that I've been hearing so much about from Susie? She's pretty. I should look so good in muddy stocking feet. Are you gonna tell Susie she came to the performance?"

"I suppose if I don't, you will?"

"That's right," she quipped lightly, turning in the seat to look at him. "You knew what she was thinking, Jordan. You could have introduced us and set her mind at ease."

His mind sure as hell wasn't at ease, why should he give Ali the satisfaction of knowing he'd ached to reach out and touch her? "Count yourself lucky she didn't have a golf club handy, or worse, use those three-inch heels to gouge out both our eyes."

"I don't know about you, but I was prepared to duck and hope for the best. If Arlan had looked at me like you were looking at Ali…"

"Leave off, Ellen."

"Okay, okay." She held up defenseless hands. "Just trying to help."

"I don't need any help from you."

"Lyin' son of a bitch," Ellen muttered the mantra beneath her breath. "You're just too stubborn to admit you made a mistake."

His fingers tightened on the steering wheel. "Don't make me stop this car and put you out."

"Well hell, it wouldn't be the first time you threw me over for another girl," she sniffed. "Mary Martin wasn't half the kisser I was. Arlan told me so."

"Arlan would."

"Are you trying to say he lied?"

"He just told you that to get in your pants."

"And still does, twenty or so years later. On a regular basis, I might add."

"Nevertheless," he pressed on with the argument that, even still now, as grown men, continued to be a point of debate between him and Arlan, "Mary Martin was the best kisser in the ninth grade. I ought to know, I kissed my way through the whole freshman class."

"Pig. So how come you ended up with society ice, then?"

Jordan spared his sister-in-law a sideways glance. "As if you'd know what went on in our bedroom."

"As if everyone in Charleston didn't know what wasn't going on in your bedroom," Ellen shot back candidly.

The light ahead of them turned red. Jordan jolted to a stop and turned to stare at her. "What do you mean?"

"Even if you did work a lot—"

"Goddammit, I'm tired of hearing about how I was always working!"

"If you'll let me finish," Ellen eyed him disdainfully, "I was going to say even if you did work a lot that was no excuse for Gloria's behavior."

Behind them a horn honked, but Jordan ignored it. "What behavior?"

"The light's green, Jordan."

"I don't give a fuck what color the light is!" he roared, continuing to ignore the irate driver behind them, who by now was leaning full blast on his horn. "What behavior?"

"For God's sake, Jordan," Ellen said in exasperation, "get a clue. Gloria's therapist packed up and left town the day after she did. On an extended vacation, I believe he called it." The driver behind them tired of waiting and whipped around the side of the Lincoln, gesturing rudely out the window as he passed.

Stunned, all he could say was, "Gloria was having an affair with her therapist and nobody thought to tell me about it?"

"I wanted to tell you, but Arlan told me it was none of my business and to keep my big nose out of it."

"Arlan knew, too? Jesus." He stomped the gas and ran the light that had turned red again, oblivious to Ellen's alarmed gasp.

"You mean to tell me you had no idea?" she asked, grabbing for the passenger handle tucked into the plush roof.

"Do I look like I had an idea?"

"Well, you paid the bills. Didn't you ever notice the hours she supposedly spent in his office, and that the hours you paid for didn't coincide? Because, Jordan, trust me, there's no way on this green Earth he could have billed you for all the time they spent together. You'd be bankrupt."

He felt like he'd been kicked in the gut. Why? Why hadn't Gloria told him there was someone else instead of letting him believe she was having a breakdown? "I was there, Ellen," he said after he'd had time to digest what she'd told him. "I was there for Susan's birthday parties and her recitals and school plays. I escorted Gloria to all those charity banquets and balls she was constantly insisting we attend."

"I know."

They drove in silence for the remainder of time it took to get home. Ellen was flying back to Savannah in the morning. She'd only come to Chicago to see the play at Susan's request. And, he'd guessed, to check up on him because he hadn't been home since moving here.

For the rest of the evening Jordan closeted himself in his study with a bottle of Scotch, going through old bills and paperwork and check stubs. Around midnight he heard Susan come in. Heard, too, Ellen greet her in the hall and was grateful that his sister-in-law was trying to give him time to come to terms with Gloria's newest form of treachery.

New to him, anyway.

Around one a.m. he removed his glasses, rubbed his weary eyes, polished off the glass of Scotch at his elbow, and flung himself on the leather sofa. Manila envelopes and the papers they contained littered his desk and the carpet around it. He'd found several paid bills from Gloria's therapist, but not near as many as there should have been. Why bother? What difference did it make now if she'd screwed her shrink's brains out while he was working his balls off to keep her in the style to which she was accustomed? The hard, cold fact was that Gloria had never loved him. She might have respected him at one time, perhaps when they were first married, but he was past trying to fool himself into believing they'd had a storybook marriage.

Maybe in the back of his mind he had known, had blamed himself, and that's why he hadn't contested her reasons for wanting the divorce. No doubt she'd determined the best defense was to elicit guilt over the long hours he put in on the job and sympathy for her delicate emotional condition, rather than risk public censure for adultery and abandonment. He could try to prove the deception in court, at the custody hearing, but to what advantage? Susan didn't deserve to be subjected to the illicit details of her mother's perfidy. Mudslinging rarely sullied only the intended victim.

But Christ, he was so tired of playing the Southern gentleman, particularly where Gloria was concerned. Gloria didn't give a damn about anyone but herself. Why she wanted Susan back under her roof when she considered their daughter more of a nuisance than a flesh and blood miracle to be cherished and loved was a mystery to him.

Staring up at the ceiling, he willed his mind to go blank. God knew he needed the rest. But even as he succeeded in pushing thoughts of Gloria aside, others crowded in. Unwanted, painful memories of the way Ali had opened her heart to Susan—a lonely teenage girl looking for acceptance from her peers, unable to embrace the imminent coming of age taking place around her and blossom. All because of insecurities Gloria had instilled through emotional neglect rife with bizarre rationalizations.

He knew Ali cared for him, why was it so important he hear the words?

I miss you, Ali.

Poor Ellen. If she only knew he had considered, for the space of two crazy heartbeats, dropping her and her expensive Vegas shoes to the ground the second he'd seen Ali standing by her car, rigidly erect, her dark, mahogany eyes snapping with accusation. He'd been so damned starved for the sight of her that most days he couldn't breathe, couldn't think, couldn't sleep. Yet when the opportunity to make things right with her had presented itself, some perverse part of him had held silent, letting Ali assume the worst, hoping against hope that she would do something thoroughly outrageous.

Not that he wished Ellen ill will—he didn't. He loved the little minx like a sister, would protect her with his life. But was it too much to hope that Ali might be beset by one of her uncontrollable urges and fly into a jealous rage?

A glance at his watch put the time at one-thirty a.m. He was still no closer to sleep than he'd been when he'd arrived home. His gaze came to rest on the telephone occupying one corner of his desk. No, it was too late to call. Ali would hang up on him.

He thought about waiting until morning, then have Susan call to thank her for attending the performance, even if Ali hadn't wished her presence known. He immediately felt guilty. Using Susan to soften Ali up before taking the plunge made him no better than Gloria.

* * * * *

The phone jarred Ali out of a deep sleep. Scrubbing at her grainy eyes, she rolled over and tried to make out the time, but the luminous numbers on the bedside clock blurred together. She fumbled with the twisted covers, knocked a tissue box to the floor, along with a glass dish full of assorted earrings—kept on the nightstand because she had a bad habit of going to bed with her earrings on only to wake later to sharp, stabbing pains where the posts were gouging holes into her head—before finally laying hands on the phone.

"Hull—" She cleared her throat and tried again. "Hello?"

"Ali." Jordan's husky voice rolled over her like velvet gravel.

Wide awake now, she sat up, huddling against the iron headboard, gripping the receiver with one hand, a knot of blankets and sheets in the other.

"Don't hang up. Please."

She could hear his uneven breathing. Or was it hers? Her heart was knocking so loudly against her chest it was hard to tell.

"Ali?"

"I'm here." She clutched the phone tighter. "What…why are you calling so late?"

"Tonight…it wasn't what you thought."

"I don't remember asking for an explanation." She fought to keep her voice even, though the Herculean effort it took made her break into a sweat.

"The woman you saw me with is my sister-in-law. My brother's wife. Susan asked her to come up from Savannah to see the play. She's leaving tomorrow."

"And your point would be?"

"I'm trying to apologize."

"Then you have the wrong number. It's your brother you should be calling at…" now that her eyes had adjusted to the inky darkness she could read the numbers on the digital clock across the bed, "one-forty in the morning."

"Dammit, I'm not sleeping with her," he ground out.

"I'm not interested in your sleeping arrangements."

"Then why the hell did you come tonight?" he demanded irritably.

"For Susan. I said I would come and I try not to make a habit of breaking my word."

"For Susan," he snorted. "Right. That's why you came late, hid in the back of the auditorium without letting her know you were there, then beat a trail for the parking lot before the applause died down. She looked for you, Ali."

"I was going to send her a card," she said, but she noticed he didn't say *he* had looked for her.

"You were trying to avoid me." His tempered tone held accusation.

"And you weren't trying to avoid me by yanking Susan out from beneath my nose without so much as a phone call to let me know she wouldn't be coming to the shop after school? I paced the floor for hours," she snapped, "thinking something had happened to her. Was that my punishment for failing to express undying love at the drop of a dime?" Ali heard his expulsion of breath and rallied to compose herself after the impulsive outburst.

"I...I didn't think you'd appreciate my taking advantage of the offer indefinitely. You're right. I should have let you know."

"That was so unfair," she breathed against the tightness in her throat.

"Ali," he groaned. "Jesus, please don't cry. I never meant—"

"I'm half of this conversation, and if my half wants to cry, it will! You don't have any right to call me in the middle of the night and...and talk to me this way. You gave me all of thirty minutes to jump on the love-wagon after dropping your little bombshell. If you think I'm going to lay myself open for the knife just because you're fabulous in the sack, you'd better think again, Finch."

"This isn't the way I wanted things to turn out, Ali."

"You walked out on me simply because I didn't say the words you wanted to hear when you wanted to hear them."

"I know I rushed things," his voice was strained. "But I was hurt that you wouldn't admit to caring, just a little."

"Well, you showed me, didn't you? Love my kid, love me. Drop and give me fifty or resign your commission. I don't know what kind of marriage you had with Gloria, but I don't respond well to ultimatums or vengeful tactics."

"I didn't give you an ultimatum!" he exploded.

"You didn't have to express the conditions verbally," she shouted back. "A blind man could've felt the change in your attitude. Hot one minute, cold the next. Is that what you did to Gloria when you didn't get your way? Freeze her out?"

Crackling silence descended across the wires, broken only by their sporadic breathing. Ali squeezed her eyes shut, covering the mouthpiece so he wouldn't hear her ragged attempts to squelch the sob building in her throat.

After what seemed like an eternity he gave a harsh, brittle laugh. "I guess I did," he rasped. "Though I never thought of myself as a cold, vengeful man. Maybe that's why she burned up the leather on her therapist's couch instead of the sheets on our bed."

No matter how she tried to hold it back, a whimper escaped. The pain in his voice magnified her own to unbearable proportion. Her chest caved in with the effort to speak. "I-I have to go."

"Ali," he pleaded hoarsely, "let me come over. Let me make it right."

God, if only he would cease saying her name like a prayer she might be able to sever the connection. She wanted so badly to tell him all was forgiven, to have him in her bed again so she could touch him and show him how much she cared. She didn't want it to matter that he'd turned a cold shoulder on her at a time when her emotions were in turmoil, when, conversely, she had been struggling to bounce back from the psychological blow dealt her by her mother. Everything had been compounded by the conflicting shock of hearing him say he loved her, all within the space of two hours.

How could she be sure of right and wrong, of his sincerity, of anything when her emotions were still raw and dangerously close to the surface?

After a choking gulp and several hard swallows she managed to get out, "You have to make it right with yourself first, Jordan. I can't... I have to go."

"Ali..."

Terrified she would break and beg him to come to her if he said another word, she hung up, then curled into a fetal position in the middle of the bed. As though turning her back on the phone would keep her from reaching out to call him back.

Chapter Fourteen

ಉ

In Monday's mail was a note from Susan thanking her for attending the performance and berating her for not showing herself, but Susan would forgive her. Included in the note was a picture of Susan and the entire cast in costume. Ali smiled as she tucked the note into her desk drawer. She propped the photo against the crystal penholder on top of the desk.

On Wednesday afternoon of the following week Ali was sitting at her desk going over the resumes of college students who had so far answered the ad she'd posted in the *Tribune*. Most were photography or theater majors. Some simply expressed a burning desire to break into the world of fashion modeling. She had settled on a graphic design firm and had met with key executives to propose her innovative ideas for the new catalogue. They were impressed and agreed to take on the project, with Ali having the last word on layouts for the magazine.

Word had also leaked to several professors at the university of what she was hoping to accomplish and they had sent letters of support, offering to supervise the students in the more technical areas, if she so desired.

Deanna poked her head around the curtain to ask, "How's it coming?"

"The response has been overwhelming, from students *and* faculty. We're really going to do it, Deanna. The design firm says if we bust our tails the first issue can be out in less than three months."

"That soon?" Deanna grinned excitedly, continuing to hover behind the curtain.

Ali rubbed two fingers along her temple where a headache was starting to build. "I was hoping you'd help me write copy for the selected photos. If we write the blurbs as we go along it will save a lot of time. Better to discard what we don't need than wade through the piles of chosen shots later trying to whip out something, don't you think?"

"I think you're a genius, is what I think. You really want me to help write the copy?"

"You're here every day of the week, you know as much about the merchandise as I do. I need someone who works with the customers and knows what sells. I was thinking we could read each other's blurbs to catch any missing details. The job's yours if you want it. If you say no, I'll have to get down on my knees and beg."

"You talked me into it." Deanna's glittering eyes belied her pleasure at the confidence Ali placed in her.

Ali tapped the butt of her pen on the desk. "Why are you hiding behind the curtain? Do I look that rabid?"

"Nope."

Deanna swept the curtain aside to reveal a cut glass vase filled with at least two dozen Blue Girl roses, baby's breath, and delicately interlaced ferns. Ali could only stare, dumbfounded. "Somebody sent you blue roses?"

"No, silly. You. Aren't they beautiful, in a melancholy sort of way?" Deanna set the crystal vase on the corner of her desk, fussing with the blooms for a moment before handing her the card.

"Must be Franny's idea of a joke." Ali took the card from Deanna's outstretched hand. "What kind of person orders blue roses from a florist?"

"They didn't come from a florist," Deanna replied absently. "A private courier delivered them."

"What do you mean a private courier?" She frowned up at Deanna, the card forgotten for the moment.

"I mean some guy in a suit pulled up to the curb in a silver Taurus, lifted the whole shebang out of a gigantic cooler sitting in the front seat, and walked them in. Didn't give his name or say who he worked for. I didn't have to sign for them or anything. He just handed them to me, said they were for Miss Allison MacPherson, and that I was to give her the card you have in your hand. Then he left. Is that weird or what? Mmmm," she bent over the bluish tinged buds that could, depending on the light, appear lavender, "they smell heavenly."

Ali leaned back in her swivel chair and examined the plain vanilla card in her hand, devoid of fancy scrolls or advertising of any kind.

"Well, what are you waiting for? Open the card. I'm dying to know who sent them."

Flipping the card open, Ali silently read the bold handwritten script with her heart in her throat, *From my mother's garden in Charleston. I miss you. Love, Jordan.*

"Ali, please," Deanna's impatient tone snapped her head up. "The suspense is killing me. Are they from that Finch guy or not?"

"Yes," Her voice was barely audible.

Deanna clasped a hand to her chest. "Oh God, isn't that romantic? Blue roses from a blue man."

Deanna hadn't asked questions when Susan had started coming to the boutique after school. Nor had she commented on Jordan's frequent, if short, visits to the shop to pick up Susan, or the equally abrupt cessation of both. She was an absolute believer that fate brought star-crossed lovers together, no matter the odds. Which was why, at thirty-nine, Deanna saw no reason to go out of her way to date around. She was still waiting for fate to drop Mr. Right into her lap.

Ali could tell Deanna a thing or two about fate. She didn't believe fate had anything to do with two people working at a relationship. People made their own fate by the conscious choices they made every day—about their jobs and their families and the code of ethics they lived by. Titanic's sinking could have been avoided. Ali would grant fate the iceberg, but not the poor judgment and arrogant assumptions of the engineers who had built the unsinkable ship. The mere addition of an adequate number of lifeboats could have spared hundreds a watery grave. Simple math, not fate.

Was it fate that had sent her mother skittering to hide behind the dining room curtains? No. Perhaps she and Jordan had been destined to cross paths at some point, him being Franny's boss, but fate had not made him insist she let him be there for her during troubled times. Then, when she'd failed to dance to his tune, to freeze her out. Not unlike her mother had done so many years ago. It was during those troublesome times that a person's true character was brought to light.

And sadly, blue roses from his mother's garden in Charleston couldn't change that.

* * * * *

Jordan contemplated his next move like a corporate raider on the prowl. In retrospect, he'd kissed his way through the entire female freshman class in high school, ditto for his sophomore year. Junior and senior years were spent perfecting sexual finesse. Though once in college he'd settled down and married, applied himself to learning his craft, and the years since had been spent clawing out a niche for himself and honing his business acumen to a razor sharp edge.

The thing was, Ali made him crave that same carefree excitement he'd enjoyed during high school. He was primed and pumped to do whatever it took to break down her resistance. To show her he could change. Had changed. And lucky for him her best friend was seated not twenty feet from his office.

"Franny, would you come in here a moment?" he called through the open door.

The normally robust Franny nearly slunk into his office. She stood just inside the door, hands folded primly in front of her. "Yes?"

"You can come all the way in. I won't bite."

Dragging her feet as though she were going to the gallows, she came to stand in front of his desk. "If this is about Susan hanging on the phone—"

"It's not about Susan." He waved away her concern impatiently. "It's about Ali."

"Ali?" She blinked at him, baffled.

"You remember, the woman who dragged you kicking and screaming to a picnic lunch in the park."

"Right. That Ali." She shifted from one foot to the other. "I apologize for the remark she made about you pinching my, er... Well, she gets nuts sometimes. It won't happen again."

"What size shoes does she wear?"

Franny continued to blink at him, the blank expression on her face slowly eroding into a frown. "I beg your pardon?"

"Shoes, Franny. What size shoes does she wear?"

She opened her mouth to speak, closed it, then said, "Did I miss something?"

He changed tactics. "Would you say Miss MacPherson is a rational person?"

"Not particularly," she answered cautiously, gnawing at her lower lip. "You're firing me," she blurted out suddenly. "I knew it. I knew this would happen when she came barreling in here like ten trucks on a two-lane highway. It's this man she's dating. He's—he's robbing her of what normally good sense she might possess."

"Ah, yes." He nodded. "The old money guy."

"Yes! Yes!" Her index finger cut an arc through the air. "That's what she wanted to talk about while she was wining and dining me in the park. Oh, sure, she apologized for pissing me off, but then she started in about this guy again. It's all supposed to be a big secret. He's in the middle of a nasty custody battle, and they have to sneak around to be together, and she said she'd explode if she didn't talk to someone about it. Jordan, I'm sorry. It's just that she—she gets crazy. I mean this thing with her mother…well, never mind about that. That's a whole other story. She wouldn't even tell me his name, for chrissake!"

"Big secret, huh?" Jordan stroked his chin thoughtfully.

"Yeah. She's worried she'll do something to hurt his chances of getting custody of his kid. You'd have to know Ali to know why she'd worry over something so stupid. I mean, if this guy wants to have a relationship with her, he should have it or hit the road. Where does he get off asking her to sneak around like she's some sort of…of…of lowlife. It's bad enough her mother's been beating her down since the day she came home from college for a visit, wearing makeup for the first time. Lord, was that a nightmare."

"What happened?" he asked curiously.

It took so little to loosen Franny's tongue. "What happened? What happened? I'll tell you what happened. She dragged Ali to the bathroom by the hair and tried to scrub the lipstick off. Called her a whore. Said she wasn't paying another dime of Ali's tuition as long as she insisted on parading around like a two-bit slut. I've told Ali for years she should just tell her mother to fuck off, excuse my language, but, well, that's why she sometimes goes a little overboard.

"I'm sorry," she said again, taking a deep breath to compose herself. "I didn't mean to go off. None of what I just told you excuses her behavior. She had no right to interrupt in the middle of a business day and put you on the spot that way. Jesus, you'd think she'd know better than to pull a stunt like that. She runs her own business. She'd have a fit if someone burst into her boutique and wreaked havoc. I'll clean out my desk."

"You're not fired, Franny. And you haven't answered my question yet."

"What question?"

"What size shoes does Ali wear?"

"Six." She frowned. "Why?"

Jordan shrugged noncommittally. "It's just that I overheard two men yesterday arguing about the correlation between a woman's shoe size and her ability to rationalize business decisions versus personal improprieties. One claimed seventy percent of women who wear a size eight or larger are hell on wheels in the office, but outside the office they tend to be self-conscious. Hiding their feet under tables and things of that nature. While women with smaller feet are just the opposite. Self-conscious in the work place, but very upbeat and confident in a social setting."

"That's the biggest bunch of horseshit I've ever heard."

"That's what I thought. The fact that Ali wears a size six pretty much nips their theory in the bud, wouldn't you say?"

"That's what you called me in here for?" She stared at him as if he had two heads. "To test a retarded theory you overheard a couple of guys, who are obviously just as retarded, arguing over?"

"Well, you did tell me Ali is a successful business woman. Then out of nowhere she came in here ready to drag you out by the hair, if necessary, over a personal matter. Kind of had me wondering if there was any truth to the possibility. They looked like professional men, I figured they must have drawn their conclusions based on personal observations of female co-workers."

Franny rolled her eyes in disgust. "Having just proved my theory that all men are pigs, can I get back to work now? Or would you like to discuss the possibility of being invaded by giant alien warrior women bearing a striking resemblance to Jane Fonda?"

Jordan suppressed the urge to grin. "No thanks. I saw that movie. Send my piglet in on your way out, would you? If I have to listen to one more sloppy conversation with Randy Peters, I'm going to throw up."

Franny hesitated in front of his desk, trailing a finger along the edge. "Er, that's kind of something I'd like to talk to you about. Not that I don't adore Susan," she rushed to add.

"Say no more." He held up a hand. "As of today she won't be staying here in the office after school. She's mature enough to handle herself at home until I get there."

"Oh. Well then…"

"And Franny?"

She paused at the door to turn and look at him. "Yes?"

"I don't think there's any need to mention our little discussion to Ali, is there?"

"Is there a sign on my chest that says 'please come charging back into the office and embarrass my boss again'?"

"I'll ignore the sign on your chest if you'll ignore the one on my forehead that says 'pig'."

"Deal."

* * * * *

Friday afternoon another delivery crossed Ali's desk. The package was wrapped in decorative silver foil covered with purple irises, a froth of lavender bows and spiraling ribbons trailing over the edges. If not for the two customers who'd entered the shop just as Deanna handed her the gaily wrapped box, Deanna would still be doing a jig waiting for her to open it.

Ali stared at the rectangular box sitting in front of her for all of ten minutes before pulling loose the ribbon. No card had accompanied the mysterious gift, but she had a pretty good idea who it was from. With shaking fingers she tore away the paper, lifted the lid, and peeled away the layers of tissue paper.

Shoes. High heels. Blue suede with three-inch heels, to be exact. Tucked inside one shoe was a folded square of paper. *For the pair you ruined running away from me. Love, Jordan.*

Groaning, Ali let her forehead bang against the desktop. As if one wore suede during the approaching summer months. He'd known exactly what he was about, deliberately choosing winter shoes. Shoes that would sit in her closet and slowly drive her insane because of the very fact that she wouldn't be able to wear them until October—September at the earliest. They probably wouldn't fit anyway, she mused haughtily, trailing wistful fingers over the smooth, supple leather. How the heck had he known her shoe size?

Well, she couldn't keep them, so it hardly mattered. If she didn't immediately return the expensive pumps he would assume…things he shouldn't assume.

Quickly, before Deanna could sweep into the back room to coo over her latest unwanted gift, Ali refolded the tissue and snapped the lid on the box, hiding it in the bottom drawer of her desk. She would deal with Finch later. This afternoon she was scheduled to meet with some of the applicants and their professors at the design firm for a meeting.

* * * * *

Poised to deliver either a blistering set-down or moderately sweet encouragement—depending on who answered the phone—Ali dialed Jordan's home number. She would have called him at the office if not for his guard dog, Franny.

"Hello," Jordan's rich tone came over the line.

Bristling, she jumped in with both feet. "Let's get something straight here, Finch. I wasn't doing the running away, you were."

"Really," he remarked casually. "That wasn't quite the way I saw it. You obviously didn't walk into an auditorium full of people with muddy feet, so I can only assume you picked your way carefully through the grassy area to the pavement on arrival. Not so during the escape."

"Excuse me, but I wasn't the one who crawled out from between the sheets with an icicle stuck up my butt, sugar."

"Let me crawl back between them and we'll make up. I hear make-up sex is unrivaled."

"In your dreams."

His voice dropped an octave. "You don't want to know what we do in my dreams. I don't think there's a rating capable of describing—"

"Stop it!"

"I made a mistake, Ali. I'm not perfect, God knows, but I'm trying to make it right. You have to forgive me sooner or later."

"Like hell I do."

"Now who's freezing who out?" he challenged. "At least I'm willing to try to work it out."

"There isn't anything to work out, Finch. You made it perfectly clear it was your way or the highway. And in case you forgot, I'm an excellent driver."

"No, what you're good at is pushing people who want to get close to you away. If your mother called you right now and said she was sorry for the way she treated you, that she wanted to start over, would you forgive her and make the effort?"

"I'm through with this discussion."

"Of course you are," he said with an air of superiority. "Running away is always easier than making a stand, isn't it, Ali? God forbid someone would actually see past the outrageousness you wear like a coat. Isn't that why you bragged about your tattoo the first night we met? To scare me off in case I got too interested? Sure, the sex was great, but when it came down to having to give a part of yourself, you froze up."

"Cool!" she heard Susan exclaim in the background. "Ali's really got a tattoo?"

"Yes," Jordan told her.

"Where?"

"On her butt."

"Finch!"

"Ohmygod!" Susan squealed. "What's it look like?"

"I don't know, she won't let me see it."

"Damn it, Finch! What the hell are you doing?"

"Can I get one?" Susan asked.

"Not until you're eighteen."

"Daddy, come on. Does she really have a tattoo?" Susan demanded skeptically.

Ali felt her face heat up. She wanted to crawl beneath the bed and hide. No, she wanted to kill Jordan Finch for exposing her to Susan. Next he would be telling her —

"She could be lying," Jordan allowed. "But I've seen —"

"Jordan, please!" Ali gripped the receiver with both hands. "You said you didn't want her to know."

"Maybe I've changed my mind."

"What! What!" She could almost picture Susan's wide hazel eyes wondering what other secrets she was hiding. The kid was probably doing a jig next to Jordan, hoping to wheedle out of him exactly what it was he'd seen.

"Don't," Ali heard herself pleading. "Please. She wouldn't understand. You'd be putting a weapon of revenge right into her hands. The minute she gets peeved with you, she'll run out and get something pierced."

"From what I can tell age seems to have little to do with peevish behavior. Besides, she's scared to death of needles."

"Needles?" Susan shrieked. "Daddy, give me the phone! Let me talk to her."

"Later, honey. Ali was just about to tell me something important. Weren't you, Ali?"

He wouldn't.

"Ali."

"I can't believe you'd — you'd — blackmail me like this," she sputtered.

"Well, if you're sure you don't care..." The warning was concealed in dulcet tones, but no less effective.

"This is insane."

"Daaaddyyy!"

"I'm waiting, Ali."

"All right," she gritted out. "I care. Is that what you wanted to hear?"

"I was thinking more along the lines of that, and dinner," his tone was unyielding, "tonight."

"You can't hold this over my head forever."

"You'd be surprised what I can do when I put my mind to it. Eight o'clock okay?"

"Just peachy," she sneered, nails digging into her palm. "But don't think this will change—"

"Ali?" Susan's breathless voice came on the line. "Ohmygod, do you really have a tattoo or was Dad just pulling my leg?"

"Yes, Susan," she admitted gravely. "I really have a tattoo. But it isn't something you should consider cool."

"Bonnie's dad has a tattoo. On his arm. It's a woman dressed like Jane. You know, from the old-time Tarzan flicks? He flexes his muscles and makes her dance. What does yours do?"

Old-time Tarzan flicks. Jeez. "It doesn't do anything."

"What's it look like?"

"Nothing quite as entertaining as Jane doing the hula on my hip, I assure you. I wish I'd never gotten it. Tattoos are permanent. They aren't something you should decide about on the spur of the moment. Believe me, I could do without it just fine."

"Yeah, but what does it look like?" Susan voice held a modicum of fascination, no doubt envisioning something medieval, with fangs and daggers dripping blood, winding around her body.

"Susan, honey, it's not important what it looks like. The point is that it doesn't enrich my life in any way, shape, or form. New experiences should affect your life in a positive way. I got the stupid thing without thinking it through and now I'm stuck with it for the rest of my life. If I was so damn proud of it, don't you think I would've shown it to you by now?"

"You told Dad about it," Susan pointed out indignantly.

"Well..." Oh God, I could never be a mother, "that's different."

"How?"

Because he's an adult and I'm an adult — most of the time — and... "Does Bonnie think her dad's tattoo is cool?"

"Kinda. He was in the Marines and she thinks that's cool. But she made him cover it up the night of the play. He was drunk when he got it."

At the risk of falling from grace in Susan's eyes, Ali said quietly, "So was I."

"Yeah, but—"

"No buts, Suz. It would be different if I'd thought it through and decided it was what I really wanted. I didn't. So whether it's flowery and harmless or gory and scaly really doesn't make any difference, does it? I told your dad because I didn't want him jumping to conclusions later on. We kind of agreed to be honest and up-front with each other in the beginning. I guess you're old enough to understand that when two people are attracted to each other, like you and Randy, they tend to...romanticize certain aspects of the other's character. You have to know where to draw the line on rash judgments, and sometimes that's really hard, even for adults."

"Hold on a second, Ali. Dad, do you mind? I'm trying to have a private conversation here."

"You can have private conversations when you're thirty," Jordan replied in a fatherly tone. "Give me the phone."

Susan let out a long-suffering sigh. "I hate when you pull rank. Ali, I gotta go. Will you be in the shop Monday? I'll stop by."

"Sure. See you then."

Jordan reclaimed his parental rights to commandeer the phone. "I'll pick you up at eight."

"You're going to pay for this, Finch."

"I certainly hope so."

Ali slammed down the phone and stalked to the bathroom to shower and change. She had just enough time to fix her makeup, arrange her hair into a pile on top of her head, don her silk robe, and as icing on the cake, slip her feet into the blue suede heels he'd thought to torture her with before going downstairs to set the table for a candlelight dinner.

Chapter Fifteen

ဆာ

"You're not dressed," he said when she answered the door.

"We're eating in," she informed him. "Nice of you to dress for the occasion though." He had on a dark gray double-breasted suit that accented his broad shoulders, tawny looks, and mouthwateringly trim waist. A lesser woman would have fallen to her knees and begged forgiveness for any number of uncommitted sins just for the chance to touch him. She, however, was going to rip his heart out and feed it to him.

He looked past her to the dining room where candlelight flickered off the cloth-covered walls, the black-rimmed Oriental plates, the silverware, and sniffed the air. "You cooked?"

"Nothing extravagant," she said as he loosed the button and shrugged out of his jacket. Ali took it from him and folded it neatly over the back of the couch. "Wine?" she offered, moving to the cabinet across the living room.

"That would be nice."

Bottle in hand, she turned to face him, pouring a generous amount. And couldn't help but feel a thrill of satisfaction as his eyes traveled over her from the titillating vee of her robe to the suede shoes on her feet.

"I halfway expected you to send them back," he said, accepting the flute to sip.

"Don't be absurd." Ali lifted her glass to her lips. "A woman never sends back the perfect pair of shoes."

"So," he sat down on the couch, "what were you and Susan discussing so intently?" His gaze slid down the flash of leg exposed as she lowered herself to the other end of the couch.

"Sex."

He didn't rise to the bait. "Really."

"She's old enough to know the facts of life. And the fact is, I'm fucking her daddy."

He regarded her silently for a moment, then asked, "Is this a test? Am I supposed to get pissed and leave now?"

Yes! her mind screamed. *Leave. Run. Stop looking at me as though you can change what I am.* "Before dinner?" she mocked lightly. "That would be rude. We haven't crawled between the sheets yet."

"We can skip straight to dessert if you prefer."

"My kind of man," she purred, rising to glide around the end of the couch. She could do this. She would do it. After tonight he wouldn't want anything more to do with her. She could put him out of her head and get on with her life.

His hand shot over the back of the couch to capture her wrist as she turned in the direction of the foyer, snapping her around. "Shouldn't we settle on a price first?"

"A price?" she lifted an eyebrow at him.

"How much does it cost to get fucked these days? It's been a long time since I've visited a whorehouse."

His silky tone sucked the air from her lungs. Ali could only stare down at him mutely. Having it put into words made it all sound so...rank.

"How much, sugar?" he repeated, rolling onto one hip to plunge his free hand into his trouser pocket, extracting a money clip bursting with hundred dollar bills. "Enough?" He held up the clip. "More? And just so there aren't any misunderstandings, I'll want every dollar's worth. Of course, money doesn't really make the transaction an even give and take. It's more like you giving, me taking. And you know what they say in business— the customer's always right."

Ali tried to jerk away, but he held her fast, dragging the edge of the metal clip down her arm, "Your mother did an excellent job pounding the courtesan act into your head. There's just one thing she forgot to tell you. Some men like it."

Outraged at herself for acting so rashly, at him for neatly turning the tables on her, for wanting him despite the fact that she'd sworn to remain in complete control, Ali asked coolly, "What makes you think you can afford me?"

"Why don't we find out?" he suggested, keeping hold of her wrist as he rose and came around his end of the couch to face her. "Bearing in mind the rate of inflation since I was a kid, I'd say twenty is more than generous for a kiss. Got change for a hundred?"

"Sorry. I'm fresh out of small bills."

"Then I guess it'll have to be five very hot kisses." He yanked her stiff body fully against his, twisting her shackled wrist behind her back, ensuring any struggle would result in contact with his groin.

The onslaught began as he pushed aside her robe to place his mouth on her shoulder, his tongue snaking out to taste the perfumed flesh, moving slowly, so slowly over her collarbone to the base of her throat. A rush of warmth flushed her body. Ali fought to control the sweeping sensations threatening to crumble her resolve. She remained stiff and unyielding, her free arm anchored tightly to her side.

"One," he murmured hotly where the pulse beat like a trapped animal at the base of her throat. "Two," when his mouth had made its way up the side of her throat, his teeth sank into the edge of her earlobe. Then his hand was on the sash of her robe, tugging the knot loose.

"You said kisses," she reminded him curtly, tugging closed the robe.

"I don't believe I specified they would follow any particular pattern. Anytime you'd like a say in how I choose to conduct this sexual transaction, I'll be happy to pocket my money."

"And if I've changed my mind? If I don't want to conclude the transaction?"

"That wouldn't make you much a of whore, would it? Three."

Ali gasped when his mouth closed over her nipple through the silk of her robe. She was losing control. Yet if she gave in and made love to him, as she wanted to do, she would open herself to more hurt, more pain. The next time he walked away she might not be able to stand it. She wasn't the kind of woman a self-assured, responsible man like Jordan Finch married. She was the kind he came to when the world beat up on him. When he needed to let go, to explore the baser side of his predictable nature.

Except nothing about Jordan Finch was predictable tonight. He hadn't been put off by her crude remarks or offensive demeanor. To end the charade would prove she'd been wrong to deny him the words he wanted to hear. To continue would lacerate her dignity as a woman to shreds, possibly beyond repair.

Moving to the other breast he sucked the taut nipple into his mouth, laving the material until it was soaked. "Four." He straightened, running his tongue over his lower lip. "Now for the tricky part. Deciding which set of pouty lips to kiss next. These," he laid a finger against her mouth. "Or these." White-hot knives buried themselves beneath her skin when his hand slipped between her legs to palm her, squeezing lightly. "One pair's as good as another. Isn't that what you said that night in the parking lot?"

"Stop it. Stop it. Stop it!" She beat at his chest with her fist. "It was good between us 'til you—you ruined it by saying you loved me. Why couldn't you just leave things the way they were?"

"Because people change, Ali. And when they meet someone they care for their expectations change. I fell in love with you, and you acted like I committed an unpardonable sin. You didn't even want to deal with it. You still don't."

"I don't know how to deal with it!" she cried, flinging herself away from him when his hold on her wrist loosened. "Don't you get it, Jordan?" She whirled to face him. "I don't...know...how."

"Learn," he said simply. "Try. That's all I'm asking. It won't kill you. I should know, I've had my feelings thrown back in my face a time or two."

"You can't love me," she snarled acidly, her voice so ragged around the edges that even she didn't recognize it. God how she hated him at this moment for so callously ripping open that putrid wound. "My own mother can't even love me!"

"That doesn't mean you aren't worthy of being loved!" he roared back ferociously. "Jesus!" He savaged the Windsor knot of his tie, and snapped open the top button of his dress shirt. "What do I have to do? What do I have to say to get through to you? You want to have a meaningless, sexual relationship with me, is that it? We just tried that. It didn't work. You want to know why it didn't work, Ali?"

"No, but I feel sure you're about to enlighten me." Ali strode to the cabinet and poured herself a Scotch. To hell with the sissy wine. She needed something with a kick to it.

"Because you're the only one who thinks of yourself as less than worthy. Somewhere along the way you forgot you were having fun and actually started to believe the things your mother told you."

Ali knocked back the Scotch and swallowed, casting a pointed gaze at his groin. "You wouldn't be saying that just because you have a hard-on, would you?"

He didn't bother to hide the fact that he was still aroused. Not that he could. "I was taught it was a sin to use a woman, not want her."

The liquor burned its way down her throat, spreading warmth and restoring some of the inner balance she'd lost. "Tsk, tsk, Finch. That can't be proper etiquette for a pillar of the community raised in Charleston society."

"You know what?" He rounded the couch to take the tumbler from her hand, refilling it with another three fingers for himself. "I don't give a rat's ass what Charleston society thinks. Or Gloria. Or some straight-laced judge I've never met. If having a relationship with a warm, loving, intelligent woman is wrong and immoral, tell me why it feels so damned right."

Ali didn't meet his gaze. Instead she concentrated on drawing circles along the polished wood of the credenza with her index finger. "I thought we were just going to have a fling. I wasn't prepared for...this. You walked out on me."

Her last statement hung in the air between them.

He took a healthy swig of Scotch before answering the charge. "I know. I was wrong. But that doesn't mean I stopped having feelings for you or that I'm incapable of changing and growing. If it makes you feel any better, Ellen ripped my ass all the way home for not introducing the two of you. Susan told her all about you. She's probably on the phone to my mother, as we speak, telling her what an idiot son she raised."

"How did you know my shoe size?"

"That's another thing." He rested one hip against the credenza. "Franny's under the impression this mysterious pig of a man you're dating is no good for you. Took every ounce of willpower I had not to tell her that pig is me. She's, uh, intimated on several occasions that he—I—made you feel ashamed of your rather unorthodox past. Is that true, Ali? Do I make you feel that way?"

"No," she whispered bleakly, studying the tips of her painted nails. "I make me feel that way. Some smart shrink would say since I can't take out my frustrations on my mother, I take them out on everyone else. Poor Franny, bless her heart, has weathered more than a few of my tantrums."

Jordan made a derisive sound in the back of his throat. "Take it from me, shrinks are overrated. Particularly when they're sleeping with your wife and charging you by the hour for it."

"Is that why Gloria wanted the divorce?"

"Maybe. Who knows." His voice had a disembodied quality to it, as though he had distanced himself from feeling any emotion over the betrayal. "I only just found out about their torrid little affair the night of Susan's play. Ellen has no compunction about announcing to the world that I'm a lyin' son of a bitch, but it didn't occur to her that I might want to know my wife was screwing her therapist."

Lyin' son of a bitch. "Ellen. As in your ninth grade steady?"

"That would be her. The one who married my brother." He frowned at her. "I thought I told you that."

"Yes...yes, you did. I guess it slipped my mind." So the brunette who'd looked at him with a twinkle in her eye and cooed in his ear as though she knew him intimately was Ellen Ginsworth. "She knew Gloria was having an affair and didn't tell you?"

"To hear her tell it, all of Charleston knew Gloria was sleeping around. Ellen and Arlan live in Savannah, so how gullible does that make me? Gloria said she was having a breakdown. I believed her. Or thought I did, anyway." He studied the tumbler in his hand. "It doesn't matter now."

Ali's disbelieving gaze flew to his. "What do you mean it doesn't matter? Of course it matters! It's leverage you can use to keep Gloria from taking you to court over Susan."

He finished off the Scotch and poured another. "The idea occurred to me, but I can't do that to Susan."

She threw up her hands in frustration. "Ellen's right. You are an idiot. If Gloria went to all the trouble to fake a breakdown in order to conceal her affair from you, she's not going to want it dragged out in front of Susan any more than you do. I'd bet Ellen's Vegas shoes that the only reason Gloria wants custody of Susan is because women like her, with money and position, are afraid their friends will drop them like a hot potato if they don't continue to retain the customary mother-child arrangement. What would Gloria's society buds think if she divorced her husband and gave up her only daughter?"

"You're assuming Gloria's friends aren't equally as shallow as she is," he grunted.

"That may be. But how many of them are cold-blooded enough to run the gamut of criticism and whispers and backbiting sure to follow? Women who willingly give up their children aren't tolerated in polite society, especially by those who view themselves as the very core of all that's moral and decent. And I know what you're going to say," she held up both palms, "that there could be damaging side effects for Susan. But either way you go, Jordan, Susan is going to be affected. If you don't fight for her, what does she have left to believe in? She already knows her mother doesn't want her. She needs to know how much you do. In a situation like this words just aren't…enough."

Jordan set the tumbler carefully on the credenza, his movements slow and precise, then turned to her, taking her face in his big hands. His gaze was so intense she felt the heat of it clear through to her bones. "Do you know how good you are for me? Do you have any idea how many nights I laid awake wishing I could talk to you about the hell I'm going through with this custody case? I told myself a thousand times not to involve you, you didn't deserve the hassle. That I should just leave you alone. And I almost had myself convinced until you showed up to watch Susan's performance."

Deanna would call the overriding urge to keep her word to Susan and attend the performance, fate. Ali termed it a conscious decision. Fate could claim the mud that ruined her shoes if it wished. She couldn't control Mother Nature.

"I can't leave you alone, Ali. Call it what you will, infatuation, obsession, love. Whatever you can be comfortable with. Just don't ask me to ignore what I feel, because I can't. Maybe we didn't start off under the best of circumstances, but we've both overcome some high-risk obstacles to get where we are in life. I think it's worth working at. We're worth working at."

Infatuation. Obsession. Yes, those were elements she understood, could work with. "Come to bed, Finch, and let me

show you just how obsessed I am with those sexy peepers of yours."

* * * * *

"That's it?" Jordan traced a blunt finger over the small tattoo no bigger than her thumb stamped high on Ali's left buttock.

"I detect a note of disappointment. What were you expecting?"

"I don't know." He lifted a shoulder, unsure if it was indeed disappointment he felt. "Something…"

"Primitive? Erotic? Downright lewd?" she threw out a few suggestions, cutting a white line down the center of his chest with one nail.

He'd anticipated something along the lines of a sleek panther or tiger with claws and teeth bared, actually. Nothing so simple as a single music note. Pink. The damn thing was pink with blue squiggles dancing around it. But that's how it was with Ali. Daring, complicated, unpredictable on the outside, soft and giving and intuitively empathetic inside.

"Dangerous," he decided, sliding his palm over the curve of her hip. It still amazed him how responsive she was to his touch. He metamorphosed into King Kong the minute she came near him. They'd only just finished making love and he was ready for her again.

"Ali MacPherson, woman of danger. Yeah, I could go for that."

He stuffed a pillow behind his back and settled her against his shoulder. "By the way, what was on the menu for tonight?"

"Hungry?" She twisted to look up at him.

"A little," he admitted.

"I'm ashamed to say you were going to dine on an exquisitely made peanut butter sandwich."

"You're shitting me."

"No. I was mad as hell you told Susan about my tattoo, then left me floundering on the line trying to explain."

"Well, you showed me."

She elbowed him in the ribs. "Want that sandwich now?"

Ali shrugged into her robe, Jordan his trousers. They shared peanut butter sandwiches at the ice cream parlor table in the kitchen. Ali ate one. Jordan ate three along with an apple.

"When I was a kid," Jordan said between bites, "I used to eat apples with a big spoonful of peanut butter."

"Did they teach you that at Charleston Boy's Academy or did you pick up that little habit off the street?" she teased, using her napkin to dab the corner of her mouth.

"Wanda, our housekeeper, turned me on to the technique. Every day at lunchtime she'd sit out on the back porch with an apple and a spoon of peanut butter. She told me never to forget to appreciate the simple things in life."

"You can't get much simpler than licking peanut butter off a spoon," she agreed.

"Wanda was the first woman, aside from my mother, that I loved. I should have listened to her when she said Gloria wasn't right for me, but then I wouldn't have Susan, so…"

Ali reached across the table to cover his hand with hers. "That business with Gloria and her shrink really does bother you, doesn't it?" she asked softly.

Jordan pushed away the sudden bout of melancholy that gripped him. "It bothers me the way she treats Susan, like she's a commodity to be traded."

"You loved her, Jordan. If you say you didn't, this, us, is only a shallow attempt at revenge. Eye for an eye."

He studied her across the table, this woman who had brought color back into his black and white life. A woman like Ali could have any man she desired. Was he deluding himself to think he could hold on to such a mercurial creature for any considerable length of time? "You haven't actually said there is an us."

"There isn't actually a man in the moon, either, but when you look up at it, he's there. Don't think so much, Finch. For every answer there's another question. Let's get you through this custody thing with Susan, then we'll hash out what exactly 'us' entails. Fair enough?"

"Why do I feel like I've just been put on the back burner?" He stood up to dump his paper plate, and hers, into the garbage.

Jordan felt her move up behind him. Her arms came around his waist. "No, we've been put on the back burner. Susan comes first."

He placed one palm flat on the counter, the other over her linked hands. "How much of a selfish bastard will I sound like if I ask when it's our turn?"

She pressed a warm kiss to his bare shoulder. "If we stop being careful now it could ruin everything. I wish you could stay, but it's getting late. You'd better go."

When he was dressed, she walked him to the door and handed him his coat. He pulled her into his arms for another kiss, one of half a dozen they'd shared while he tried to make himself presentable enough to pass inspection in case Susan beat him home from Bonnie's, where a group of kids had gathered for a one last study session before finals.

She tasted of peanut butter, reminding him of simpler times, simpler days, when he hadn't had the responsibility of fatherhood or the constraints of a strained marriage or disgrace of divorce hanging over his head. There was no doubt in his mind that Wanda would like Ali.

"I'll call you tomorrow," he promised, brushing his lips over hers one last time.

She folded her arms under her breasts, casting him a nefarious look from beneath winged brows. "That's what you told Ellen Ginsberg."

"Yeah, but Ellen didn't have a snazzy belly ring and a music note on her ass."

"Get out of here." She laughed and pushed him out the door.

* * * * *

The tune Jordan had been whistling died in his throat the second he recognized Randy Peters' car parked along the street curb. Three houses up from theirs.

He knew a moment of panic as he killed the lights, pulled into the drive, and cut the engine.

They're just studying.

Yeah, right. There's actually a man in the moon, too.

She wouldn't. She's only fifteen.

Yep. Fifteen, and ripe for plucking.

Oh God.

Don't blame God. He's not the one whose high school ring is hanging around her neck. Didn't you give Mary Martin your high school ring in junior year?

Shit!

Jordan bolted from the car like a rocket. If that giant hormone in pants had laid one hand on his little girl…

"Susan!" he thundered the second he cleared the door.

"In the kitchen!"

Angry strides carried Jordan through the foyer and down the hall, where he drew up at the kitchen door. Susan was sitting at the table munching on potato chips. Randy Peters was nowhere in sight. His eyes raked over her, searching for some sign she'd been violated, but she looked the same as she had when she'd left the house. Innocent.

"Where is he?"

She looked up. "Who?"

"Peters," he snapped. "And don't play games with me, young lady. I saw his car parked down the street. You *know* better than to bring a boy into this house when I'm not at home! Now where is he? Hiding in your room?"

"No!"

But Jordan wasn't listening, he was already taking the stairs two at a time.

"Daddy!" She pounded up the steps behind him.

He burst into her room, scanned the bed for signs of recent use, then stormed down the hall, checking the spare bedroom, and his own—God help the little bastard if he'd dared that far.

"What are you doing?" Susan wailed, following in his wake as he clomped down the stairs and began a search of the first-floor rooms. "Randy's not here! Daddy, what is the matter with you?"

"What's the matter with me?" He whirled on her halfway through the great room. "I leave you alone for five minutes and the next thing I know you're—you're sneaking behind my back with that boy!"

"I was not sneaking around! Randy drove me home from Bonnie's and his car stalled. I let him use the phone to call his dad. Is that a crime?"

"I suppose his car just conveniently stalled three houses up the block? Please, that's the oldest line in the book, Susan. There are any number of ways an engine can be fixed to sputter out when you don't plan on going far. He could have called his dad from one of the neighbor's houses."

"Well, I don't know all the neighbors around here yet," she pointed out. "What is the big deal?"

"The big deal is you were alone with him in the house."

"Ah!" She clapped a hand over her mouth, a look of disbelief on her face. "You think we had sex?"

"Did you?"

"I can't believe you're asking me that!"

"Believe it," he growled. "I don't know how wild your mother let you run before you moved here with me, but in this house we have rules. First, and foremost, you will not have boys in this house when I'm not home. For any reason."

"Daddy, you're doing it again," she howled, stomping her tennis shoe-clad foot. "You're jumping to conclusions and judging Randy unfairly. You're judging me unfairly!"

"What I'm doing is grounding you. Indefinitely." Though he had just left the arms of his lover he would not draw parallels between himself and his daughter. He was a grown man, married, divorced. Susan was only fifteen. She had no idea of the pitfalls that awaited her. To hell with teetering on the brink of discovery. She could learn about the perils of casual copulation in sex education class, not firsthand under the tutelage of Randy I'll-trade-my-school-ring-for-your-virginity Peters.

She gaped at him, horrified at the prospect with school's end just around the corner. "Grounding me? But—"

"Until school is out you can park your behind in Ali's shop. And I don't want you calling or speaking to Randy Peters. If he shows his face at this door again, I'll deal with him. Is that perfectly clear?"

"But we didn't do anything!" Susan's eyes misted with tears that spilled over the rims and ran in rivulets down her cheeks.

"What you did," he pointed an irate finger at her, "was jeopardize your very precarious position in this house. Do you know what would happen if your mother were to get wind of how you cozied up with Mr. Peters in my absence? We talked about this, Susan. I thought you understood the necessity of restraint. How important it is, with this custody hearing hanging over our heads, to exude an air of propriety. Apparently, I was wrong."

"Daddy, I'm sorry—"

"Sorry won't make a sack full of difference to a judge," he bellowed, unable to rein in his temper. "I may not have been able to control your mother's urge to gallivant all over Charleston like a hoyden, but I sure as hell won't allow you to follow in her footsteps."

"What are you— What are you talking about?" she sniffed, scrubbing her palms over her cheeks.

"Nothing," he snapped, irritated with himself beyond belief. "Go to bed."

"Daddy—"

"Go to bed, Susan." His tone left no room for further argument. He needed to be alone. He was more furious now than he'd ever been in his life, and not just because he'd removed himself to Chicago to escape the painful memories of Charleston and the auspicious future that had once been in his grasp, but because he'd come very close to alienating Susan on more than one occasion.

She let out a shuddering sigh and turned away, shoulders slumped, to leave the room. He heard her heavy footfalls on the marble tile of the foyer, then silence as she ascended the carpeted staircase.

Susan was all he really had aside from his work. Hindsight being what it was, he realized she was all he'd ever had that truly belonged to him. And to think he'd stood by and let Gloria make the decision of where Susan would live based on her own selfish desire for freedom. He should have taken Susan with him when he left the house on Wimple Street. In a sense he had abandoned her to a mother who had no use for her, except as a trinket of divorce, one that would enable Gloria to retain her plastic pedestal among her peers.

Well not this time. If Gloria took him to court and somehow managed to win, he would use every bit of influence he'd managed to procure over the years, both in judicial and law enforcement circles, in order to wrangle frequent visitation and vested interest clauses into the settlement contract. He would petition for joint custody. Failing that, he would use whatever means available to insinuate himself into every aspect of Susan's upbringing, so that even the most minor of parental decrees would force Gloria to consult and include him in his daughter's day-to-day life.

He would squeeze until Gloria crumpled. Then they would see which meant more to his faithless ex-wife, their daughter or her freedom.

Chapter Sixteen

೫෨

Ali knew something was wrong the minute Susan set foot in the boutique. The brightness was missing from her hazel eyes, replaced with misery, worry, and something else Ali couldn't quite pin down.

"School's almost out," Ali said, following Susan to the back room. "Shouldn't you be doing a whoop and a holler?"

"What for?" Susan tossed her book bag onto the divan, and plopped down next to it. "I'll just have to spend all day in the house twiddling my thumbs."

"Why would you want to do that when you could be out with your friends? Just because you won't see them every day at school doesn't mean you can't keep in touch over the summer."

"Yeah. Right. When Dad gets finished being a prick about Randy."

Uh-oh. Ali picked up her mug from the desk and walked to the coffeemaker in the corner. "I, uh, thought things were a little smoother now that he's gotten to know Randy a little better."

"He thinks we had sex," Susan blurted out.

Caught off guard by the abrupt confession, Ali sloshed the hot coffee over the rim of her cup. She reached for a paper towel to halt the crawl of the splattered liquid before it could spill over the edge of the counter onto the floor. "Does he…er…have any reason to think it's true?"

"No," Susan denied emphatically. "He wouldn't even listen to me, Ali. I tried to tell him how Randy's car conked out down the street when he drove me home from Bonnie's last night, and that I don't know all the neighbors yet, so I let Randy in to use the phone to call his parents. Dad freaked out, said it was just an excuse for us to be alone in the house. Then he said he wasn't going to let me run all over town like a hoyden. Now I'm not allowed to see or talk to Randy, and I have to stay here after school."

Hoyden? Anger, quick and hot, scalded through Ali's veins. It was just wrong to compare Susan's behavior with her mother's previous indiscretions. And how dare he—no matter what the argument with Susan had been about, or how upset Jordan had been at the time, or whatever licentious conclusions he'd jumped to concerning Randy Peters—use her offer to supervise Susan after school as a means of punishment? She could understand his concern, it was only natural, given—if the events transpired as Susan claimed—Jordan had probably spotted Randy's car parked a suspicious distance from the house when he'd arrived home.

But to enlist her as Susan's jailer without first discussing it with her was beyond contemptuous. By condemning Susan to Ali's watchful eye, he was pushing the boundaries of their relationship, reshaping it to the point that she and Susan would become adversaries instead of friends. The look on Susan's face said the punishment declared very clearly, to both her and Ali, where Ali's loyalties lay, or, rather, where Jordan expected them to lie.

What was it he'd said last night about someone you care deeply for? Expectations change. He expected her to back him up, no questions asked.

Ali carefully wiped dripping coffee from the bottom of her mug, walked back to her desk, and turned her chair to face Susan. She sat down, crossed her legs, rearranged her skirt, and took a sip of the steaming brew to quiet her lashing tongue before it yammered out of control.

"Let me see if I have this straight. Randy drove you home from Bonnie's. His car stalled out down the street from your house. You don't feel comfortable enough with the neighbors yet to ask if you can use their phone, so you let Randy into the house to call his parents. Is that right so far?"

"Yes. But Dad —"

"Let me finish," Ali forestalled her with a raised ringer. "I have to get this straight in my head. Okay, so your dad comes home and he sees Randy's car parked in front of a neighbor's house and assumes Randy is still there with you, alone. I can see where he might have been a little upset."

"I knew it!" Susan jumped to her feet. "I knew you'd take his side."

"I'm not taking sides, Susan. Sit down and let me finish. Please. I was fifteen once, I know what it's like to try and explain an innocent situation to an irate parent. They don't come any more irate than my mother. Did I ever mention that my mother and I don't speak?"

"At all?"

"At all," Ali confirmed.

Susan sat back down on the divan, folding her hands between her knees. "How come?"

"Because every time I did something she didn't approve of she went on a rant, wouldn't give me a chance to explain or tell her why I did what I did. She didn't *listen* to me. And because I was so sure I was right all the time, I didn't listen to her." Oh, hindsight was a bitch. "Your dad didn't listen to you last night and you're mad. You have every right to be. But did you listen to him? Do you understand why he reacted the way he did to the thought of you and Randy being alone in the house, especially when he didn't have any reason to expect Randy would be there?"

"But I *explained* it to him."

"You didn't answer my question. Do you understand *why* he got bent out of shape?"

"Yeah. He thought we had sex."

"Yes, but that's not what scared him."

"Scared him?" Susan scoffed. "He wasn't scared, he was pissed."

"He was scared, Susan. He's had you to himself, sort of, since you were born. The only other men he's ever had to share you with are family. He wasn't scared so much that you might have sex with Randy as the fact that Randy might take you away from him. I'm not saying he handled the situation the best way he could have. He's under a lot of pressure right now, worrying over this custody case. And if he won't tell you that the courts most often lean toward giving the mother full custody in a divorce, I will. That means he has to work doubly hard to convince a judge he's the better choice."

"That's what he said, kind of," Susan admitted in a small voice. "That if Mom ever found out she could make a big deal out of it. It's so unfair," she whispered, hanging her head to study the toes of her shoes. "Why does some judge get to decide where I should live instead of me?"

"That's the good part." Ali reached out to smooth her hair. "The judge will take your preference into consideration. But you have to be responsible enough to back up your choice with solid reasons. The fact that you love your dad and want to live with him isn't enough. They'll look at how much he works and compare it to how much time he spends with you. Whether he takes an active interest in your schoolwork, supervises outside activities, and how you spend your time when he's at work. They're going to look at what kind of friends you have, and what kind of friends he has, and how he spends his free time."

"Gosh, they have to know all that?"

"They're worse than the IRS, honey. They'll want to know what you had for breakfast, and whether or not he puts the toilet seat down when he's done. Ha, made you smile."

"Okay, I get it." Grinning ruefully, Susan fell back against the divan, folding her hands across her stomach.

"Well, that's about all the free advice I have for the day. Go home."

"Home?" Susan echoed. "I can't. Dad said I had to stay here 'til he picks me up."

"Yes, well," Ali waved a negligent hand, "I don't have to do everything he says. He's not my father."

"So you're like...ordering me to go home?"

"Ah, technicalities. Yes. I'm ordering you to go home. If you want to come in and hang out tomorrow, that's up to you."

Unconvinced, Susan chewed on her lips. "What about Dad? He'll be really mad if he finds out I left without permission."

"Mmmm. I see what you mean. Want me to write you a note?"

"Ali."

"Here," Ali pulled out the bottom drawer of her desk and took out her wallet. "Go down to Mo's and get us a couple of sodas. I'll call and get the official okay from 'father knows best'."

Susan folded the notes and stuffed them in her jeans pocket. "I thought we weren't supposed to let Franny know you and Dad were an item."

Ali slanted her an indignant glance. "For your information, young woman, I certainly do check with the parents of minors who wish to purchase clothing from this boutique with their father's credit cards."

"Oh, man, and I'm gonna miss it," Susan complained, shuffling toward the curtain.

Ali got up to check that Susan had indeed left the shop before returning to her desk to place the call.

* * * * *

"Jordan?" Franny peeped around the door of his office. "Ali is on line two. Says she recognized the last name on the credit card Susan handed her and wants to verify a purchase."

"Oh." He breathed a silent sigh of relief even as a different kind of tension gripped his insides. "Sure." Jordan had the sudden urge to wipe his sweaty palms on his pants before picking up the phone, but resisted. "Miss MacPherson. How nice to hear from you. My daughter isn't giving you any problem about calling to check on her purchase, I hope?"

"Not at all, Mr. Finch," she replied sweetly, guessing correctly that Franny was hovering close by.

His tone immediately softened when Franny closed the door and retreated to her desk. "Ali, honey, I'm sorry. I meant to call earlier, but I was stuck in meetings all morning. I guess Susan told you what happened last night after I got home."

"Yes, it seems her prick of a father got her mixed up with her hoyden mother and forgot to tell his new whore that she would be pulling warden duty."

"Now wait just a minute—"

"No, you wait just a minute," she hissed furiously. "How dare you use our arrangement after school as a...a...jail sentence! Do you know the position you put me in? I am not Susan's mother, I'm not her nanny, I'm her friend. And that friendship is not based on our sleeping arrangements. It existed before I even knew who you were. You could very easily have broken the trust she has in me."

"Ali—"

"Don't say another word unless you want me to march down to that office and bang your thick head against a wall. I am sending Susan home. If she wants to come here after school or over the summer to help out, I'm glad to have her. But I won't be your enforcer. And before you leave the office today, Mr. know-all-see-all, you might want to call Randy's parents and verify Susan's story like a reasonable human being, instead of letting your mind wander in the gutter. Have a nice fucking day!"

The phone slammed in his ear. Jordan surged to his feet, stalked to the door that separated his office from Fanny's desk, and flung it open. It wouldn't do any good to call Ali back, she'd just hang up on him again.

Honest to God, the woman made him crazy.

"I'll be out for the rest of the day. Give Dale any problems. Don't beep me unless it's an emergency."

* * * * *

Franny leaned sideways around the corner of her desk to watch her boss stride purposely down the hallway. Upon reaching the elevator he rammed an agitated finger against the call button several times. When the elevator doors shushed shut she leaned back in her chair, dropping her head back to gaze heavenward in prayer. "Please don't let Ali be responsible for his foul mood." Ali had a way of bringing out the demon in a person, then bashing them over the head with a dose of bluntness.

Thank God she, herself, was a completely rational human being. Reaching for the phone, she dialed the number to Ali's boutique.

"What have you done to my boss?" she demanded the second breath was detected on the other end of the line.

"Not a thing," Ali answered airily. "I told you, I called to verify a purchase his daughter wanted to make. Why?"

"Because he just stormed out of here looking for someone to kill. I just wanted to be sure he wasn't going to decide halfway down the elevator shaft it was me."

"How like you to be unconcerned for me."

"Dollface, I'm calling to warn you, aren't I?"

"Yes, sweetness. I'm marking it down on my calendar as we speak."

"Swear to me, Ali, that you didn't make some perfectly inappropriate remark about his daughter or me or my ass."

"I can promise I made no such remark about any of the three."

"Well...that's something of a relief. Maybe he was already out of sorts and I just assumed it was your fault. Not that it would be easy to tell either way, these days. One minute he's growling, the next he's whistling. And Susan, his daughter, is driving him to distraction with her new boyfriend."

"Jealous?"

"Of what?" Franny asked indignantly.

"The fact his daughter, what is she, about sixteen or so, has a boyfriend and you don't?"

"Huh," Franny snorted. "What truly amazes me is you haven't been able to run off your latest disaster in pants."

"On that we agree. It is amazing. He's very tenacious."

"Bulldogs are tenacious."

"Yes, but they have atrocious manners. Mine's only atrocious in bed."

"Dare I hope for details this time?" Franny spun around in her chair to find Dale standing in front of her desk, a hostile expression on his face. "Hold on a second. What is it, Dale?"

"Dare I hope to get these contracts copied sometime this afternoon?" he inquired sarcastically.

"Why, Dale, can it be a college-educated man like yourself never mastered the rudiments of operating the simple, yet complexly intricate, copy machine?"

"Oh, Franny, that was good," Ali praised, blatantly eavesdropping and enjoying every minute of it.

"Thank you."

"Speaking of college-educated men," Ali murmured when she caught sight of Jordan striding past the plate glass window of the boutique. "Mr. Finch is here now, Franny," she said loudly as he appeared across the counter from her. "I'll be sure and pass along your message."

"What message?" Jordan frowned as she hung up the phone.

"Franny's concerned about Dale."

"Why, what's the matter with him?"

"Prevalent indications suggest his education was less than stellar."

"That's ridiculous." He frowned. "Dale graduated first in his class at Ivy Tech."

"Then either Dale failed copy machines 101 or he's just plain sexist."

He ignored the comment, leaning over the counter to glower. "Miss MacPherson, might I have a word with you? In *private.*"

"Of course, Mr. Finch." She favored him with a brilliant smile meant to set his already simmering temper to a boil. "But you do realize it's the middle of a business day and my free time is extremely limited." She rounded the corner of the counter and swept past him, indicating with a wave of her hand that he should follow her. As if there was any danger of that not happening.

Once behind the curtain that separated the storage room and her office from the main show floor, Ali seated herself at her desk and crossed her legs. "Now, then, what can I do for you, Mr. Finch?"

He stood near the coffee machine, silent, the muscle in his jaw ticking, considering his words before speaking. He unbuttoned his double-breasted jacket, crossed his arms over his chest, then said, "Why is it every time I think we've come to an understanding one of us takes a detour?"

Ali studied the toe of her high heel as it bounced up and down. "The difference between you and me, Finch, is that I take detours because they're there. You take them because someone throws up a roadblock, ordering you off the main highway."

"This from the woman, who, just last night, said if we weren't careful it could ruin everything. I take it you blame this episodic breakdown of communication on me, so decided to retaliate by sending Susan home after I specifically requested she remain here. We are not, then, of the same mind that what she did could result in serious repercussions."

"Wrong. We are of the same mind. This isn't about Susan's failure to comprehend the seriousness of the matter, or the possible far-reaching ramifications. Though, I did explain to her that she does bear the responsibility of scrutinizing her own actions beforehand to determine how those actions might be interpreted by a court."

He relaxed a little at that, a note of relief in his tone when he spoke. "You backed me up."

"In a manner of speaking, yes."

"I see. So, whizzing past Franny to call me a prick was just for fun, then."

"I wanted to get your attention."

His eyes smoldered enigmatically. "I don't recall you've ever had a problem getting my attention, Miss MacPherson."

"Pay attention, Mr. Finch. This is the tricky part. The prick—by the way that was Susan's description of the crazed man she knows to be her father—not mine. My word isn't in the dictionary. Anyway, the prick, just last night, proclaimed he lay awake nights wishing he could talk to me about the changing events affecting his and his daughter's lives. Yet, here I am the next afternoon, minding my own business—thinking everything is fine and dandy with the world in general, as much as it can be at the moment—when who should come dragging her heels into my boutique but the accused herself, expecting to have the irons clapped on by none other than," she executed two neat flourishes with her hand, "me. Tell me, Finch, darling, do you see anything wrong with this picture?"

"Yes, Miss MacPherson," he responded gravely. "Frankly, I do." He moved to stand in front of her, trapping her crossed legs between his thighs. Placing his hands on the arms of her chair, he bent to put his mouth a hair's breadth from hers. "I said I would call, and you're very, very angry with me for not doing so immediately, if not sooner. Did you, perhaps, write something derogatory about me on the bathroom wall during this sudden bout of despondency?"

Despondency? Ali was so stunned by the glint of satisfaction she glimpsed in his eyes that she was momentarily speechless. He was seriously suggesting she had reacted pettily in a moment of girlish uncertainty, trying to twist the circumstances to assuage his own guilt. She had done no such thing. The very idea was ludicrous.

Yes, she had wanted to get his attention, but for the express purpose of exposing the way he'd chosen to handle the delicate situation with Susan, notwithstanding negative effects such measures could have on her own fragile relationship with the girl, not for the reasons he had indicated. She had every right to resent his arrogance in assuming that she would fall in with his unspoken plan of action, even though she had, in the end, managed to contain herself and deal with the problem while extricating herself as an accomplice in Susan's eyes. A feat narrowly accomplished. And one she had no desire to perform again in the near future.

"Once again," she said tightly, determined to ignore his closeness and the scent of male that vibrated through her senses, "you fail to grasp the point of the exercise."

"Really. I thought I grasped the point quite brilliantly." He touched his lips lightly to hers. "My expectations were that once regaled with Susan's tale of tyranny you would require no immediate explanation. Nor were you seeking confirmation of the facts as presented to you when you called my office. And you just informed me that, despite your rabble-rousing disposition and the fact that you think I handled the situation indelicately, you explained the basics to Susan."

"You did handle the situation indelicately."

"That's what fathers, do, sweetheart, when faced with a crisis concerning the chastity of errant daughters."

"Hypocritical fathers, you mean."

"Are there any other kind? No, I feel sure I'm on the right track, here. Carefully employed phrases including such words as prick, hoyden, and whore," he continued, "were meant to incite contrition on my part while obscuring the true motive behind your verbal attack. Really, Allison darling, there's no need to play coy. Chastisement in any form, coming from you, is nearly always stimulating."

The timbre of his voice as he said the word "stimulating" sent an excited shiver down her spine. Ali licked her lips, ordering her body to ignore the warmth pooling in her lower regions. He wasn't right. She wouldn't let him be right. She had controlled the outrageous responses beating against her brain at his high-handedness for Susan's sake, not because of any feelings she may have for him.

Well, dammit, she couldn't think with him breathing down her neck at such close quarters. Where was her normally snappy, inciting vocabulary when she needed it? Had every scrap of twisted repartee suddenly fled her brain simply because he'd admitted to trusting her with the shaping of his daughter's morality when her own was so glaringly questionable?

"You were testing me?" she asked, almost afraid to hear the answer.

"Hardly." He straightened, dragging a forefinger over the sheer silk encasing her thigh. "Did it ever occur to you that I sent Susan to you because I knew, in your own unique way, you could get through to her in a way that I can't?"

"What's so hard about leveling with her?" Her eyes fixed on his finger where it toyed around her kneecap.

"You're in a position to be objective, whereas all I could think about at the time was what perverted schemes were hatching in Randy Peters' mind. I mentioned I was seventeen once, right?"

"Mmm. I'm beginning to wonder just how wild a life you led during those willful teenage days. And please, spare me the crap about how it's different for boys than it is for girls."

"It is different. Teenage girls think of sex in terms of romance. Boys at that age are just one big sex gland looking for gratification. I can't change hundreds of years of primeval conditioning, but I can try to keep my daughter from falling prey to the lecherous clutches of hormonally imbalanced peter packers. So? Do I break his face the next time he shows up on my doorstep?"

The oblique equivalent of asking, Did they have sex?

Ali lifted one shoulder. "I didn't actually ask."

His finger stilled on her knee. "How can you have a conversation about sex and not ask if they had sex?"

"The conversation wasn't about sex, *per se*. It was about your irrational reaction to the thought of their having sex."

"What is the damn difference?" He glowered at her.

Now that her feet were back on familiar ground, her thinking process was quickly reestablishing itself. "The difference is it's none of my business unless Susan chooses to tell me, in which case I would advise her to proceed with extreme caution."

"You'd tell me, though." The statement was somewhere between a question and a demand.

"I don't know that I would, Jordan. I don't imagine Susan would confide something so personal to me without first requiring a promise to keep her confession confidential. And this really isn't the time or place to discuss it. I'm sure you need to get back to work."

"I took the rest of the day off."

"Well, I don't have that luxury. I have a catalogue to put together, orders to place, deliveries to unpack—"

"Fine." He shrugged out of his coat, tossed it onto the divan, and began to loosen the cuffs of his shirt to roll the sleeves up over his forearms. "We can continue the discussion while I help you unpack."

Ali placed a hand to her breast in mock distress. "What, and leave your defenseless daughter alone in the house without protection against peter packers running amuck in the streets? I'm shocked at you, Mr. Finch. Why, at this very moment Randy

Peters might be launching an assault at the gates of your unguarded castle with intent to defile."

Jordan pulled her from the chair with little care for grace or finesse. "I swear to God you enjoy driving me to the edge."

She placed her palms flat against his chest for balance. "Truth be known, Finch, I think we're both riding close to the edge. There's no point in making an issue of something that may never come to pass. Susan isn't stupid. Sooner or later she's going to suspect we're sleeping together. Thanks to TV programming these days, children, even young ones, are all too aware of what goes on behind closed doors. It's no longer the lure of mystery or even a case of healthy curiosity that leads them to question lectures on the evils of sex. If you make too much of this thing with her and Randy she'll throw your own actions back in your face and then where will you be?"

He rested his forehead against hers, toying with a loose curl at her shoulder. "What do you expect me to do, Ali? Let her run wild?"

"Let her know you trust her. Listen to what she has to say before jumping to conclusions. You place too much emphasis on what might have happened instead of what did happen. If she did have sex with Randy — and I'm not saying I think she did — you can't do anything about it. You can't stop her if that's what she really wants to do. But I think she has a little better perspective on things now. I don't know what you can tell her about Gloria, though, because I steered clear of that subject."

"Okay," He kissed the tip of her nose. "I'm going to let you off the hook this one time. Now come on, I'll help you unpack those deliveries."

For the next two hours they worked together, side by side in the receiving room, unpacking boxes, checking invoices against materials. Ali unwrapped and hung up each piece on the transport rack, examining every detail for flaws. Anything with the slightest irregularity was put to the side to send back to the manufacturer later. She would tolerate nothing but the best on her boutique racks. The extra work was a drain on her time, tedious at best, but in the long run it saved on customers returning the merchandise for refunds or exchanges and the accompanying headaches and hassles.

"Guess I'd better get home," Jordan finally said, straightening, working the kinks from his back. "You're a slave driver."

"That'll teach you to offer your services for free."

He collected his coat from the divan in her office and pulled her close for a hard, brief kiss. "I'll call you later."

"That's what you said last night."

"Yes, but I said I'd call today and today is still today, so technically I'm in the clear."

"Get out of here." She buffed him on the shoulder. "I'll be here late as it is, playing catch up."

"Don't stay too late. If Susan has plans tonight—shit. I forgot. She's grounded."

"Nice going, Romeo. You couldn't just give her a lecture and let it go at that. I guess that means you won't be climbing up my balcony anytime soon, huh?"

He bent to nuzzle her neck. "Where I'd like to be climbing is up your skirt."

"Sorry, pal." Ali breathed in the scent of his aftershave, instinctively arching her neck to give him better access. "You screwed yourself. Think of me while you're playing the reluctant tyrant."

"There isn't an hour that passes I don't think of you. Give me five minutes behind one of those boxes in the storage room and I'll show you."

"Jordan, please," she groaned.

"I'm going. I'm going," he sighed heavily. "Christ, now I have to put my jacket on to walk out of here."

Ali didn't bother to hide the bubble of laughter working its way up her throat as he shrugged into his coat and buttoned it to help hide the bulge at his crotch. He gave her one last kiss and strode out.

She wondered, as she watched him leave, if Jordan had any idea how adorable he was when he was aroused.

Chapter Seventeen

📚

Jordan arrived home to find a contrite Susan waiting for him.

"Ali said for me to come home," she defended her position before he had a chance to do more than take his coat off and loosen his tie.

"Yes, I know. She called the office to make sure it was okay."

"Daddy, I'm really sorry. I didn't— I mean I wasn't thinking how it might look when I let Randy use the phone. I promise it won't happen again. I'll be responsible from here on out, you'll see."

"I'm sorry too, sugar." He pulled her against him and pressed a kiss to her hair. "I shouldn't have jumped on you without giving you a chance to explain. Dads don't think like normal people, especially when it comes to their baby girls." He leaned down to look her in the eye. "Forgive me?"

"Only if you forgive me," she sniffed.

"Deal. Want to go out for supper or stay in?"

"Let's order pizza and veg out in front of the TV."

"I can dig that."

"Huh?" Susan frowned up at him.

"Forget it. Go order the pizza while I get changed."

They spent the evening watching sitcoms and laughing and stuffing themselves with pizza. Susan drank soda. He had a beer. Tonight's binge would require an extra hour's workout on the weights later, but he didn't care. He was just happy he and Susan had gotten past the rough patch and were on friendly ground again. She hadn't asked how long she was grounded for, nor did she beg off in lieu of their apologies to one another, which made him even prouder of the young adult she was becoming.

They lounged on the couch in the great room with feet propped on the coffee table, something Gloria had gone absolutely ballistic over the few times she'd caught them at it. Even his den's coffee table in the house on Wimple Street had been strictly off-limits. Now that he wasn't expected to conform to house rules made by his very proper wife, Jordan realized how stifling it had been to come home from work and be denied the simplest of unwinding routines such as sipping a highball while reading the paper, propping his feet up on the table, or just plain flopping down on the couch in his den to watch the news or a baseball game.

Dinner at the Finch house was at seven on the dot, when he could make it home for dinner. Otherwise he had to leave directly from his office to meet Gloria at some fundraiser or other, which tied up most of his night. He had divided his time between work and Susan as evenly as he could, but had, admittedly, grown resentful and tired of the constant whirl of social soirees Gloria scheduled without consulting him. Before long he had started working later, and she had begun to attend the parties and banquets alone.

He hadn't minded so very much when Gloria had gone without him. It had given him more time with Susan in the evenings. Which had been, approximately, around the time Gloria had started experiencing emotional and mental stress. God knew she'd never admitted to being physically incapable of volunteering to lead the hordes on another charitable crusade. Physical exhaustion he could have understood, but then that particular diagnosis wouldn't have aided her need to stay out every evening until midnight or later.

Though he had fought the divorce, believing in the vows he'd spoken fourteen years earlier, in retrospect, perhaps divorce had been the best solution all around. For himself and

Gloria, anyway. He wished things weren't so strained between Gloria and Susan, but there wasn't much he could do about that, either. Gloria had brought that malady on herself.

At ten o'clock Susan unrolled herself from her slumped position and kissed him on the cheek, hiding a yawn behind her hand. "Night, Daddy."

"Night, honey." As she entered the foyer he called out, "Hey, Susan." She turned to look at him over her shoulder. "You don't have to go to Ali's boutique after school unless you just want to."

"Does that mean you believe I was telling the truth when I said nothing happened between Randy and me?"

"Yeah," he grinned wryly, "something like that."

"Daddy?"

"Hmmm?"

"Do you believe me because Ali told you to, or because you really think I'm telling the truth?"

So much for subtlety. "I beg your pardon. Ali's not the boss of me."

"Yeah. Right." Susan made a production of rolling her eyes, grinning cagily as she left the room.

When Jordan was sure Susan was in bed for the night he retired to his own room and flopped on the bed, reaching for the phone to call Ali. "Hey, it's me."

"Hi me. Boy, you sure know how to cut close a deadline, Finch."

She was referring to his promise to call today. Technically, it was still today. "In my line of work it's considered an advantage. Thought you'd want to know Susan and I made up."

"Oh, Jordan, that's great."

He propped his arm over his head, bending one knee to get more comfortable. "Then she wanted to know if I believed her because you told me to."

"Well, you can't win 'em all, slugger."

"I miss you," he said huskily. "Have lunch with me tomorrow."

"Jordan, I'm not sure that's such a good idea."

"What is that, your mantra now? I told you, I don't care what Gloria thinks. Let her think it. Hell, at least I'm on the level and not shacking up in some seedy motel."

"I know, but—"

"When you get right down to it, asking Susan to keep our dating under wraps is like asking her to lie. Who says the judge won't question her about my social life?"

"Yes, I understand that, but—"

"What kind of example am I setting by restricting her sociable activities while secreting my own?"

"Will you please let me get a word in?" she bid intractably. "There's Franny and the people you work with to consider, along with the fact we met at a party."

"Company get-together," he corrected. "Whole different atmosphere from nightclubs and parties where you were invited by a friend of a friend of a friend."

"I was invited by a friend."

"Employee. Besides, if we hadn't met at the party fate would have brought us together through Susan."

"I don't believe in fate."

"Honey, if you hadn't been standing in the foyer when Susan came down the stairs in that dress you sold her, you can bet your ass fate would have found me on your doorstep the next morning. Give it up, Ali. Have lunch with me."

Still hesitant, she said, "I'd feel better about it if you'd check with your lawyer first."

"My lawyer and I have an arrangement. He doesn't tell me who to date, I don't bitch about how much he charges for phone calls. It works for us."

During the lull that followed they listened to the hum on the line and each other's breathing. Jordan crossed his ankles.

Uncrossed them. Placed one foot flat on the mattress and picked at the lint balls on his sweat pants where the material stretched across his thigh. He could almost picture her chewing on her lower lip.

"Ali…"

"It's just not a good idea, Jordan!" she exploded in a rush of breath.

"Why?"

"For one thing you don't even have a court date yet. For another, you and Gloria aren't exactly on the best of terms at the moment."

"What does any of that have to do with you and I having lunch?"

"Honestly, Jordan," she blew out, "you can be so thickheaded at times. What's come over you? Why are you suddenly so…so determined to drag this out in the open?"

"Maybe the question, Miss MacPherson, is why are you so set against coming out? Ever since I told you how I feel about you, you've tried to put restraints and conditions on what should be a natural maturing of our relationship. I know I was cautious about publicizing our association at first, but you're no longer a stranger to me, Ali. Or to Susan, either. We've spent time together, gotten to know each other, involved ourselves in each other's lives. Susan's nuts about you. I'm crazy about you. Ellen called me an idiot. We're past the point where there's a need to censure every move we make."

"I'm only thinking about what's best for Susan."

"No, you're not." He hauled himself up against the headboard. "The best thing for Susan would be for all of us to spend more time together. She admires you. She trusts you. You're a good influence on her. But you're not sure of your feelings for me so you're trying to pretend mine for you aren't serious. Listen to yourself, Ali. You dragged me out of my pretentious little box of do's and don'ts, shattered my preset notions of right and wrong and parental etiquette, and made my life fun again. I'd forgotten how to have fun. How the simplest things like spitting out the window can bring back memories of when I was a kid, and how Arlan and I would see who could spit the farthest when Mom wasn't in the car.

"Your spontaneity made me realize how structured my whole routine has become over the years. And just when I'm starting to unwind and enjoy the surprises you throw at me, you start…sounding like your mother, lecturing me on the evils of sex and what other people might think if they see us together, and what time to go home."

She sucked in a breath, held it, then released. "That's not funny."

"Ironically, I think your mother would approve of me and the sobering effect I have on you. Wouldn't she be proud to know you've come to your senses of late, enough to control those nasty little outrageous urges you're prone to? I mean, at least you have the decency to be discreet about your newest sexual encounter. God only knows what the pillars of Charleston society, ergo, Gloria's friends, would think if they knew I'd latched on to a tart who hasn't any better sense than to keep herself hidden, like any good mistress should do."

Her voice stretched tight over the wires. "Are you trying to piss me off?"

Jordan dug his thumbnail into his leg. "For someone who doesn't believe in fate, you certainly have predetermined how this thing with Susan will work out. Can't you see you're using the situation to recreate yourself into this…this image you think is more respectable and accepted? That's wrong, Ali. I didn't fall in love with a woman who says and does all the right things at the right time and conducts herself accordingly at the appropriate moment. I fell in love with the woman you are. The funny, sensitive, impetuous, unpredictably uncommon woman who turned my world upside down and shook it loose. The one who took my gawky teenage daughter under her wing and turned her into a swan, then pulled floss out of her purse at dinner, waiting for me to crack. The one who wants me to make love to her with my glasses on, and drives ten golf balls down the fairway before she starts counting her score, and feeds me peanut butter sandwiches in her kitchen, and calls my office to tell me I'm a prick."

"All right! Fine! We'll have lunch! Are you happy now?" She sounded out of breath, as if she'd been pacing the floor while he yammered on about the virtues of impropriety.

His muscles, which, during the diatribe, had tensed one by one until his whole body was stiff as a board, relaxed. "Very. I'll pick you up at noon. Is that okay?"

"I-I'll have to check my schedule when I get to work. I have meetings with the graphics firm I hired to oversee the catalogue, and students to interview, and the shipment you helped me unpack today to get out on the floor."

The anger came out of nowhere, coiling in on itself, twisting through his innards. He sat bolt upright, flattening a palm against the quilt. "You do that, Miss MacPherson. You check your schedule and see if you can fit me in."

"There's no need to get snippy. It's just that this catalogue is going to require a lot of extra hours if I want to get the first issue out for the fall. And I do, Jordan. This project is very important to me. It's something I've wanted to do for a long time, and now that I've committed to doing it, I can't waffle on the details. Being a businessman yourself, I would think you'd understand. I wouldn't expect you to put off an important meeting with a client or your architects just to suit me."

She was right. He was acting like a jerk. She wasn't trying to put him off indefinitely, it was just that she was approaching a critical point of expansion in her business, where her time and skills must be utilized wisely in order not to lose, what for any entrepreneur, especially a small business owner, was a gamble.

"I do understand. If lunch is a problem, how about dinner? Here. With Susan and me."

"Could I let you know in the morning?"

"Sure. Yeah. I'll give you my cell number. After you look over your schedule beep me and I'll call you. I don't know why I didn't think to give it to you before." He waited for her to find pen and paper and then rattled off the number.

"Well, it's nice to know you don't give out your cell number to just anybody. I'm flattered."

Goodbyes were stilted. Jordan hung up and strode to the bathroom where he ripped the floss from its container and attacked the plaque on his teeth, then squeezed the toothpaste from the middle to brush. Oh, yeah, he was a rebel, all right. Who gave a diddly damn if he squeezed the tube from the middle? There was no one here to care. He could squeeze from the top if he wanted. Or the bottom.

He and Gloria had never even shared the same tube of toothpaste. She had used some fancy tooth polish. He, Crest kid that he was, continued to slog through life fighting cavities the old-fashioned way. Next trip to the store he was going to replace his standby light blue paste with a minty gel.

Better yet, he was going to hit Ali where it counted most. In the sensory glands.

* * * * *

Ali tried to concentrate on the mound of work piled on and around her desk, but her mind kept wandering back to last night's conversation with Jordan. What he'd said wasn't true. She wasn't trying to recreate herself. She wasn't like her mother. Her mother had laid guilt trips on her for the express purpose of getting her way, not because she'd been thinking of what was best for Ali.

Checking her watch, she discovered it was already ten and she still hadn't called Jordan to tell him lunch was possible. Her meeting with the graphics firm wasn't until two. She'd already lined up a photographer, chosen the first batch of outfits to showcase in the catalogue, and scheduled four students for a final interview tomorrow, after which she would arrange with one of the volunteering professors for a stage shoot. The theater department at the university had been only too happy to provide props and materials. Just this morning they had faxed her detailed sketches and couriered over several photographs of strategic spots around downtown Chicago that would work nicely for evening apparel.

All in all, everything was advancing much more smoothly than she'd anticipated. So, why did she feel as though there was an inflated balloon wedged in her chest? If Jordan didn't care what Gloria or his lawyer or a judge thought, why should she? Susan wasn't her daughter. She had never claimed to be mother material. She had been honest with Jordan from the beginning and the damned fool had gone and fallen in love with her anyway.

Deal with it, Ali. He's a responsible, caring father – he knows what he's doing.

"I'm good for lunch at noon," she told him when he returned her call minutes later.

* * * * *

On his way out at eleven-thirty, Jordan stopped in front of Franny's desk and said, "Okay, here's the thing. I'm the old money guy Ali's been seeing on the sly. You can have your little shitfit later, right now I'm on my way to take her to lunch. What does one of her picnic in the park lunches usually consist of?"

"Champagne and chicken salad," she answered when she was finally able to work her jaw closed. "So when did you sneak out and get a social life?"

"I didn't sneak."

"You most certainly did."

"I prefer to think of it in terms of necessary precaution."

"Ali doesn't do cautious, Jordan, except when it comes to business."

"I'm not asking your permission to date her, Franny. I just wanted to know what she likes for lunch."

"If I weren't miffed at you for keeping me in the dark after the way I've gone on and on about her lately, I'd ask if you had the foresight to bring along a quilt for today's outing. But since I am miffed, you're on your own."

"I did bring a quilt."

"Bully for you."

* * * * *

"A picnic?" Ali looked at him in surprise when he took her elbow and led her out of the boutique to the car, where he unpacked the necessary items from the trunk of his Lincoln.

"That's the idea." He folded the blanket beneath his arm and picked up the basket, then took her hand and led her across the street to the children's park. Casting about for a place to drop his booty, he chose the shade of a large maple tree along the wooded edge of the picnic area. "Franny sends salutations. She hopes we're swamped with biting ants and permanent grass stains."

"You told her?"

"Uh-huh." He let go of her hand to spread out the blanket, then sat down to unpack the basket.

"What did she really say?" Ali accepted the wrapped sandwich he handed her, pleased to find chicken salad between the wheat slices.

"I'll let you know when she starts speaking to me again." He produced a bottle of red wine and two fluted glasses, lending himself to the task of popping the cork over the grassy area beside the blanket in case of spillage.

"You should have let me tell her. Franny can be…" Ali broke off, sniffing the air when she caught a whiff of the familiar scent guaranteed to jump-start her hormones. Lifting her head, she scanned the immediate area for the guilty party, but it was only the two of them nestled in the shady glen behind the litter of empty picnic tables.

"Something wrong?" He poured the wine, pressing the flute into her right hand.

"What? No, no, I…nothing. What was I saying?"

"Franny can be…" He took a bite of his own sandwich, chewing methodically.

"Oh. Right. Stubborn. She hates it when I keep secrets from her. So this ought to be good for at least three months of the silent treatment."

There it was again. Carried on the faintest of breezes, that distinctive, stimulating scent that had her olfactory senses on instant alert.

"How's the chicken salad?" he asked.

"Good. What gave you the idea to have a picnic?"

He washed down the food in his mouth, and stretched out his legs so that they sat facing each other. "I watched you and Franny from my office window the day you came to take her to lunch. Thought you might enjoy sitting outside instead of in a crowded restaurant. This is nice. Being out here like this. With you. Can't remember the last time I went on a real picnic."

"Nice."

"Something wrong with nice?"

Ali studied the sandwich in her left hand. The glass of red wine in her right. Nice. Somewhere along the way she had turned into a nice girl. She had learned how to confine her switchblade tongue and conduct herself in a ladylike manner under fire, such as the night Ellen Ginsworth and Jordan had happened on her in the muddy parking lot at the high school. She had sent Susan on a fake errand, and slid past Franny with calculated ease before blowing her top at Jordan over the after school incident.

She hadn't intentionally recreated herself, but instead, had unwittingly refrained from acting and reacting rashly because, for once in her life, she cared about someone else, two someone elses, more than she cared about herself.

"Ali…" He set down his sandwich and scooted closer, until his right hip brushed against her left. "What's wrong?"

"Nothing." But though she tried to keep the moisture contained, her eyes filled with tears. Jordan was wearing Brut. He'd remembered the remark she'd made about her weakness for a man wearing that particular aftershave—cheap as it was. Insistent, straight-laced, quietly desperate Jordan Finch, who could make her pulse race wildly one minute and fire her temper the next, had picked up every challenge she'd thrown down thus far. Now he'd stooped to using her self-proclaimed flaws against her.

He leaned his forehead into her temple, speaking softly. "It's not 'nothing', it's something. Tell me. Does it have anything to do with the catalogue you're working on? Didn't your meeting with the graphics people go well?"

"It's not the catalogue, it's you. Us. Me. You said this could be infatuation, or obsession, or whatever I wanted to call it, but it's not either of those things. It matters, now. It matters what people think of me, and how they perceive us as a couple. All this time I thought I was in control, but I'm not. You've been leading me around by the belly ring, pulling me into respectability one step at a time. I've spent my whole life trying not to be a nice girl and…well just look at me!"

He raised a finger to graze the underside of her jaw. "Is that what I've been doing?"

"You know it is."

"We're pretty much shielded from prying eyes out here." He touched his lips to her cheek. "The picnic tables and the shade of these trees provide adequate cover. We could be a little bit bad if you want."

Ali let her head drop onto his shoulder. He curled his elbow around her neck and hugged her closer, massaging the muscles there with his fingers.

"Ah, Ali," he sighed quietly into her hair, "I can't help how I feel about you. You make me feel alive. I had meetings scheduled this morning, too, and for the first time in my professional life all I could think about was how to finagle around them so that I could be here with you. I'm supposed to survey a site for a new client later this afternoon, but if you asked me to take the rest of the day off so we could spend it together, I'd call Franny and tell her to rearrange my schedule. And for once she wouldn't talk back, because she's not speaking to me."

"I think I do love you," she mumbled miserably against the lapel of his jacket, "but I don't want to say it until I'm sure. And I resent how you planned this romantic picnic and purposely wore cheap aftershave in an obvious attempt to break down my defenses."

"Objection duly noted. Truthfully, I was hoping you'd want to rip my clothes off, tart that you are, and have at it on this blanket."

That got a laugh out of her. He loosened his hold on her neck, palming her jaw to guide her chin up so that their eyes met. "Are you serious? Do you think you might love me?"

"It could just be the wine and chicken salad talking. Then again, it could be the Brut."

He rubbed her bottom lip with his thumb. "What if it's not?"

"Oh, Jordan," she sighed, closing her eyes against the glimmer of hope she saw in his. "I've made so many mistakes in my life. Made so many wrong choices without thinking them through. I need to be sure. I love the time I spend with you. I love the way we fit together in bed. The way you touch me and look at me like I'm someone special."

That same thumb lingered at the corner of her mouth. "You are special."

"But is loving those things really the same as loving the whole person, the complete package?"

"What do you want from me, Ali? A resume? A list of rules? You can't choose whether or not you fall in love with someone, it just happens. Christ, that's like saying there's no difference between other men you've dated and me."

"Of course there's a difference," she rushed to say. "I know what not loving someone feels like. I know the difference between wanting to be with someone in bed and wanting to be with them out of it. It's not a matter of which is more important. I want…" She swallowed and looked away, letting her gaze sweep over the picnic tables, the playground where stay-at-home moms were watching their children swing and bounce up and down on the see-saws and whoop with joy down the slide to land on their rumps in the dirt.

"That's the problem, I guess," she said, feeling his eyes on her. "I don't know what I want anymore. I used to know. Now it's all jumbled around in my head and I can't think straight. I need to be sure, Jordan. Because no matter how…impetuous…you think I am, I feel like saying the words implies commitment, at least insofar as the immediate future is concerned."

"Mmm." He flattened his hand on the other side of her hip, caging her into the hollow between his arm and chest. "And you do your best to keep your word when you give it, like when you said you'd attend Susan's play. You came even though you knew there was a chance of running into me. That's one of the reasons I trust you. You've already proven you wouldn't intentionally steer Susan wrong, or ignore her, even if you and I aren't on the best of terms.

"But, Ali, sometimes you just have to close your eyes, hope for the best, and jump in with both feet. I appreciate your candor and seriousness, I really do. You got a bad start with your mother, and that relationship, or lack of it, tends to color your perspective. You're a good person. Honorable. Trustworthy. Sexy as hell. You made a go of a your own business, which is no small accomplishment. Everything you do, you do with a sense of purpose and style and exuberance. I wish I could say the same for the last ten years of my life."

He turned to look out over the playground and Ali knew he was remembering the last several years of his marriage, the pain of divorce, how he'd struggled to understand Susan a little bit better during these last months. It was amazing to her that after all the recent changes in his life he was still willing to take yet another chance. He had so much to lose by opening his life to her. And while boxing herself inside a relationship she wasn't sure she could handle scared the bejesus out of her, neither did she want to walk away.

Maybe she was trying too hard to put a label on something that couldn't be labeled. She'd never felt for any other man what she felt for Jordan. If it wasn't love, it was certainly a comparable emotion.

"Yes," she spoke at length, a note of conviction in her tone. His hazel eyes swerved back to hers, holding her gaze for several heartbeats before she said, "I think I do love you. Now what?"

"Come home with me."

Chapter Eighteen

✍

"Home?" she echoed. "Now? In the middle of the day? Jordan, be sensible. I have a meeting, and you said you had to survey a site—"

"Not my house," he cut her off. "Home. To Charleston. Jeb called this morning. He arranged for an informal hearing with a favorable judge to establish temporary custody until Gloria returns from Europe."

Ali had to wrap both hands around her glass to keep from spilling red wine all over both of them. "You...you want me to go home with you and...meet your parents?" she squeaked. "Isn't this a little sudden?"

"The hearing is Friday afternoon. We could stay the weekend and be back Sunday evening. I think Ellen and Arlan are coming in for the weekend, too, so you can meet everybody, including Wanda."

"You mean in a hotel? I'd stay in a hotel and you and Susan would stay at your parents'?"

"No, I mean we'd both be staying at my parents'. The place is practically a mausoleum. It could hold Sherman's army. You won't find a hotel with better service."

"But I have this catalogue to get off the ground and Deanna doesn't work weekends. I haven't hired a part-timer yet. And—"

His mouth on hers cut off further protest. Why, she wondered, as he wrapped his arm around her waist and drew her against his chest, did she become so weak-minded when he kissed her like that? As though she was the center of his world. Her lips parted beneath his. He took his time, kissing her thoroughly, his tongue abrading hers, beseeching, tempting, promising tomorrow would be a little less scary if only she'd let him inside her heart.

His fingers roamed her face, brushed over her eyelid, her cheekbone. But meet his parents…

He anticipated the terror that was welling in her throat and deepened the kiss, keeping her close to him, rubbing the tension that had settled between her shoulder blades away with his hand. At some point during the drugging kiss he set his glass aside and took her face into both hands without breaking the mouth-to-mouth contact.

Through it all Ali had kept a firm grip on her wine glass. He pried her fingers from around the fragile stem and tossed it aside. She heard a dull thud as the flute landed in a clump of grass.

"Say yes," he entreated against her mouth.

She placed her palm flat against his chest and felt the harsh thumping of his heart beneath the crisp linen of his shirt.

"Say yes, Ali. Let me take you away for the weekend and pamper you and introduce you to my family. I know you think I come from a bunch of stiff-necked high-waisters, but they're not really as snobbish as I sometimes make them sound."

"Yes, yes," she heard herself whisper into his mouth. Her hands slid up his lapels until her arms were wrapped tightly around his neck. "Don't let me think. Just don't let me think."

* * * * *

Between the boutique and overseeing shoots for the catalogue Ali stayed fairly busy that week. As luck—or fate, as Deanna would say—would have it, Franny dropped in on the lingerie set. After touring the bedroom setup she stretched provocatively across the rumpled silk sheets of the tester bed, arranged herself amid pastel pillows, and aimed a sultry smile at the confused photographer, telling him in that sassy tone of hers, "Let's see how good you really are, sugar pie. Make me into a goddess of love."

The photo, which started out as a joke, came out fabulous. Originally, Ali had planned to hire a local model for the lingerie shoot, but after seeing how photogenic her best friend was, badgered Franny until she agreed to give herself over to wardrobe and makeup and pose for another picture. Then another. And another. The results were astounding. From the batch of scintillating proofs the photographer proudly displayed during their next meeting Ali chose the one that would grace the cover of the catalogue.

By picking Franny as the cover model Ali accomplished three things: atoning to the Dematos for being mean to Franny, avoiding another grudge that could last into the next century for not telling Franny the old money guy she was dating was none other than her boss, and a knockout, gorgeous cover for the first, and most important, issue, which would either boost sales up several tax levels or have Ali scrambling to balance profit and loss sheets. Not that making up to the Dematos over fried chicken and linguini noodles in clam sauce in Gladys' homey kitchen was a hardship. Making nice with Frank Demato required little more effort than letting him rub her head and call her Alicat. With Gladys, well, if you let the woman feed you some form of pasta, all was forgiven.

To prove her mother's theory — that she was no decent kind of daughter — she stopped sending money. She couldn't have imagined the feeling of relief that swept through her at finally accepting that it was physically, emotionally, and spiritually impossible to fit the mold her mother had tried to force on her during childhood. Thank God.

When Ali passed around the photos of Franny during dessert, Frank Demato said, "Who's the babe? She looks familiar."

Ali broke into a grin. "She should. It's Franny."

"Franny?" Frank echoed unbelievingly, his ruddy cheeks flushing deeper with embarrassment. "My Franny freckleface? Impossible. This woman is — My God, it is Franny!"

Franny slung a spoonful of vanilla pudding at him. "Mom, tell him to stop."

"Frank, stop. Franny, don't throw food at the table. So, when do we get to meet this Dale you're always griping about?"

"As soon as he sees this picture of my daughter posing in the nude," Frank predicted dourly.

"I'm not nude."

"Close enough," Frank grumbled.

"Mom."

"Frank."

Franny had the hots for another of the architects in Jordan's firm, though she didn't want to admit it. Ali didn't really believe Dale was a sexist pig. Franny would never fall for anybody like that. Indulge in a one-night stand, maybe. But not for the long term. She was pretty sure Dale was pushing Franny's buttons purposely—like with the copier incident—to get her attention.

Franny was back to speaking to Jordan, but strictly on a professional level, leaving Ali to tell Jordan during one of their nightly phone conversations that Franny was modeling for the catalogue in her spare time.

"Meanwhile, the cleaning lady who takes care of our offices is giving me suspicious looks," Jordan informed her wryly. "The women's room wall is doubtlessly covered in graffiti depicting the baser side of my character."

"You flatter yourself, I think. It's far more likely that Dale's name graces those hallowed stall walls."

"Just what I need, an in-office romance," he grunted. "Am I going to get to see you at all this week?"

"You should know there's no rest for the expanding entrepreneur."

His voice lowered an octave. "I could show you something that's expanding."

"I detect a pout coming on."

"I am not pouting."

"Sounds like pouting to me, Finch."

"If you'd come home at a decent hour we could have dinner together or clean out the drawers in my study."

"Before or after Susan goes to bed?"

"After."

"A quick roll on the desk?" she asked lightly.

"The desk. The couch. The floor." His voice was thick with undisguised need. "Wherever I can get my hands on you."

"Way to set a good example for your very impressionable daughter, Finch."

"What she doesn't know, I don't have to explain."

"She might be thinking the same about you," Ali pointed out.

"We've already established all fathers are hypocrites at heart. I could explain it to her until I'm blue in the face, like my parents tried to do for me, but she won't get it until she has kids of her own to worry over."

"Then again, maybe you'll find yourself explaining it to a judge. You're not out of the woods yet, Finch, darling. You may look like a saint compared to Gloria, but it's too soon to know what she has up her sleeve. You don't know where she is, but she knows exactly where you are."

"I have a number she can be reached at in case of emergency. Jeb called with it this morning. Somewhere in France. That's what prompted this hearing with the judge. He wants to interview Susan privately. Then me. Get a fix on how things are going at present. Jeb thinks Stonewall will grant me temporary custody without a fuss, especially seeing as how Gloria won't be there to protest in person."

"Jordan, her lawyer will have notified her of the hearing."

"If she's so worried about the outcome, she can rearrange her schedule to show up."

"What if she does?" Ali threw out for consideration. "What if Gloria shows up, repentant and ready to take up where she left off? Jordan, you know the courts lean toward the mother in most cases."

"I know," he sighed tiredly. "And I've thought about this. A lot. Especially since Susan threatened to run away if they ruled in Gloria's favor. I know you think I should use Gloria's infidelity to sway the courts, but I don't want Susan caught in the middle. I don't want her to be left with more bitter memories than she already has. If the hearing doesn't go in my favor, or if it does and later down the road when Gloria returns and the judge makes a final decision that grants her custody…I'll have to move back to Charleston. To be close to Susan. Strengthen my case for an appeal. If nothing else, to be an integral part of her life. And I hate telling you this over the *damn telephone*."

"No, it's…it's all right. I mean, of course you want to do what's best for Susan."

"I don't know what's best anymore, Ali. Is it worth it to drag Susan through all this when in another two years she'll be able to choose for herself without interference from the courts? I could probably get joint custody or unlimited visitation with no problem. Then I have to ask myself am I fighting for Susan to get back at Gloria or because I don't want to be alone or because it really is in her best interests?"

"Jordan, why are you doubting yourself now? You know Susan wants to stay with you."

"God forgive me for saying this, Ali, but as long as I'm a single father and Gloria keeps the heat on, my life isn't my own. Everything — my relationship with Susan, with you, the demands of my job — will continue to be scrutinized. I want Susan with me, no two ways about it, but I don't want to have to look over my shoulder every day. I don't want to have to impose stricter rules on Susan because Gloria's waiting in the wings for me to fuck up. And the hard truth is…you're important to me. You don't deserve to be treated like a potential hazard by the courts or Gloria's watchdogs or — " he broke off, cursing beneath his breath.

"Godammit, Ali, I need to be with you to discuss this. This isn't right. We're looking at trying to make a long-distance relationship work here, and I don't hear you saying that's okay by you."

Jordan could almost feel her pulling away from him, emotionally distancing herself, because though Ali put on a brave face to the world, projected an attitude that had served her well in business, she still doubted her self-worth. She would believe she was making it harder for him instead of easier. The thought of losing her made his gut tighten. He should have waited, he bitterly chastised himself. He shouldn't have gone into this over the phone – the only link he'd had to her for more than a week. And Jesus, he was feeling the strain.

"Ali," he said her name reverently in the silence that stretched out between them, "talk to me."

"Let's just see how things go with your family first, okay?"

* * * * *

By Friday morning Ali was one big nerve. She'd packed and unpacked her suitcase seven times, removing outfits that seemed outlandish and replacing them with simpler, classical styles that showed less cleavage. No flamboyant colors. No short skirts. No clingy blouses.

"Less is more. Less is more," she repeated over and over to herself.

She exchanged bangles for gold links, geometrical costume earrings for sedate posts, bulky necklaces for a string of pearls and a few broaches. Spiked heels were out, sensible pumps in. Then, in a fit of frustration, she swiped the whole business onto the floor.

"They're going to take one look at me and know."

She threaded out her belly ring and stored it in her jewelry box. No way in hell was she getting busted by Charleston's elite. It was imperative that she make a good impression on Jordan's family.

Susan had come into the boutique every day and was a tremendous help in getting the newest shipments out onto the floor. She also assisted Deanna with customers, which left Ali free to tie up loose ends.

After two more meetings with the graphics firm Ali had a working timetable, manageable budget, and had, from those students interested, chosen her models. A last-minute decision to include a tuxedoed male to complement the models in evening wear left her shuffling through pictures of the young men available to set aside in a separate stack for consideration later. Gratefully, she left the task of choosing set designers, prop assistants, makeup artists and the like to the very capable hands of volunteering, extremely cooperative, excitable professors. After all, they knew their students' strong points better than the students themselves.

Having used every available minute of free time this week Ali wandered the boutique with her final list of approved clothing, including the models' sizes, and coordinated outfits with accessories. Deanna offered to write up the blurbs over the weekend and tend the boutique on Saturday.

Ali wouldn't have believed it possible, but all that was left to do for the moment was to pack for the trip to Charleston.

Doomed. Just like the Titanic. What difference would it make what she was wearing when they discovered she had a tattoo on her ass?

"Ali!" Jordan's voice boomed up the stairs, followed by a clumping of feet that proved to be Susan.

"Up here!"

"Hey, great place!" Susan was all eyes as she entered the disaster of a bedroom. "How come your clothes are all over the floor?"

Jordan stopped in the doorway to survey the mess of discarded clothes and shoes and purses and upside down suitcases. "I brought Chinese."

Ali stood in the middle of the mess she'd just made. "I was packing."

"So I see. Well, everybody has their own system."

His was no doubt perfect. He probably had one of those all-in-one travel organizers for the businessman on the go. Shirts would rest in a plastic sleeve, guaranteed not to wrinkle. Shoes placed in their own specially made compartment. Hangers for coats and ties. A nook for his shaving kit.

"Can I use your bathroom, Ali?"

"Sure, sweetie. Jordan, why don't you go ahead downstairs and get out the plates. We can eat in the dining room or the living room, it doesn't matter."

He advanced into the room as Susan was shutting the connecting bathroom door, and placed a comforting hand around the back of her neck. "You're not going to chicken out on me at the last minute are you?"

"I'm thinking about it," she replied sullenly.

"You promised."

"Well, you were wearing Brut and kissing me like a madman at the time. I can't be held accountable."

"There's nothing to be nervous about. They're people, just like you. And I've hardly seen you this week with all the hours you've put in. I'm thinking very seriously of checking us into a hotel so we can have five minutes alone."

The toilet flushed. Jordan brushed a quick kiss over her lips then stepped back. "A word of advice. Do *not* let Susan help you pack. She's been packing all week and still isn't finished. I'll dish up the food. Susan, shake a leg in there, I'm hungry."

"Coming!"

Jordan left the bedroom. Ali waited for Susan, heard the water running in the sink, then silence while Susan dried her hands and was probably leaning into the mirror inspecting her makeup like all women did when a moment of privacy and a mirror presented itself.

"Done," the teen announced, swinging open the door.

Ali leaped at her like a tiger on raw meat, grasping the teen by the shoulders. Susan's eyes widened in alarm, but the girl had to understand that she was desperate.

"Here's the deal. You don't tell anyone I have a tattoo on my butt, a tattoo period, don't even think the word much less say it, and I won't tell your dad you and Randy had sex."

Susan's mouth fell open in astonishment. Her face flushed. Her eyes darted nervously toward the door in terror, lest they discover Jordan was still near enough to overhear them. When she could speak, her voice was barely a whisper. "How did you—"

"Never mind how I know, I just do."

"Oh, my God."

"I'm sorry to spring it on you this way, you know I think the world of you, but this is important."

"This is blackmail."

"Yeah, well, life's tough."

"Ali, it's just a harmless tattoo."

Her eyes narrowed. "One word about my harmless tattoo and you're toast. Got it?"

Susan nodded so hard she should have developed whiplash. "Got it."

"Okay then," Ali straightened, absurdly relieved.

"Ali, you swear you won't tell Dad? He would, like, freak out or go bonkers or something."

"I just said so, didn't I? Wait!" Ali gripped Susan's shoulder again at the door, spun her around. "You used something didn't you? Please, God, say you didn't have unprotected sex."

"We used a condom."

Ali wasn't sure which caused her more apprehension, the fact that Susan had admitted to having sex with Randy and that she, Ali, had not only suspected but kept the information to herself, or that the young couple had obviously planned their illicit encounter. Another possibility was that Randy ran around with a condom safety tucked in his wallet, waiting for the right opportunity to present itself.

What if Randy hadn't used the prophylactic correctly?

Susan was only fifteen. Fifteen. Good God, at fifteen Ali hadn't been able to comprehend what sex entailed, much less mature enough to understand the risks accompanying the unfathomable act. She'd been a virgin until the ripe old age of nineteen.

"Hey, are you guys coming down to eat or what?" Jordan called from the bottom of the steps.

"We'll talk more about this later," Ali said out the side of her mouth. "Come on. Paste a smile on your face and act like we've been talking about clothes."

The food tasted like ashes to Ali, who was now beset by a guilty conscience. So long as the subject of sex went unmentioned between her and Susan, she had been able to convince herself Susan's business was her own.

Now that her suspicions had been confirmed, Ali felt like a felon.

Jordan would expect her to give Susan up, for her own good, of course. Susan was counting on her discretion. If she told Jordan, Susan would never trust her again. If she didn't, and Susan continued her close encounters with Randy Peters, Susan could end up pregnant, contract any number of venereal diseases, or worse, AIDS. Jordan would blame Ali for not coming to him with the truth when she had first learned of Susan's aberration.

Susan slipped off to the living room to watch TV after dinner while Ali and Jordan cleared the table. He rinsed, she shoved plates and silverware into the dishwasher. When they were done Jordan rested his hips on the counter and pulled her to him for a warm, delicious kiss. Her guilt over Susan made her painfully aware of just how easily she could lose him.

Ali relinquished herself to his tender lips, giving as much pleasure as she took. When had he become such a vital part of her life? During the nightly phone calls in which they shared bits and pieces of their days? The steamy bouts of lovemaking when he touched not only her body but her soul? Over lunch in the park? While eating peanut butter and apples here in this very kitchen?

Dear Jordan. Dear, brave Jordan. His quiet strength had too often been the target of her discontent. He stayed when he should have run. Introducing her to his family was a complication he could do without. A complication she could do without.

When he reluctantly lifted his lips from hers, she stood in the circle of his arms, letting her uncertainty show in her eyes. "Jordan, are you absolutely sure this is a wise move, me going home with you? I mean, you have the hearing Friday afternoon, and you haven't seen your parents in quite awhile. They might not appreciate having a stranger thrust on them with no warning."

"I warned them. They're expecting us. They'll probably pin a medal on your chest for agreeing to come along so I won't be tempted to fly out again right after dinner Friday evening."

Eyeing the kitchen door in case Susan came back through, he slid his hands beneath the front of her shirt, caressing the underside of her breasts through the lace of her bra. His knuckles grazed down her ribs, over her belly to the snap of her jeans. Then suddenly he leaned back against the counter and lifted her shirt.

"You took it out," he said of the missing belly ring, his accusing tone liberally laced with irritation.

She jumped back a step and yanked her shirt down.

"Why did you take it out?"

"Because I don't want your family to think I'm some sort of freak or something."

"They can think whatever the hell they want. Put it back."

"I'll put it back in when we get home."

Stormy hazel eyes glared back at her. "Put it *back*."

"You're being ridiculous," she hissed low. "I'm not going to meet your family with a ring in my navel."

"They won't be acquainting themselves with your navel," he shot back, voice near to a growl. "I don't want you changing to suit them. You suit me just the way you are, belly ring, tattoo, and all. Is that what that mess of clothes on your bedroom floor is all about? Finding the right attire to impress the gentry?"

"It's just a stupid navel ring! Why are you making such an issue of it?"

"Because every man should have a fantasy about the woman who turns him on, and that's mine. I like knowing it's there, under your clothes where no one else can see it. Some men read Playboy or Hustler for a thrill, mine is fantasizing about that damn belly ring. And if you pack one damn skirt longer than mid-thigh I'll take a razor to the hem. I mean it, Ali."

Fantasy. *Fantasy!* Was that what was she was to him? A living, breathing, flesh and blood fantasy? Oh God, in retrospect it all made a horrible, sick kind of sense in her mind. His obsession with her belly ring. Indifference to his parents' approval. The way he had deliberately avoided properly introducing her to his visiting sister-in-law that night at the high school. Hadn't he safely swept Ellen away to the car before returning with the paltry offer of a towel to clean her muddy feet? And telling Susan about her tattoo. He'd been expecting dangerous—he'd gotten a simple music note instead.

Red flags everywhere and she hadn't seen them. Hadn't wanted to see them. She'd been such a fool to let down her guard. Jordan Finch wasn't looking for a permanent, lasting relationship, he was indulging in a full-fledged midlife crisis. A torrid affair to ease the boredom and loneliness brought on by the disillusionment of divorce.

I warned them, he'd said. *They can think whatever the hell they want.* In other words, it didn't matter if she made a good impression on his family because they would instinctively comprehend that she wasn't the kind of woman he would get serious about. Not the type of woman he would ever consider marrying.

He reached out to hook two fingers in the waistband of her jeans. Ali slapped his hand away, moving out of reach.

"Honey, come on, I don't want to argue." He reached for her again and caught her around the waist. Ali twisted so that the hard band of his forearm clamped over her stomach. He tenderly tucked a swath of hair behind her ear. His tawny head bent into the curve of her neck from behind.

"I'm sorry," he said low against the lobe of her left ear. "I know I'm being selfish. It's just that I want you so much I can barely stand it. Lately, it seems like everything and everyone has a piece of you but me, and spending time alone this weekend will be damned near impossible. I never thought the day would come when I'd be jealous of my own daughter."

Ali could feel his erection pressing into the cleft of her buttocks. His arm was wrapped around her middle possessively, palm cradling her left hipbone, while his other hand slid over her shoulder, beneath her arm pit, hovering along the side of her left breast. His breath was warm against the sensitive skin of her nape. He nipped at the pulse beneath her jaw, his grip on her tightening as his breathing grew uneven.

Footsteps from the hall sent them scrambling apart. Jordan turned into the countertop to hide his condition, grabbing for the dishrag that lay folded over the double sink to polish the brass fixtures. Ali moved to fuss unnecessarily with the centerpiece on the table by the bay window.

Susan sauntered around the kitchen island, leaning into the corner with a grin on her face. "You guys don't have to pretend you weren't playing kissy-face. I'm not a baby, I know you're doing it."

"Doing it?" Jordan arched his daughter a look over his shoulder.

"Yeah—it. You know, going all the way. Sex. Don't worry, I'm won't tell anybody. But it's nice how you try to set a good example and don't make up stupid stories to get rid of me like Mom used to do when she wanted to sneak out and be with her therapist."

Jordan went stone-cold still. Ali's hands froze amidst the leafy greenery of the centerpiece. She was tempted to deny the accusation, but kept silent. Her emotions were still swirling in confusion. It would be interesting to see how Jordan handled Susan's enlightened proclamation concerning not only her mother's escapades, but Jordan and Ali's as well. Not that the girl had proof of any kind to back up her assumption, but as Ali had warned Jordan before, Susan was bound to figure it out sooner or later.

He could hardly admit to a sexual relationship without painting himself in a hypocritical light.

Jordan's eyes turned hard. "Excuse me, young lady, but is there a purpose for that crude remark, other than the obvious attempt to embarrass Ali and myself?"

"I wasn't trying to embarrass you!" Susan objected. "Honest! I just...well, heck, Dad, I'm not three years old, anymore. I know you guys are attracted to each other that way and...and...oh, forget it. I'm screwing it all up. I just wanted you to know that you don't have to include me every time you go out to, like, a movie or dinner. I'm old enough to understand you want to spend some time alone, that's all."

Ali noted the whiteness around Jordan's tightly pressed lips, the glimmer of guilt in his expression. Her earlier anger faded slightly in the face of his uneasiness. He had just finished telling her he was jealous of Susan and the time she spent with Ali, and here was Susan, having picked up on those vibes and generously offering to step aside so as not to interfere.

Ali didn't know whether to applaud Susan or smack her. She knew a ploy when she saw one. Typical teenager that she was, Susan was attempting to circumvent a future lecture from her father should circumstances bring to light her own indiscretion with Randy Peters. The girl figured what was good for Father Goose was good for Susie gosling. And hadn't the conniving little Jezebel been shrewd to procure Ali's promise to keep silent before boldly broaching the subject of sex in mixed company.

Idiot! You're the one who put the idea in her head by making a big deal over your tattoo.

Ali turned to face Susan and folded her hands in front her. "I feel obliged to point out that you're doing the same thing to your father that you accused him of doing to you not so long ago, when he assumed you'd had sex with Randy Peters." A guilty expression not unlike Jordan's twisted Susan's features. Heedless to the girl's sudden discomfort, Ali pressed on. "Let's cut to the chase, shall we? As you say, you're old enough to know the facts of life."

"Ali..."

She waved away Jordan's warning and continued. "No, it's all right. The best way to clear this up is for Susan to ask outright if you and I are having sex. Go ahead, Susan. I won't lie to you. But be aware this type of personal discussion is a two-way street. Come to think of it, maybe the best thing would be to sit down and discuss the risks and pitfalls of entering into a sexual relationship with someone you hardly know."

She paused to look from one to the other. "You two have had the sex talk, right? About heavy petting and venereal disease and contraceptives and the signs of pregnancy?"

Susan blanched white around the gills at the thought of being forced to answer questions about her own sexual experiences. "P-pregnancy?"

Ali made a sympathetic gesture. "A sad but all too often result when contraceptives fail—which they occasionally do. Only abstinence is one hundred percent effective in that respect. Then there are the sexually transmitted diseases, like herpes, which aren't fatal—unlike AIDS—but on the other hand aren't curable either. I knew a girl once who contracted herpes from her boyfriend, who swore he'd been faithful to her. Duh.

Anyway, she's married now, but she and her husband have to be careful to use condoms or avoid sex altogether when she has a flare-up." Ali glanced askance at Jordan. "They can cure syphilis and gonorrhea now, right?"

His reaction was to close his eyes, as though fending off the mental images Ali's words conveyed of his baby girl falling prey to one unholy malady or another.

"Gosh, you guys, I-I wasn't trying to butt into your business or anything. I didn't really want to know if you were… That's disgusting!"

Ali planted her palms on the counter. "Honey, you haven't experienced disgusting until your hind end is propped up on a gynecologist's table while he swabs at weeping sores on your gentalia. You know the old saying 'it only takes one time'? Well, ask Sandy Logan, my friend from high school. She'll be only too happy to tell you a quick thrill in the sack isn't worth the pain and humiliation of a lifetime. Her so-called *faithful* boyfriend spread the rumor throughout school the next day that *he* had no such disease—it must have been Sandy who was promiscuous. I don't think I have to tell you that Sandy was shunned after that, not to mention the horrible jokes and razzing she endured."

"What—What happened to the boyfriend? Didn't anyone razz him?"

"Nobody ever does, honey. Society in general considers it to be the girl's fault if she ends up pregnant or diseased."

Susan was appalled. "That reeks. She couldn't have known he was infected if he didn't tell her."

Ali affected an indifferent shrug. "Her tough luck. That's why it's so important to be informed about these things beforehand. It might not be romantic to discuss venereal disease when your hormones are screaming, but nowadays, not asking the tough questions can cost you your life. Did I mention Sandy had to have her babies by cesarean? You know what cesarean is, right?"

"Yeah, it's where they have to cut the baby out instead of delivering it...you know, the regular way."

"Sandy's kids were delivered cesarean because to deliver them vaginally increased the risk that her baby would contract the herpes virus on its way out."

"Gross!"

"Hey, nobody ever said sex was all fun and no work. You take on a tremendous amount of responsibility when you have sex with someone you aren't sure you can trust." Ali was reminded of the first time she and Jordan had made love. She could feel his eyes on her and knew he, too, was remembering how he had trusted her when she'd told him it was safe to proceed. And she, in turn, had trusted that he had remained faithful to his wife throughout their marriage.

Talking with Susan so openly about the risks of casual sex put her in mind of Gloria's faithlessness. Perhaps they had jumped the gun. Could Jordan be a hundred percent sure Gloria had taken precautions with her therapist? That Gloria hadn't unwittingly exposed him to any number of social diseases during the course of her affair?

While Susan pondered the information imparted to her by staring at the toes of her tennis shoes Ali chanced a questioning glance at Jordan. *It's okay*, he mouthed, inclining his head almost imperceptivity. But her emotions were still in turmoil.

Ali jerked her gaze back to Susan. "So do want to know if we're having sex or what?"

"No!" Susan's head snapped up, startled by Ali's candor. "Jeez, just forget I even mentioned it. I really only came in here for a soda." She opened the fridge and wrestled a Pepsi from the six-pack Jordan had brought with the food.

Jordan pounced on Ali the second Susan cleared the door, catching her arm to drag her up next to him. "I had a physical before leaving Charleston. There's nothing to worry about."

"I'm relieved to hear it. Then you won't mind if I ask to see the results of the blood test?"

"You don't believe me," he said, stunned.

"Whether I believe you or not isn't the issue. It just makes good sense for both of us to be completely sure. I was tested six months ago and haven't been with anybody but you since. We should have discussed this the night you told me Gloria had an affair behind your back."

"I was already gone from the house, and her bed, by the time I got tested."

"My test results are upstairs in the beside drawer. Where are yours?"

"On file at my doctor's office in Charleston," he snapped. "I didn't think I needed to carry them around with me to whip out on short notice. Which gives you every reason to accompany me home, doesn't it?"

She peeled his fingers from around her arm. "As your fantasy lover or your sweetheart?"

"What the hell is that supposed to mean?" He towered behind her as she moved around him to the sink, where she retrieved the dishwashing crystals from beneath the counter and opened the dishwasher to fill the cups.

The hurt and anger welled up inside her again. Ali straightened, careful to keep her voice low. "Cut the shit, Jordan. We both know the only reason you want me to go home with you is so you can prove to everyone in Charleston that you're not just another cuckolded shmoe whose wife dumped him for another man. Otherwise, it would matter what your family thinks of me. And while I don't pretend to be a stuck-up prude, I certainly don't intend to parade my tattooed ass around your mother's dinner table."

He wasn't rising to the bait, seeing the tactic for what it was, an attempt to put distance between them. "I sincerely hope not. My mother frowns on the flaunting of body parts until after dessert. Bragging is done after dinner, in the study, in true Southern fashion. Over brandy and cigars."

Chapter Nineteen

ഔ

Ali slid closed the first cup, filled the second with crystals, closed the dishwasher, and turned the knob to the start position. She hadn't really allowed herself to think through the rash decision to accompany Jordan to Charleston. The nervous jitters had claimed her while she was trying to pack.

"I'm not ready for this."

"Ali, we've passed the fling stage."

"No, you've passed the fling stage. I'm still working on it."

He grasped her shoulders and turned her to face him. "Now, who's having trouble keeping up? I'll pack my Brut," he offered as enticement.

"It's not just that."

"Then what is it?"

She licked her lips saying low, "What if I want more?"

"More what?"

"Than this. What we have now. What if I want marriage? Children?"

There. There it was, flashing in his eyes for the briefest of seconds before he managed to mask it—the fear, the panic. "What's wrong with what we have now?"

"Nothing, if that's the way you intend for us to continue indefinitely. But eventually, just like any other woman, I want those things. I want the option to want those things. If you don't, then…well, I'm not getting any younger, now am I?"

His hands dropped away from her. "What are you saying? That you won't see me anymore unless I want the same thing?"

"Do you?"

He plowed a hand through his hair. "I haven't really thought that far ahead."

"Then you don't need to be dragging me to your parents' house for the weekend just so you can thumb your nose at Charleston society," she said stiffly.

"Are you dumping me?" he finally asked, murder in his eyes.

"I'm doing you a favor, Finch."

"Like hell. This is just some trumped up excuse to avoid making a commitment so you can...what...date around? Keep your options open?" He was shaking with anger, but so far had managed to keep his voice low.

"Well, there is that."

"You want an answer about marriage and kids now, is that it?"

"That's about the size of it. What, you didn't think a woman like me would ever consider settling down with a husband and kids? Or maybe you didn't think a guy like you would ever need to worry about settling down with a woman like me."

His jaw worked as he considered her somewhat veiled ultimatum. "I can't talk about this right now."

"Then maybe you'd better leave. Good luck at the hearing."

He opened his mouth to speak, then jammed his jaws shut. Without another word he turned and strode out, ushering Susan along with him as she volleyed questions at him, clearly confused at the turn of events.

* * * * *

"I thought you were going to Charleston for the weekend?" Deanna said in surprise when she entered the boutique Friday morning to find Ali at work in the back room.

"Change of plans," Ali announced brightly. Smart lady that Deanna was, she'd learned early on what Ali's forced gaiety portended, so went about her business as if it were any other ordinary day.

Ali wouldn't think about the wounded look in Jordan's eyes when he'd left Thursday evening. The disappointment in Susan's. Wouldn't think of how much it had hurt to lie in bed that night thinking of them cozied around the family table at his parents', eating dinner, laughing, sharing amusing stories. She would work. And did. Until late Saturday evening, when she continued to compose blurbs for the magazine layout at home, designate which clothes were to be worn by which models, jot down notes on ideas for future reference, scan the male students for possibilities, all while washing down a peanut butter sandwich with milk when what she really wanted was the false courage a glass of Scotch would give her.

She went into the boutique Sunday and worked another twelve hours. It was killing her to wonder how the hearing had gone. She wanted Jordan to call. Didn't want him to call. Wanted Susan to rush through the door with good news come Monday morning. Prayed she wouldn't. Jerked her wandering mind back to the task at hand a thousand times during the day.

She was just about to call it quits for the night when the buzzer at the back door sounded, causing her to jump nervously. The back door was used only by Deanna and herself or delivery personnel. Deliveries were scheduled for Monday through Friday. Sometimes a late shipment slid in on Saturday, but never Sunday.

Her palms were sweating before she even stood on tiptoe to look through the peephole.

Jordan stood on the other side of the metal door, hands shoved deep into the pockets of his Dockers. Mostly to keep from banging down the door. It wasn't a matter of having the willpower to stay away from Ali, he didn't intend to walk quietly out of her life. And he wasn't going to make it easy for her to walk out of his. She'd said it herself, she was prone to moments of insanity.

The weekend had given him time to think. Though he still wasn't sure about marriage and kids, by damn he was sure of one thing, he hadn't asked Ali to go home with him for the mere purpose of parading her on his arm while thumbing his nose at Charleston society or his family. He wasn't desperate, he was choosy. If his family didn't approve of his choice, that was their problem.

The metal door opened and he looked into the face that haunted his dreams. She was dressed in jeans and a light sweatshirt, hair pulled back into a messy ponytail. Sneakers on her feet. No customers today. She would have had the boutique to herself.

"May I come in?"

"Jordan, what are you doing here?"

He rested a foot on the step. "I thought you'd like to know how the hearing went. Or have you suddenly developed an aversion to the little girl who sings your praises to anyone who will listen?"

"Where is the runt?" she asked as he brushed past her and made his way to her office.

"At home. Celebrating with Bonnie."

"It went well, then." She breathed a sigh of relief, closed the door, and followed him back to her office, leaning one hip against the corner of her desk to fold her arms.

"I was granted temporary custody until the final hearing in August."

"Congratulations," she said softly, and meant it. "Gloria didn't protest?"

"She protested out the wazoo." He turned his back on her to pour himself a cup of coffee, using one of the insulated cups kept stacked beside the machine for special customers. "From an airport in France via her lawyer. Judge Stonewall wasn't impressed with her plea for understanding. He was, however, impressed with Susan during their private interview. But that doesn't mean we're in the clear." Facing her again, he took a sip of the hot liquid. "I missed you."

She said nothing, just stood there, running a thumbnail along the edge of the desk. Jordan could tell by her expression that she didn't want to hear that he'd missed her, thought about her, lay awake nights aching to hear the sound of her voice, but that was just too bad. He'd been miserable for the last three days. Ungraciously, he hoped she had been miserable right along with him.

It was his turn to push the envelope, indulge in the madness she had loosed in his blood. "You missed me too, but you won't admit it. Let's work this out."

"There isn't anything to work out."

"You cut me off at the knees with a 'thanks, it's been fun' and expect me to be happy about it? I don't think so, Ali." Why bother to sugarcoat it? Why strive for calm when inside he was raging. He set his cup aside on the counter and went to stand in front of her. She wouldn't look him in the eye, but instead fixed her gaze on the rack of clothes against the wall to her right.

"I have something for you." He reached into his pocket and pulled out a folded piece of paper.

She stared at it like it was a coiled snake. "What is it?"

"My test results."

She took the paper he placed in her hand, scanned it briefly, then refolded the sheet into a neat square. "Thank you."

"Now, let's see yours."

"I...they're at home."

"No problem. I'll follow you in my car."

She looked up at him, frowning. "You want to see them right now?"

"I don't think that's asking too much under the circumstances. You raised a valid concern about the perils of sleeping around. We put it to rest and both breathe a little easier."

He knew she couldn't argue with the logic, especially since she'd been the one to lecture Susan on the risks of casual sex. Jordan waited while she tidied up her desk, filled her briefcase with work she wanted to take home, and turned out the lights. He stood with her while she set the alarm and locked the back door, then walked her to her car, holding the car door until she was seated behind the wheel.

She murmured a polite thank you. He slammed the door and walked to his Lincoln, slamming that door as well. When they reached her condo she set her purse on the hall table and said, "They're upstairs in the beside drawer. I'll be right back."

He didn't wait in the foyer, but trailed her up the stairs. She seemed to sense he was near the edge of letting his temper fly, so didn't argue the point. Her scent, *their* scent, still lingered in the bedroom. It hit him full force as he entered the room. There were no clothes strewn haphazardly about this time, Ali had returned her Sunday-go-to-Charleston clothing to its designated drawers and closets.

She walked around the bed and opened the drawer, rifling through the contents. Straightening, she silently held out the envelope to him. Jordan flipped open the lip and removed the lab results, barely registering the negative stamps before tossing the papers aside on the coverlet.

"Handy to have within reach when interviewing prospective fathers." His arrow hit the mark. She flinched. It was a cruel thing to say but he didn't much give a damn. He hadn't been able to let loose the fury and hurt he was feeling Thursday evening because of Susan's presence. But Susan wasn't here now. It was just the two of them, staring at each other across the corner of the bed.

"Okay." She wrapped her arms around her waist in a defensive gesture. "I guess you think I deserved that. It would be best if you leave now."

"Best for whom?" he grunted. "Not me. Did the sheets have time to cool before you went out scouring Chicago for likely candidates?"

Her chin came up. "I'm not going to dignify that question with an answer."

He sounded like a jealous lover. Which was exactly what he was. The thought of Ali sleeping with another man made his teeth grind. "Good. Because I'm not really interested in the answer. I am not fucking expendable, Ali."

"This isn't any easier for me than it is for you!" she cried.

"Bullshit."

"What do you want from me, Jordan?"

His eyes shot sparks at her. "You know exactly what I want. I want things the way they were."

"Things can't be the way they were." She tapped at her breastbone. "I want more, and I'm not going to let you make me feel guilty for it."

"Oh, that's right." He settled a shoulder against the six-and-a-half-foot bedpost separating them. "You had an urge."

"It's not an urge, it's what I want out of life."

"Funny, all those times we were together, in bed and out, you didn't know you wanted a husband and kids. Right now I'm having an urge myself." His hand shot out to grab her wrist and haul her up against him. "I was there for you," he growled. "There when you doubted yourself and what I felt for you. When you didn't know how to separate your own self-image from the twisted image your mother pounded into your brain. When you needed to talk or cry or throw one of your little temper tantrums, or just needed to be held and touched. I thought we had something special."

"It was special," she insisted, pulling at the hold he had on her, but he reined in tighter.

"Yeah, it was so special you can't wait to get me out of your life like yesterday's news."

"I was there for you, too."

"You were there for Susan. Not me. Never just me. I needed you with me in Charleston and you panicked. You don't want to be married, Ali. Marriage involves compromise. You don't get to hold all the cards and make all the decisions."

"Why do you always have to make it sound so ugly?"

"Because a bad marriage is ugly. Divorce is ugly. And I don't intend to go down either road again."

Greed and anger warred within him. Why did she have to be so stubborn? Why did she have to throw marriage and kids at him now? Now, when he was fighting to salvage the only good thing to come out of his and Gloria's ill-fated union. Now, when he needed her support, her touch, her understanding and patience.

Jordan had tried to picture in his head what the future might hold for them. The only vision that came to him was one of watching her walk out on him down the road and taking the kids, their kids, with her. Of starting over again. Child support. Weekend visits. Custody battles.

She had laid it all out on the table for him, and still, he couldn't walk away. Couldn't let go. Some dark, primal need deep inside him had clawed its way to the surface and wouldn't be ignored.

"Stop looking at me like that."

"Like what?"

"Like you want to hurt me."

"Maybe I do," he snapped irritably. "Maybe I want you to hurt like I hurt. Or maybe, just once, I'd like for you to quit pushing and pulling, manipulating the circumstances, rationalizing the reasons, and throw your arms around me, tell me you love me, want me. That I'm as good for you as you are for me. That I make a difference in your day, your life."

"Oh, Jordan."

Though he remained unyielding, the tears welling up in her eyes tore through him like hot knives. He rode out the urge to thumb the droplets from her cheeks as she swiped at them absently, turning, tugging, trying to get free. Jordan didn't tighten his grip on her wrist, but neither did he loosen it.

"Let go…" The plea wasn't only for physical release, but emotional.

"So it will be easier to turn your back on me? A clean, fast break? No way in hell, baby. It's not over until you can walk away without a second glance. Over," his voice grew husky while thumbing the underside of her wrist where her pulse was beating out an unsteady rhythm, "is when you don't tremble when I touch you."

"Why are you doing this?" she whispered raggedly, raising her tear-stained face to his, eyes begging silently for him not to go any further. To stop what had already started when he touched her—the changes in her breathing, from shallow to choppy, the darkening of her mahogany eyes to near ebony, a complete awareness that transcended the physical, all signaling arousal.

So, he had surprised her by coming to the boutique this evening. She had expected him to brood in exile, long enough, at least, to have her defenses in place when they met again. It pleased him to know she was just as vulnerable as he at the moment.

"I love you," he stated baldly. "I want you. I'm not willing to be noble and give you up without a fight."

He pivoted, pushing her down on top of the down comforter, meshing their bodies until he could feel every lush curve from chest to thigh. Even through their clothing the heat of her need seared him to the bone.

"What will it prove?" she panted, yanking at the waistband of his pants, loosing his belt to drag down the zipper. "Except that I can't say no to you right now, this minute."

And that was his edge. The fact that she couldn't say no.

* * * * *

Ali wept with joy when Jordan spilled into her body for the last time. Their lovemaking was, at turns, desperate, achingly tender, ruthless. No one else had ever made her feel so loved, so cherished, so utterly, unequivocally desirable. She forgot she could never fit into his life and clung to him. He held her tightly, whispering how much he needed her, how he'd missed her.

When he rose from the bed to dress she leaned back against the pillows, watching, admiring the play of muscles in his back and shoulders as he pulled on his trousers. "We can't go on like this, Jordan."

He angled his chin to look down at her, his expression cloudy. "Yes we can."

"I'll find a way," she warned. "Despite my own weakness, I'll find a way to make you stay away."

He scooped up his shirt and sat down on the bed beside her. "You don't want me to stay away."

"Nevertheless, you can't expect me to put my future on hold. Women don't have the same advantages as men when it comes to conception. I want to have children while I'm young enough to enjoy them." It was a matter of emotional survival. If she continued to give in to the madness that had gripped her only moments before, she would have nothing in the end but bittersweet regrets.

He looked away, offset his teeth. "Does that mean you intend to start seeing other people?"

"It means I want the chance to find out if marriage and family is in the cards for me."

"And you want to fall into bed with the first guy who fits the mold with my permission?" he snorted unbelievably. "Forget it."

"What about Susan?"

"What *about* Susan?"

"I...I'd like to continue a friendship with her, but if we aren't able to at least be civil to one another—"

"Screw civil." He yanked his shirt over his head and stood to shove the tail into his waistband. "Why don't you just ask me to pull up a chair and watch the winner deliver stud service."

He bit off a string of savage curses, chilling and electrifying the air around them at the same time. Fists clenched, he squeezed his eyes shut, letting his head fall back on his shoulders. "Jesus, I didn't think it was possible for a woman, any woman, to drive me to the point of violence. Goddamn you, Ali."

Ali wallowed in her own misery after Jordan stormed out, leaping from the bed, naked, to rip the sheets from the mattress. She screamed out her frustration to the four walls, smashed a porcelain figurine shaped like an Italian urn against the door, sending jagged chards of pottery flying in all directions. She hated herself for hurting him, for being able to cut him so deeply after he'd rushed straight to the boutique to share the news of the custody hearing, his triumph, his test results.

Yes, he'd been angry and resentful over her attempt to break things off. Still, he knew she had an emotional investment in Susan and the not knowing was killing her. He'd wanted her to know he was telling the truth when he'd said sleeping with him was safe. That he cared enough about his own health and her peace of mind to produce proof.

Then she'd gone to bed with him and kicked him in the gut. Again.

How was it possible to go forward into the future when she couldn't get past the present? How could she be so strong and sure of herself one minute, yet weepy and weak-willed the next?

Because she loved him with all her heart and soul and the thought of bearing any child but Jordan's left her feeling sick and empty inside.

Because Allison MacPherson needed a piece of paper that made it legal to enjoy the rights of parenthood.

And because Jordan Finch, from the minute he'd stepped into her life, had made a difference.

Chapter Twenty

୫ଚ

"You're killing me, you know that..." Franny slammed the door and staggered to the couch. Toeing off her heels she collapsed on the cushions, propping her tired, aching feet on Ali's freshly dusted coffee table.

"Drink?" Ali held up a bottle of Scotch she'd just pulled from the cabinet.

"Love one." Franny accepted the tumbler and sipped. "So, what's on the agenda for tonight? Please, God, let it be something tame like a movie. These late nights are catching up with me."

"I'm sorry. I'm wearing you out."

"No, you're killing me." She held her glass up in salute. "Dale is wearing me out."

"Wait 'til he gets a load of you on the cover of the catalogue. Then he'll wear you out."

"Here's to genius photographers who can make a tired broad like me look good in nothing but a sheet of velvet."

"Amen."

They drank in companionable silence.

Franny had the hots for Dale, though the hussy didn't want to admit it. While *she* had fallen into the most disgusting habit of waiting by the phone. Wondering. Hoping.

You don't want me to stay away. But in the end she hadn't needed to find a way to keep Jordan at arm's length. It had been Jordan who had walked away without a second glance, leaving Ali to discover just how agonizingly empty the days and nights without him could be.

No calls. No surprise visits to the boutique to glare at her over the counter.

No blue roses from his mother's garden in Charleston. No fancy wrapped boxes.

Susan's visits to the boutique continued, but were becoming sporadic at best. When the teen did visit, their conversations were fraught with gaps because both avoided the subject of Jordan and the impending custody case and Randy Peters, which left only the most frivolous of daily events to fill gaping holes. It was as if Susan were comparing Ali's sudden disappearance from her father's life to her mother's, afraid to let herself get too close, to trust in and depend on their friendship too heavily.

Franny bent over her tumbler, studying the way the light reflected off the cut glass as though it were the most fascinating of enigmas.

In an effort to throw off the pang of longing that gripped viciously at her insides Ali splashed another three fingers into her own glass. "Thinking of asking for a raise now that you're a supermodel?"

"The custody hearing is next week," Franny blurted out.

Ali's heart clamored against her rib cage.

"It doesn't look good."

"What…what do you mean it doesn't look good?"

Franny took another healthy swallow before answering. "You didn't hear any of this from me, but mother dearest went and got herself married up good and proper. Came back from Europe with a doting husband and a statement from some quack doctor she found over there, diagnosing her with some sort of thyroid disorder which, it seems, accounts for her 'uncontrollable emotional distress'. What a load of shit."

"How do you know all this? I thought Jordan was closed-mouthed about his personal life at the office."

Franny lifted one shoulder in a half-assed shrug. "I listened in on his telephone conversation with his lawyer."

"Franny!"

"What?" Franny didn't seem particularly bothered by the fact that she had invaded her boss' privacy. "You think he's going to tell me anything now that you two are on the outs? Christ, you look at him wrong and he charges like a wounded boar."

"My God." Ali pressed her glass to her forehead. "He must be going out of his mind."

"It gets worse."

"Worse than you eavesdropping on his private conversations?" *Oh God, oh God, he's seeing someone.*

"Please. A misdemeanor at best. If he loses the case he's packing it in and moving back to Charleston. To be near Susan. He's already entertaining bids from other developers."

"That would be like starting all over again for him."

"Not entirely. Jordan has a good, solid reputation in Charleston. Old ties, former business associates."

Along with an ex-wife settled nicely back into the bosom of her peers, who'll rub victory in his face every chance she gets. And a brokenhearted daughter who'll put him through hell because he failed to keep his promise.

"Judges tend to lean toward homes where there are two parents," Ali murmured more to herself than to Franny.

"That's a fact," Franny agreed. "How much do you know about Jordan's ex?"

"Susan resents her. She cheated on Jordan with her psychiatrist. Then served him with divorce papers and took off for parts unknown."

"Nice."

"Oh, Franny, why did I push marriage and kids with him? Why didn't I just leave well enough alone and enjoy what we had? He's been through so much."

"Hey." Franny's stocking feet hit the carpet. She sat up straight as a poker, jutting a crimson fingernail at Ali. "I don't want to hear that kind of talk. You deserve to have the brass ring as much as anybody else if that's what makes you happy."

"No." Ali slumped into the overstuffed chair and covered her face with her hands. "No, I wanted the brass ring so I could shove it up my mother's nose. I committed, essentially, the same sins as Gloria. I involved myself in Jordan's life, played mother to his child for awhile, then announced I needed freedom to explore my options with other men."

"Yeah, you're a regular Christopher Columbus, you are. What other men? Jordan's been out of the picture for almost two months and you haven't as much as looked sideways at anything in pants. My mother clearly explained the facts of life to me at the tender age of fourteen—you can't get knocked up with a padlock on your panties. No, wait, that was Dad. Mom told me to stick a quarter between my knees and call if it fell out."

"I hurt him, Franny," she stated quietly through trembling fingers.

"He hurt you too, Ali. He made you believe anything was possible. That the two of you had a future together, and when you reached out to grasp that future he left you hanging. For Chrissake, you don't cultivate a monogamous relationship with a woman then invite her home to meet your family unless you're pretty damn sure she's 'the one'. That precept has been in the rulebooks since the beginning of time. You had no way of knowing he wasn't prepared to go to the wall."

"He was there for me."

"You were there for him, too."

"Not when he needed me most." *You were there for Susan. Not me. Never just me.* "I could have gone to Charleston with him like he wanted. Met his family. Provided emotional support for him and Susan. Instead I drew lines in the sand. I was more worried about making a good impression and proving my mother wrong than just being myself. He was worried about losing his daughter. Up until I fucked it up, we were making strides, Franny. Moving in a positive direction. He's right. I don't do compromise well. He came to me…he wanted to work it out…and I…" Ali trailed off, pressing her fingers to her lips.

"Why did I have to make every issue about Susan, her well-being, her wants, her needs? Why couldn't I get past all the problems and concentrate on us? When he told me about the custody suit, I empathized with Susan. When she started dating Randy Peters I took her side on almost every issue. When he learned about Gloria's infidelity I stole his limelight and ranted about my mother." Ali explained what had happened the day she had gone to see her mother and was refused entrance to the house she'd grown up in. "You know what he told me that night? He said all the things my mother despised about me were the things he loved. He had a shitfit when he found out I'd removed my navel ring for the trip to Charleston. That's what started the whole mess."

Franny rose and went to the sideboard to pour another Scotch. "When did Jordan Finch become your best friend?"

"What?"

"Well, you didn't come running to me to kiss your hurts. I've been telling you for years to dump the old broad. Your mother has never been a happy woman and she did everything she could to make damned sure you weren't happy, either. To the best of my knowledge you've never discussed your mother with anyone but me."

It was true, she'd never admitted the heartbreak and disillusionment she'd dealt with throughout those childhood and early adult years. Not even to Franny. She'd always pretended it didn't matter. Franny knew it mattered and did her best to boost Ali's morale after a demoralizing visit home. But though she would eventually break down and tell Franny the details, she never expounded on how those hurtful instances made her feel. Inadequate. Resentful. Blaming herself for not being smart enough, worthy enough, successful enough to earn her mother's love and respect.

As a child she had tried to please her mother. Failing that, she had dedicated four years of college to building a moat around herself that her mother couldn't cross. Then graduated to royally pissing off the woman she couldn't please. Guilt demanded she play the contrite daughter and keep sending money, but her pride wouldn't let her acknowledge that what she was really trying to do was buy what her mother wouldn't — or couldn't — give. Love and acceptance.

So when Jordan had tried to give her those gifts she had automatically assumed there was a price attached. That he wanted her to be a certain way, act a certain part, when all along he had already accepted her for who she was.

"Oh, shit, Franny, what have I done?"

"You stood your ground, Ali. You want a husband and kids. Jordan obviously doesn't want to be the father or the husband."

"Yes, but I didn't want those things until Jordan came along."

"So, do something about it."

"Like what?"

"I don't know." Franny waved a helpless hand. "Storm the Bastille or something. If that doesn't work, try crawling on your knees and begging."

"Like that's going to happen."

* * * * *

Charleston was a lovely old city and Ali would have liked to have taken the time to explore, but there was work to be done and not much time left. She rang the bell at Jordan's childhood home and waited patiently, noting the beauty and grace and charm that surrounded her.

An older version of Jordan answered the door. "May I help you?"

"I'd like to speak with Jordan, if possible."

"May I say who's calling?"

"Ali MacPherson."

The man's mouth dropped open for a fraction of a second. "You're her."

"Who?"

"Her." Almost as if he couldn't help himself, the man's gaze flew to her ass, then back to her face. Embarrassment caused him to become red-faced. "Jordan's girlfriend."

Busted. So much for tact. "That's right, I'm her. Can you be intrigued and amazed later? I really need to speak to Jordan."

"Oh. Sure." He backed up, indicating she should step inside. "He's out back in the rose garden. This way." But he stopped dead, turned to face her and thrust out his hand. "By the way, I'm Arlan, his brother."

She took his hand firmly. "Ah, yes, Ellen's husband."

"You've met Ellen?"

"Yes." If the rest of the house was like the foyer, she was in trouble. Marble and polished walnut collided to thinly mask old world style and elegance. Silk hangings and gilt frames lined the sweeping staircase. Pocket doors separated the offshoot rooms. "In a dark parking lot with Jordan's arms around her. You said he was in the rose garden?"

She left him staring after her as she made her way down the hall toward what she hoped was the kitchen or close to it. "Wanda?"

The older woman jumped, turning to stare at her while reaching for her apron to wipe her flour-encrusted hands. "Heavens, you startled me, dear. Can I help you?"

"Yes. Yes, I think you can." Five minutes later she headed out the back door toward the rose garden, armed with an apple and a spoon of peanut butter. She followed the cobbled path, enchanted with the colors and scents, stopping when she came across the Blue Girl roses, which Jordan had sent her in hopes of…

They smelled heavenly—like love and life when all was right with the world. When she looked up again, the epitome of Southern grace and style stood before her. Jordan's mother wore a floppy hat on her head to keep her white skin from exposure, gloves to protect her hands against cuts and scrapes, and held in her arms a bouquet of freshly cut roses. Still, she couldn't have appeared more elegant. Mrs. Finch eyed the apple and peanut butter, then smiled, nodding her head toward the back of the yard. "He's back there, waiting for life to kick him in the gut again."

"Susan…"

"Judge Stonewall was very interested in hearing all about how she suddenly found curves and breasts in your boutique. But he determined that it couldn't be any worse than playing doctor in the cart shed at the country club."

Ali let out a breath, relieved more than she could say. "He's a good father. He didn't deserve…this."

"My dear, life rarely hands us what we think we deserve. Otherwise, I would have been crowned Miss South Carolina and Missy Sternwood would have dropped dead of envy."

"If you're going to object to my being part of Jordan and Susan's lives, say so now."

"Will you turn around and leave if I do?" the older woman wondered aloud.

Their gazes met, clashed, acknowledged. "No."

The Finch matriarch smiled, kindness and hope and understanding in her hazel eyes. "If Arlan asks to see your tattoo, tell him you want to see his birthmark first."

"Why? Is it disgusting?"

"It's shaped like a penis." And with that she sailed off toward the house, humming to herself.

When she could breathe normally again, Ali made her way to the back of the garden, where Jordan sat near a waterfall, his back to her, watching the coy fish swim lazily beneath the water lilies. He turned when she reached around and stuck the spoon of peanut butter in his face. "Wanda didn't have the crunchy kind on hand, you'll have to make the best of it."

He took the spoon and licked the sticky paste. When he spoke his tone was deadpan. "What are you doing here, Ali?"

She seated herself next to him, bit into the apple and chewed, taking her time before answering. "I came to help you, Finch. God knows someone has to."

"If you help me anymore, I'm liable to slit my wrists."

"Cheer up, it could have been worse. Susan could have told the judge how you sniffed after me like a dog while denying her the simple pleasures of prom night."

He wasn't going to make this easy. "I hardly sniffed after you."

She turned to him, offering a bite of apple. "Finch, you're an idiot. You can't help it, that's why it's so sweet and why I can't continue to hold it against you."

He eyed the apple, deciding it would be best to stick with the peanut butter. "Should I fall to my knees and thank you now, or is there more?"

"Hold off, there's more. Now, I'll admit, I was a bit abrasive in the beginning and that probably gave you cause for hesitation. But you weathered it well, which means you weren't always such a stuffed fish. See where I'm going with this?"

"No, but please, continue. It's fascinating."

"The point is, I could learn to like Charleston."

He took the apple from her hand, bit into it and regarded her silently for several minutes. "You're not very good at this, are you, Ali?"

"No, Finch," she admitted with a sigh, "I'm not. In fact, what I am good at is not being good at it. You knew that when we started down this path."

He lifted her hand, studied the smooth skin, and investigated the dips with his fingertips. "You're one of those people who irritates the hell out of a person, but when you're not around boredom sets in."

"Well hell, I wouldn't want you to be bored."

As if he'd come to the end of all that was good about the conversation, he released her hand and turned to stare at the pond. "You can't show up here and do this."

"Do what?"

"Act as though you want to make this work, then run off with the circus when things don't go your way. I haven't changed my mind about the marriage thing. I'm not ready for that, Ali. I don't know if I'll ever be ready to risk so much again." He stood, shoving his hands into his trouser pockets. "So, I guess you were right. I wanted a fantasy. Something that wouldn't threaten the future with complications. I guess that makes me a bastard."

"Yeah, I guess it does," she agreed, rising to her feet to put all her strength behind tossing him off balance. He landed in the pool with a hardy splash, sending the coy shooting into the darker regions of the pool for safety.

"What the hell is wrong with you?" he roared up at her, picking at the water lilies that clung to his wet shirt.

"You jerk!" Growling, she scooped up the half-eaten apple and threw it at him. It bounced off the arm he held up in defense. "I have shoes smarter than you. I come down here and bare my soul to you and what do you do? Try to make a fool out of me."

"You haven't bared shit. And if anybody's been made a fool of, it's me! I should have listened to you when you said you were a fast girl."

She looked around for something else to throw and spotted a watering can. "I'd rather be fast than too slow to catch on, like *some* people." Aiming, she let go the tin can. He caught it and threw it ashore.

"Oh, I caught on, all right. Just before you tried to put my head in a noose."

"How smart can you be? You're still sitting in the fishpond. And I never said we *had* to get married and have kids right this minute. I simply wanted to know that it *could* happen. That you could love me enough to— I never wanted those things until you came along and shoved them in my face! You made everything about family look and sound so good, so...worthwhile. So..." She couldn't breathe. Her chest hurt. It was better if he didn't see how deeply she'd been cut.

Jordan shot up from the water, dripping debris as he lunged onto the bank. Damn her, but she was ripping his guts out yet again. He caught up to her as she reached the cobbled walk, swinging her around by the arm. His mouth crashed down on hers, wanting, needing, taking every bit of emotion she let out. Her arms came around his neck, holding him tightly. Finally, he needed to speak. "I do love you, Ali. I love you so much I'm sick with it."

"I didn't come down here to argue with you or make you say things you don't want to," she said against his chest. "I came because you need all the support you can get. I came because when you care for someone that's what you do, and I haven't been too good at doing that lately. But you know what, Finch?"

"What?" he uttered hoarsely.

"No matter what the judge decides, Susan's going to be okay. And so are you. She's not a baby, anymore. She's smart and determined and she's grown up a whole lot living with you. She's got an excellent support system in you and your family."

He let out a breath, knowing deep down that she was right. Maybe he'd equated losing Susan in a custody battle with losing her as a daughter. Maybe he'd simply been afraid he'd failed as a parent. "I know. The trouble is I've gotten used to having her around all the time and I don't want to go home to an empty house."

"So move to Charleston and get a dog."

"I figured you more for a cat person."

"I am, but then you'd make a fuss over the cat hair and footprints on the countertop. No, you're definitely dog material."

He pulled back to look down at her. "Somehow, I suspect there's an insult hidden in there somewhere." He dropped a kiss on her lips, lingering over the taste. "Would you really consider moving to Charleston?"

"For the chance to torture your brother on a regular basis? How can I resist?"

"You met Arlan, huh?"

"He answered the door."

"He checked out your ass, didn't he?"

"Yep. Wait 'til he finds out about the navel ring."

A flash of long denied desire rushed through his veins. His fingers crept down her simple dress to the belly region. "You wore it?"

"Please. Would I come all the way down here without every weapon in my arsenal?"

"Seriously, Ali, are you okay with waiting? I can't do this again if you aren't. Besides, you really suck at trying to make up when the shit gets deep."

She disengaged herself from his hold, stepping back to face him square on. "I can do anything I set my mind to, Finch. And since I've already set my mind on you—unsuspecting fool that you are—you don't stand a chance in hell."

"All right, then. My mother has a gardening shed behind the garage. Care to take a tour?"

"Love to."

Why an electronic book?

We live in the Information Age—an exciting time in the history of human civilization, in which technology rules supreme and continues to progress in leaps and bounds every minute of every day. For a multitude of reasons, more and more avid literary fans are opting to purchase e-books instead of paper books. The question from those not yet initiated into the world of electronic reading is simply: *Why?*

1. ***Price.*** An electronic title at Ellora's Cave Publishing and Cerridwen Press runs anywhere from 40% to 75% less than the cover price of the exact same title in paperback format. Why? Basic mathematics and cost. It is less expensive to publish an e-book (no paper and printing, no warehousing and shipping) than it is to publish a paperback, so the savings are passed along to the consumer.

2. ***Space.*** Running out of room in your house for your books? That is one worry you will never have with electronic books. For a low one-time cost, you can purchase a handheld device specifically designed for e-reading. Many e-readers have large, convenient screens for viewing. Better yet, hundreds of titles can be stored within your new library—on a single microchip. There are a variety of e-readers from different manufacturers. You can also read e-books on your PC or laptop computer. (Please note that Ellora's

Cave does not endorse any specific brands. You can check our websites at www.ellorascave.com or www.cerridwenpress.com for information we make available to new consumers.)

3. *Mobility*. Because your new e-library consists of only a microchip within a small, easily transportable e-reader, your entire cache of books can be taken with you wherever you go.

4. *Personal Viewing Preferences.* Are the words you are currently reading too small? Too large? Too… ANNOYING? Paperback books cannot be modified according to personal preferences, but e-books can.

5. *Instant Gratification.* Is it the middle of the night and all the bookstores near you are closed? Are you tired of waiting days, sometimes weeks, for bookstores to ship the novels you bought? Ellora's Cave Publishing sells instantaneous downloads twenty-four hours a day, seven days a week, every day of the year. Our webstore is never closed. Our e-book delivery system is 100% automated, meaning your order is filled as soon as you pay for it.

Those are a few of the top reasons why electronic books are replacing paperbacks for many avid readers.

As always, Ellora's Cave and Cerridwen Press welcome your questions and comments. We invite you to email us at Comments@ellorascave.com or write to us directly at Ellora's Cave Publishing Inc., 1056 Home Avenue, Akron, OH 44310-3502.

THE
✝ ELLORA'S CAVE ✝
LIBRARY

Stay up to date with Ellora's Cave Titles in
Print with our Quarterly Catalog.

TO RECIEVE A CATALOG,
SEND AN EMAIL WITH YOUR NAME
AND MAILING ADDRESS TO:

CATALOG@ELLORASCAVE.COM

OR SEND A LETTER OR POSTCARD
WITH YOUR MAILING ADDRESS TO:

CATALOG REQUEST
C/O ELLORA'S CAVE PUBLISHING, INC.
1056 HOME AVENUE
AKRON, OHIO 44310-3502

*Please be advised Ellora's Cave website and books contain explicit sexual
material and you must be 18.*

Cerridwen, the Celtic goddess of wisdom, was the muse who brought inspiration to storytellers and those in the creative arts.

Cerridwen Press encompasses the best and most innovative stories in all genres of today's fiction.

Visit our website and discover the newest titles by talented authors who still get inspired—much like the ancient storytellers did...

once upon a time.

www.cerridwenpress.com